Dead Ends and Damnation

The Charon Contract: Book 1

Christopher K Fielder

First paperback edition April 2022

Cover Art by

ISBN 979-8-98688353-0-2 (paperback)
ISBN 979-8-98688353-1-9 (ebook)
ISBN 979-8-98688353-2-6 (audiobook)

Published by Redlief Publishing
www.CKFielder.com

For Lily and Desmond:
The Inspiration to fight Hell itself

The Boundaries which divide Life from Death are at best shadowy and vague.
Who shall say where one ends and the other begins?
-Edgar Allen Poe

I hear a tale the road to Hell is paved with good intentions, and Mama my intentions were the best.
-Randy Travis

I

A single spark.

It's funny how often something as mundane as a single spark is all it takes to ignite the chain of events that lead to the moments that change us forever. Think about it. The single spark as it came from our cave-dwelling ancestors as they slammed rocks together, giving us control of fire. The first spark of ignition that drove crude engines and set us on the path to one day reach the stars. Even in the dawn of all that would ever be it was that one lonely spark in the great nothing that set the big bang in motion. It all began with just that one simple spark. In the here and now of course it was something a little less poetic. It was the small spark from an antique piece of flint as it struck against a stone fireplace that blew an entire room of angry overpaid assholes into little chunks of smoldering meat.

I stood at the center of the charred room and did my damnedest to organize my shell-shocked thoughts. I kept focusing on that little detail, just how much destruction could come from one spark. I played back the footage in my mind. Making connections to piece together how the hell this happened, which was ridiculous since I already knew the answer. I had the memory. I had witnessed it all from this position and watched it unfold in real-time.

It wasn't like I ever planned on getting involved in some weird underground occult pulp novel bullshit. I didn't wake up this morning thinking "You know what would make this day really special? Getting the shit kicked out of me by an angel." Hell, on my list of things to do today, that one wouldn't even make the top 100. I'm not a thrill-seeker or someone who cares about adventures, I just wanted to do my job and work off my debt. Then maybe if it wasn't too much to ask, I could find some small sliver of peace in things I somehow still found joy in. I wasn't a genius by any stretch of the imagination but that seemed perfectly reasonable as far as I was concerned.

I looked around the room thinking back to a week earlier, a week before all this began. My eyes glanced over the crispy lumps of human flesh. The final earthly remains of the well-paid morons who moments before had been baited into trying to kill me. There was nothing much left, nothing that could be ID'd at least. They were almost completely unrecognizable, and as my overwhelmed mind began to wander back down memory lane, I couldn't help but think just how much they looked like...

One Week Earlier

Scrapple. It's a food whose popularity seems to fade a little more with every generation. A bold statement considering it was never on the verge of taking the country by storm. A jellied mixture of pork parts that are generally considered too low-end for even the shittiest hot dogs. It was all this meat, by loose definition only, that was ground together into a paste and shaped into a loaf to settle. I know I'm not winning any converts with my description, but it's actually pretty damn good. Tonight it was sliced extra thin and served alongside another half dozen breakfast meats and a few eggs that made up the Black Moon Diner's infamous Noah's Ark breakfast platter. The tongue-in-cheek description on the menu advertised it as containing at least two of every animal.

"The Arc" was the standard 3 am communion that kept me worshiping at the altar of the greasy spoon for more than forty years. For anyone else that would have totaled up to a drawn-out suicide by breakfast, but I had the secret advantage of no longer being alive and therefore not giving a shit. That's right by the way, not alive. Not dead either. Just kind of here. Perpetually thirty-something for more than half a century. My body stalled in the same state I was in on the day I died. No amount of exercise would ever make me leaner and no amount of grease could ever do damage. Two sides of the same coin I played to my advantage. I'd tell you more, but I don't understand all the details myself.

The diner was in its usual state of calm. The informal atmosphere where the only rule was "mind your business." Combine that with the fact that it was the only all-night spot in the city that catered to those of us who were generally unwelcome anywhere else and you understood why everyone kept to themselves. You know the late-night types. Sure the Junkies and losers that this city is so fond of producing, but also the witches and warlocks, the possessed and enthralled, the restless non-living. Anyone or anything that most people believe shouldn't exist in this world. The diner welcomed them all as long as they kept a low profile and had cash to spend.

"Everything turn out alright?" asked the sweet voice from behind the counter. I finished chewing what was left in my mouth before looking up at the smiling face of Benny standing almost eye level. Still as comforting and familiar as ever in her standard uniform of blue jeans and a well-faded t-shirt. Like the Archangel of caffeine, she poured me another cup of coffee without asking. "Steaks a little chewy," I replied as we succinctly turned towards the small short order cook who looked a good 40 years past his "best by" date. Never turning to face us, he lifted a free hand and extended a stubby middle finger before returning to scramble eggs. Benny's smile grew as she held the coffee pot, changing the subject. "How's the night going so far?"

I've known Bernice, or Benny to anyone who didn't want to get on her bad side, for more years than I could recall and she's remained unchanged since day one. She was "cute" defined. Standing a little over 5 feet tall, lean and youthful with deep black eyes and matching shoulder-length hair she wore in a careless ponytail. The girl next door who was always stunning without ever putting in effort. It was one of those things that made her more endearing.

Tonight her t-shirt had more battle scars than most of her others, aged to a thinness that only came with years of wear and tear and a cracking white graphic of a tusked skull that read "Motorhead" along the top. If a t-shirt could be described as looking "tired" then this one needed to be taken behind a shed and shot. Still, she wore it with pride, and not because it was some amazing thrift store find or overpriced designer reproduction. Because this, like all her others, was a true original. One she bought in the heydays of the heavy metal explosion and probably purchased directly from the band. A weird thing to consider when the shirt looked twice as old as the girl wearing it. Then again, not many people knew Benny the way I did. Not the 21-year-old art student she claimed to be, but as her true self. The half-demon succubus who's hid from the world for over a century.

I put the fork down on a napkin and stretched while sitting on my usual stool. "Not bad, kind of slow," with all the nonchalance I could manage. "Made a couple of trips north earlier in the evening, had to drop some dumb kid that OD'ed

4

off at the Gray. Pretty uneventful for the most part." Reaching for my coffee, I saw the dejected look creep across her face and paused for a dramatic sip. "There was the one south-bound fare I had about an hour ago." Her expression sparkled as her eyes lit with intrigue. "Who was it? What was it, man or woman? What'd they do?"

Benny loved hearing about the southbound. The passengers who had earned a one-way ticket to Hell. Not a big surprise since it was only in her nature. Like a shark sensing blood in the water, she couldn't help her excitement but did her best to control it. "A woman" I teased, "I think she was what the papers call a black widow" Benny folded her arms on the counter and knelt to rest her chin against them "No way!" She exclaimed with eyes the size of pancakes.

I often told Benny about the southbound just to see the excitement in her face. Admittedly, I even went as far to make up a few when I wanted to keep her entertained. I think in some ways it helped her. As a Lilin, she was the offspring of a demon and a human. A succubus whose purpose in this world was the seduction and corruption of men. Unfortunately for the schemers of destiny, things don't always go to plan and Benny didn't have it in her to corrupt anyone. Even confessing during one of our late-night conversations that the idea turned her stomach from guilt. A hard road to travel, being a succubus with a conscience. Yet you could tell her dark thoughts were always right around the corner. So she tried her best to sweep them to the back of her mind, and the stories from my transports hopefully kept them at bay.

I nodded along with her enthusiasm. "Seven husbands. Killed them all over 20 years. Different names, different cities, large insurance settlements, and no one ever caught on." There was a flicker in her eyes that felt familiar, like a cat moments before it pounces. "It's like I've always said. You can outrun the law, you can hide all your secrets, but in the end..." She lifted her head off of the counter and with a wave of her hand boomed in a deep mocking voice, "you can't outrun death, and you can't hide from judgment." She rolled her eyes at me "I've heard the COPs theme song enough, just give me the juicy parts" She stared me down with eager interest. "Did you do the eye thing, like, did you see it all?"

Yes, the *eye thing*, one of the tools of the job. Somewhere high above my pay grade they had a very formal name for it but I just called it "The Sight." Like a superpower I was given, but where the powers in comic books usually lead to super strength or speed this didn't do shit for me; other than give me one hell of a headache. It was designed to let me see life itself through the eyes of the deceased. To observe every moment they had experienced, from all of their virtuous highs to all of their sinful lows. all it at once like a shotgun blast of memories. If you think about how something like that could screw your day sideways, you'd be almost right. Luckily for me, everything I see gets dumped into some short-term pocket of my memory. After a good night's sleep even the sickest images get blown away like a fart in the wind.

"Yeah, I saw it all. Wasn't as exciting as you're hoping for. Crimes of passion are exciting, they're the raw acts of human nature. This one was just oddly routine, like mowing a lawn or folding towels." Benny rolled her eyes again. "You saw a murder, firsthand, through the eyes of a murderer and you're calling it routine. Come one, give me something here..." I tossed back the last bit of coffee and smiled as I held it out for another fill. We both knew I was going to cough up the story. "Just a little old lady you'd never think twice of, only this one was a total sociopath. She'd marry some lonely old guy with a good-sized life insurance policy. As long as they had, you know, cancer, Alzheimer's, heart issues. If they were suffering then they were perfect." Steam billowed from the fresh cup. "She'd spend about a year or so practicing their handwriting.

Perfecting every pen stroke before the big day came. Then those poor bastards would get a nice big meal, a relaxing nap and for dessert a bullet under the chin." I folded my fingers into the shape of a gun and mimicked blowing off the top of my head.

"A suicide as far as every investigator was concerned. A frail old man and a grieving widow, a sappy suicide note detailing his undying love and refusal to put her through the pain of watching him waste away. It never added up to anything more than a tragedy and a closed case." Benny shook her head in disgust. "It's so obvious. I bet those lazy assholes never put more than five minutes' worth of work into the investigations," she had all the righteous indignation of someone who still cared about the world. "You can't blame them, think about it. You see this small grandmotherly type crying and clutching the last love letter from her dead husband. The first thought that comes to mind generally isn't going to be *murder*."

"Old ladies get away with murder," she smiled. "Good to know, I'll keep that in mind whenever I start aging." Something at the other end of the diner caught her eye, breaking the smirk. I turned to see three men huddled together in a booth at the far corner of the diner, their bodies obscured behind stacks of ragged books. Through the gaps I could make out their identical brown sweatshirts, their hoods up to hide their faces with only long unkempt beards exposed. The one to the outside of the booth had his arm extended into the air, coffee cup in hand and gesturing towards Benny. She gave him a quick nod, his signal to bury his face once again in his book.

"Damn Druids," she said under her breath with palpable irritation. "You know, I don't care that they come in all the time with armfuls of books that smell like a dank basement. I don't care that three of them take up a whole corner booth even when it's crowded. Hell, I don't even care that they only ever order coffee," she continued. "I mean, they stopped conjuring demons in the bathroom." Her whisper grew louder and more deliberate. "But the way they demand refill after refill and always tip like shit. That's what really pisses me off." She emphasized the last few words before turning to face me again. "Let me go top them off and I'll just leave the damn pot because once I'm back you're gonna finish with the details."

"Not much left to tell." I reached for my wallet. "Besides, I have to get moving. Got another pickup here in the next few minutes." "fiiiinnnneeee", she drew out like an exasperated teenager, "but you're full of shit. Getting a first-hand view of seven guys getting their brains blown all over their recliners and you're trying to tell me that you don't have any better details. You owe me something good tomorrow." I gulped down the last bit of coffee. From the wallet, I pulled a pair of twenties and slid it back into my jeans as I stood up. With both it would mean the tip was more than the price of the meal, but Benny always provided endless coffee and some of the best company you could get on these long nights. She deserved it, and it wasn't like money meant much to me anymore. It might as well go to someone who could use it. I tossed the bills onto the counter as I saw her walking towards the intense set of beards. As she bent over to refill the furthest cup, I could see the outline of the tail she kept tucked into her jeans as it pressed against her outer right thigh. I couldn't help but smile at the commonly uncommon you grew accustomed to when the people were just the right shade of odd.

The loud clang of the cowbell tied to the door of the diner rang through the quiet night as I stepped outside. River City was the booming metropolis of the southern US, a place with the same piss-stained streets of New York but populated by the good ol' boy culture of the south. It was a place where you could find any food you would ever want to eat, buy any pointless crap you would never really need, and hate any of the people you've ever been inclined to hate. It was crowded, dirty, and had a truly rotten core. It was also home.

The nights were different, peaceful in a way you never thought a city like this could be. I know they lump this place in with a few others as "The cities that never sleep." That was just a stupid marketing gimmick designed to lure tourists here with promises of more fun than could be delivered. Sure you could find a club or street with pockets of insufferable nightlife, but the city as a whole pretty much threw in the towel around midnight. It's one of the reasons I've never minded the night shift. I pulled a small metal tin from the chest pocket of my beat-up black peacoat and withdrew one of the few remaining mini cigars from it. I may still have lungs, but I could only describe them as decorative since breathing wasn't a necessity for me anymore. Take that lung cancer, chalk another one up to the benefits of not being alive.

I struck a match from a book floating around in the pocket of my jeans and lit the cigar. Eyes closed I drew a deep mouthful of the rich smoke, holding it in for a few seconds longer than necessary and turning back to the world around me. Sometimes the best breaks you get in life are only a few seconds long, but they're the ones that keep you moving. I enjoyed a few more puffs of the cigar, then with a familiar concentration that warmed my body and a slow heavy blink, I willed the car into existence.

A black perfectly polished 1948 Austin FX3 now sat idling at the curb. A thin stream of white exhaust slowly billowed from the tailpipe of the cliché British cab as I took a final puff of the cigar and blew the smoke towards the bumper. The two clouds intermingled in the silent night sky while on the street I flicked the stump of stogie into a pool of sidewalk runoff. The engine revved of its own accord before the small yellow light nested on the roof flickered to life and gently illuminated the word *Taxi*. "Yeah, I know" I reassured the cab as I ran my hand along its side, petting it like a tired old hound. "We're not going to be late. You know that by now." The right-side driver's door popped open and with one last deliberate crack of my back, I crawled into the perfectly worn driver's seat.

To the left of the steering wheel, the wooden glove compartment door hung open as I peered into its empty interior. "You know," I said aloud to no one, "It would be a lot easier to make these pickups if I had some idea of where I was going." I snapped the glove box shut and listened for the familiar smack of paper hitting the tray. With a pop of the latch, a small manila envelope now sat inside fresh and crisp. I pulled the package out and turned it over. The flap sealed shut with a large red wax seal embossed with the winged shoe of mercury, the symbol of the messenger spirits. Profoundly ironic since the damn things always seemed to be late.

I peeled back the seal and pulled out the small form within. The standard passenger requisition form wasn't a surprise, and just like all the others this one had to be completed for every passenger. I licked my finger and turned past the cover page to the main form where the name "Andrew Gregory" was printed in bold black letters along the top. I skimmed through the description looking for the important stuff. "Self-Inflicted," and "Hamistagan." stuck out before finding an address printed at the bottom. "See, I told you we wouldn't be late," I said with a little touch of smugness since the apartment complex was only a few miles from where we sat. Flipping the page over, I noticed the small red "x" printed at the bottom of the sheet. It sat in stark contrast to the monochrome text and highlighted the words "approval for apperception of soul."

With a sigh I refolded the paper before placing it back into the envelope. "I hate using the sight on these sad sacks,", speaking only to myself as the envelope went back into the glove box. "Sometimes I wonder if watching their screwed-up lives is just my eternal punishment." The seat belt stretched itself firmly around my waist as I placed both hands lightly on the steering wheel with my eyes hesitantly dropping shut. " Ok, let's see what this one has to offer."

II

It's called a stoma, an easier way of saying gastrointestinal stomata. In Latin, I think it meant mouth but honestly my Latin was never very good. That didn't change what it actually was and Latin terms or not Andy only ever knew it as the small one-inch knob of pink intestine that hung from his lower abdomen and slowly dribbled shit into the clear bag constantly taped to his waist. It was his trusted companion, his sidekick, and no matter what name they attached to it, just another in a long line of medical humiliations he endured throughout his life. It came with the territory, a lucky bonus from the birth defect that made his digestive tract almost useless. Even something as simple as food led to the most painful decision in his daily life. Don't eat, starve yourself through the hunger pains, maybe even die; or force yourself to eat and deal with the excruciating pain that would follow. It was one hell of an existence, and it was his.

His name was Andrew or Andy since that's what the Doctors always called him when they were about to give him more bad news. My hands tightened into clenched fists as every moment of his life flooded my mind like a tsunami of memories. Every medical diagnosis and surgical hope, each lonely night in his government-furnished apartment. I felt every second and understood what brought him to his final decision.

It was infected again, itching and burning. Even when he sat almost perfectly still in the old recliner that was donated to him, the damned thing still burned. He wasn't sure how many times this had happened before since he lost count somewhere in the twenties. It didn't matter, nothing mattered. There In the loneliness of his small, darkened apartment, he instead did his best to focus on one last task. "57," he said quietly to himself as he downed another of the opiates from the heap of pills he had been stockpiling.

His head rested against the back of the chair; his face lit only by the small mute television as he reached out to the dirty side table. Fumbling he grabbed a few more pills from the spilled bottle. "58," he continued as the next one went down. The plan was simple, there were almost 70 in the pile he had created. Start swallowing, do it quickly to avoid the pain of digesting them, and don't stop until the table is empty or they have done their job. "59." He swallowed again, "59," another down, "59." Did he already say 59? He kept his eyes closed as his ears began to ring and his head swam. Nausea had set in a few minutes before and would have been overwhelming had it not been locked in battle against the opiate-induced numbness that was just as powerful. He was just at the point where he could no longer feel his limbs when the simple task of putting another pill into his mouth became impossible. Time paused and skipped. He made one last attempt to lift his hand back to his mouth, and that was all.

I always hated having to watch the fuckups pull the plug. I mean, I get it. Especially for this guy. I see where he was coming from, but my shift was almost over and this is always such a damn depressing way to end the night. I parked on the sidewalk of the tall rundown apartment building that hosted Andy's last moments and checked my watch. According to the paperwork, his time of death was officially declared by the bosses upstairs six minutes ago which gave me 4 more minutes to relax.

I always like to give the fresh ones a little alone time, a chance to work out for themselves exactly what just happened. Sure in my earlier, and I guess eager days on the job I rushed to get there as soon as they separated from their bodies. Bad idea since the situations usually involved a lot of screaming or crying, sometimes panicking, and then there's the yelling. All that emotional crap that I just don't get paid enough to deal with. Through trial and error, I found that about 10 minutes was the right amount of time to let the situation sink in as realization took hold. Any sooner and you could walk in on them curled up like a dead shrimp, still going through that weird "Why God!" moment; any longer and you risk them starting to wander out on their own. So for the next four minutes I turned the radio up and drummed softly on the steering wheel.

When enough time had passed to get this show on the road I stepped out of the cab and into the dark street. "Your carriage, my dear," I said softly to myself as I reached back through the driver's side window and leaned heavily on the horn for a beat. I gave it a good 30 seconds of staring up at the third-floor apartment with no response before deciding I needed to be a tad more aggressive. I held against the horn for a drawn-out 20 count as the blast shook intensely through the street, and just as my hand lifted from the horn I saw the small frail head of Andy poke out of his window. "You know, that's very loud," came the timid voice that would have been inaudible if it weren't for the silence of the streets. "That was the point," I said, leaning back against the cab. "Now if you don't mind, you've got somewhere to be, I want to call it a night, and there's nothing good on the radio. So could you please get your ass down here so we can get going?" He shook his head slowly in confusion. "I... I don't have anywhere to be. You've got the wrong guy," he tried to assure himself as he ducked back into the darkness of his apartment.

He was still confused and I could understand, so I gave him another moment before yelling up at him. "You're dead you know..." with a dramatic pause, "you're probably starting to figure that out by now." He poked his head out again "How do you know that?" He asked as if he could no longer trust the world around him "How do I know?" I pointed to myself as if there were anyone else on the street. "That's a long story, but I can tell you how you know. Take a look at that pale thing stretched out in the dirty chair behind you. You know, that thing that looks oddly familiar. Well, guess what, that's you, or it was 10 minutes ago." He questioned a peek over his shoulder as the truth set in. If he had any blood, this is the point where it all would have drained from his face. "You're not crazy you know," I attempted to reassure him. "Nope. Not crazy, just dead."

He murmured again as if I wasn't there, "I don't think this is right. I've made a mistake." "Wrong again," I interrupted his monologue. "You can call gobbling down a half-pound of painkillers a lot of things. *Regrettable, unfortunate, a waste of perfectly good narcotics*, hell, I guess even *pathetic* would work, but with the amount of planning you put into this I would say *mistake* sure isn't what I would call it." His eyes locked onto me with suspicion. "So what happens now?"

I lifted myself off of the cab. "Well, the way I see it you have three options." I gave him my best football coach impression and extended three fingers in his direction "One, I could leave you as you are and you can spend the next few days playing *guess the liquid* as you watch it start to leak from your old body" I ticked off the first finger. "I would advise against that one since you may get a little self-conscious watching your landlord puke on himself when he finally finds you." A look of nausea flashed on his face as I continued. "Two, you can accept that this is how things have played out. In which case you come down here and I can take you where you need to go." I ticked off the second finger. "The good thing about that one is that you get to maintain a little dignity and I promise to answer any questions you've got." "And three?" He asked hesitantly. "Well, three I come up there and take you out. I don't like to do it but it's something that can happen."

Despite sounding like a threat it was another tool of the job, but one that I tried to reserve for the really hard cases only. "I don't think a bright kid like you would want that option since it involves saying your last goodbyes to this world from the trunk of my car." I patted the roof of the cab as an audible pop of a latch echoed through the street. Without touching it the trunk lid fell open revealing a small dark compartment within that should have held a spare tire. Andy apparently resigned to his fate. "Do I need to bring anything with me?" I reached back and pressed gently to fold the trunk shut. "Remember the part where I said you were dead? I think you'll be ok without your toothbrush."

For someone who had spent the last 20 years as a medical invalid, I have to say the guy was fast. It took him less than 30 seconds from the time he pulled his head back into his small apartment before he was down all three flights of stairs and out of the complex's front door. As he stepped into the street, I held the rear passenger door open for him like a true chauffeur. He turned for one final time to view the building before crawling in. "I'm never coming back here, am I?" A tinge of regret stained his voice. I placed a less than comforting hand on his head to guide him into the back seat. "I've seen your memories kid," I admitted while shutting his door. "Even if I told you that you could, we both know that you wouldn't want to."

Settling back into the driver's seat, the engine came to life as his scared voice crept up from the back. "There aren't any seat belts back here." I could see him looking around at his hands nervously. "Don't need 'em" I reassured him. "What are you worried about, double death?" He nodded and hung his head in embarrassment. "Don't worry about it," changing the subject. "Now I promised you I would fill you in on all the details, and since we have a few minutes before we get to where we're going, let's start easy." Through the rearview mirror I could see him lift his head again as he paid attention. "So as we've discussed, yes, you are dead. As in dead-dead. Really dead. I don't think I can stress that enough right now to get my point across." I lowered the mirror so our eyes could meet. "Not dreaming and not hallucinating. Not one of those near-death experiences that you can write a book about. This is the big one. The no going back one."

He rested his head in his hands. "I don't feel dead," he said after a long pause. "Well, what exactly does *dead* feel like?" It took him a moment to find the right words. "I don't know, but I know I don't feel like what I thought death was. I mean I'm still here. I'm talking. I know what's going on. I still feel like me." He continued to shake his head "That just doesn't seem like death. I guess I just don't get why this is all happening." I reached into the left pocket of my pea coat and removed the small steel flask I kept there for times like these. "Ah, so we're getting existential now. That's a path we could go down that we might never return from. It comes down to this though, how do you define yourself?" I passed the flask back to him. "If you think that the concept of *you* revolves around that 120-pound corpse uncontrollably blowing its last farts into that adjustable lazy-boy, then you're wrong. You're something more, something intangible, something that goes beyond death. That's why it's so hard to understand." I saw him tilt his head back and take a long gulp from the cheap whiskey in the flask.

He shuddered as it passed through his throat. "Ugh, that tastes like shit," he coughed. "Yeah, but it'll relax your nerves which might help a little."

That was a lie. Alcohol doesn't affect the dead, but the power of suggestion was second to none. "I'm dead, I'll accept that." I could already see him relaxing, "but what am I now, a ghost?" slumping back against the seat. "Nah, you're a spirit. A soul that has separated from its body and is in transition to the next level. A ghost is a soul that's just kinda stuck." "So what are you then? An angel" He asked a little calmer as he passed the flask back to me. "Do I look like an angel?" I took a long pull, nearly emptying the flask as he smiled in response, "I don't know what an angel looks like, but I guess not. A demon?" I tapped my forehead, "Nope, no horns." "What the hell are you then?" He asked with increased confidence that made me laugh. "Just another asshole with a job."

"I'm assuming you mean my job title though. That depends on who you ask. The official title for the job is ferryman. As in someone who pilots a ferry. You know, a boat. It's an allegory for crossing people over the river of life. I've always hated that term. I mean first, look around you. This is an awesome cab, but it would make a shitty boat, and second, with a title like that you wouldn't believe how many times I've had to explain that I'm not some sort of magical fucking fairy." He found that to be particularly amusing. "I prefer to describe myself instead as a Charon, pronounced *Shar On*. I got it from the myth, the servant of Hades who moved souls across the River Styx." "Hey, I remember that from an old movie. Ray Harryhausen, right? The stop motion skeleton in a cheap robe" Andy interrupted. "Yeah, that's the one but they're all just fancy words. It boils down to picking up the fresh spirits like you and taking them to their next stop." "Fresh spirits?" He asked. "Yeah, souls in transition. It's kind of hard to explain. Let's put it like this. I know this girl, or not a girl, I mean she looks like a girl except for the tail. Anyways, I know what we'll refer to as a girl, and she lives her whole life on her cellphone. I'm telling you I've watched her with this damn thing and I honestly don't think she'd be able to live without it. She's always texting someone or doing whatever internet stuff people do. Hell, she's even shown me how she deposits her paychecks and pays her bills from this thing without ever having to go to a bank. Can you imagine? It's like paper money doesn't even have a purpose anymore. This world is getting insane..."

"You don't stay up to date with technology much, do you?" He asked, amused. "Have no reason to, but anyway, one day she's carrying this stack of plates and her phone falls out of her back pocket. The moment it hits the floor the screen smashes into about 100 little shards and the thing is just done for. Well, the next night I come in and she's got a new phone, and I watch her as she punches in a few numbers and sets the two phones beside each other. I couldn't see anything happening, but after a few minutes of whatever techno-magic-nonsense goes on these days, everything that was on her old phone; even though it's completely broken and unusable, is now on her new one. Just kind of floated from one side to the other." I wiggled my fingers in the air to punctuate the movement. "You can think of that as kind of like what's going on now. That old phone is dead, and we're floating your data over to the new one."

The cab became silent again, and from experience, I knew exactly what he was thinking. I decided to give him time to process his thoughts before he finally asked. "Am I going to Hell?" The words came out serious as if he already knew the answer. "I was wondering when you were going to get around to that." I popped open the glove box and pulled out his paperwork. "The short answer is no. You're not heading south." I could see the growing relief in his face. "I thought it was a sin to do, you know, what I did. I mean I wouldn't have done it had I known any of this." His eyes were wide and if crying were still possible in his condition his shirt would be soaked. "Kid, life isn't easy. Sometimes you're dealt a rough hand. I don't know all the answers but from what I've seen I think something higher than me understands in some cases your only option left is to fold." He looked up and nodded a thank you. "Don't get too excited though, I never said you were going upstairs either."

I passed the paperwork back to him, tapping on a small checkbox printed beside a single word. "Hamistagan" he pronounced slowly, "what is that?" "Limbo," I said plainly, "Or what you can think of as the closest thing to limbo. Most of the souls there just call it The Gray. You'll see why." His face looked panicked. "Don't get worked up yet, let me finish. The Mother Teresa types, the goodie goodies, they get an express pass straight to the light, that white tunnel you hear everyone going on about. The bad boys and girls on the other hand, the real assholes, I have to drag them to the pit." "The pit" he repeated. "Yeah, literally a giant pit. I have to walk them to the edge and just..." I made a shoving motion with my hands "push 'em over. Now you wanna guess where they end up?" I gave him a second, "everyone else though, the oddballs like you and me, we're the ones who haven't done anything bad enough to head south but the maitre d' upstairs isn't ready to seat us yet either. So we get routed to The Gray where you'll work until you've earned your ticket through the tunnel." "What kind of work?" "Who knows?" I shrugged "Whatever you get assigned, could be anything. I'll tell you this though, just hope you don't get stuck answering questions as you shuttle spirits for the next 60 plus years."

III

I've never had a problem with silence. Silence was a relaxing welcome when you spend half your time playing uber driver to spirits who never managed to take the hint and shut the hell up. Andy was different though, and as a uniquely uncomfortable silence filled every inch of the cab, I started to feel genuinely sorry for the guy. The tingling itch of sympathy made the silence unsettling as I looked back a few times to nudge him along and ask anything else that might have been on his mind. At this point, I'd even endure the usual eye-rollers I get a half dozen times a night. "Is everyone going to be there?" "What about that dog I had as a kid?" The common ones when the reality of an afterlife hits you like a freight train. Each time I looked back at him though, he seemed content, silently staring, finding something in the nothingness beyond the window. The vast expanse of silent fog that led to the Gray and stretched for eternity between the trapdoor to Hell and the tunnel of light.

I gave up and let him be, peaceful in the back as the glow of a neon sign grew in the distance. "Hey, check it out" I called to grab his attention. "We're almost there." You could just begin to make out the blinking words through the mist ahead. "Hemistigan," Andy read as a yellow arrow flashed, pointing towards nothing of interest. I didn't bother explaining the name but pulled the cab up to a curb that seemed to be built in the midst of nothingness. Beyond us sat what looked like a newly constructed and unrealistically clean bus terminal. "That's the entry gate," I said, pointing to the center of the terminal where a line of maybe 30 people stood. Some were still trying to figure out what was happening as they slowly filtered their way through a turnstile. "What do I do now?" He asked somewhat in awe. "Well, you start by getting out. Then you do the same thing you do any time you see a line of people." I pointed to the group. "You join in, stay behind the guy in front of you, and hope that everyone hurries the hell up." We watched the front of the line as a shaggy-haired attendant in a boxy sportscoat used a small tablet computer to check each person before they moved through the turnstile. "Eddie knows what he's doing," gesturing towards the attendant, "he'll have you processed through in no time." The rear passenger door opened itself and Andy began to climb out, "yeah, makes sense, I guess. Here goes nothing." He rallied himself with courage as he turned towards me. "I know it's your job and all, but for what it's worth, thanks for the ride," he said as he began to shut the door. With all the people I've met, all having just taken their last breath and all so wrapped up in where they were going next, it shouldn't be a shock that getting a *"thank you"* was few and far between. How often does an EMT get a "thank you" from someone having a heart attack? When it happens, it sticks with you.

"Hey, Andy!" I yelled, surprising him. He grabbed the door just before it shut. "Listen, they're going to take good care of you in there. Just relax and things are going to work out for the best. Plus, I've seen your life. I know what you've been through. Compared to what you've just left, this place...," I circled my finger towards the terminal. "This place is going to be Heaven." He gave me an unsure smile and as he began to walk towards the line something must have dawned on him. He turned back towards me mouthing something unintelligible. I opened the driver's side door and stepped halfway out, "Do what?" He cupped his hands into a makeshift megaphone "I said, I don't know your name." I gave him a pleasant shrug before sinking back in the driver's seat muttering to myself. "Yeah. Neither do I." With the passenger window rolled down, I leaned over slightly. "If you need me for anything, ask for Austin." I shifted back into the comfortable portion of the seat as the car took off. "See you around."

I've made this trip thousands of times, to the point where the entire routine has become muscle memory. Get the file, make the pickup, cross over for the drop-off. A glorified supernatural delivery boy and nothing you would consider complicated. There were drawbacks, however, like the solo trips back through The Gray. They say that space is lonely. An endless expanse with countless lifetimes' worth of vacuum interspersed by the occasional star and planet. I call Bullshit on that because I've seen satellite pictures of space, I've stared into the sky during countless slow nights, it was awe-inspiring; and if space is God's great masterpiece, the gray nothingness between existence must have been the extra canvas he or she never got around to using. A truly silent and emotionless apathy given form that was so painfully "blah " that every moment I was in it by myself I rushed to get the hell out.

You see, I could cross over from the living realm to the Gray from anywhere on the planet if I wanted. Any place on Earth, any time of the day, it didn't matter. All I had to do was start driving and visualize myself there and we were over. The same couldn't be said for the way back. In the whole of the great void of the Gray, there were only a few landmarks. The pit of despair on one end, the heavenly light on the other, and the city that laid beyond the terminal smack in the center. Then, in one small, unmarked spot that sat equidistant from all those landmarks was an unassuming stone archway. The portal back to the living realm. Death's small secret escape hatch.

Annoying of course, but purposely designed. An insurance policy that in the event some pissed-off souls managed to make their way into the Gray rather than their final destination, they could wander for countless lifetimes and never find their way back to Earth. A needle in an infinite haystack that despite its complete obscurity I also had the sixth sense to always find based solely on instinct. I think it was another one of those job-related superpowers that I just hadn't gotten around to naming yet. Maybe cabbie-sense? I floored the gas pedal as I made my way through the soul-crushing emptiness of the Gray. To pass the time and occupy my mind I started going through the alphabet and naming a fruit that began with each letter. A calming exercise I read about in a meditation book. "A, Apple," I said aloud, "B, Banana..."

I made it to Uglyfruit this time before I hit the archway between worlds. Springing from the flat slate ground that covered the entirety of the Gray, it stood like the entrance to a tunnel that didn't exist and radiated the faintest blue light from its center. I pressed down on the brakes to slow the cab and with a muted flash of light found myself back on the same empty street I had crossed from earlier, the speedometer still reading 70 mph as I adjusted to the new surroundings. It was always a shock to the system to flash from a point of absolute desolation into a major metropolitan jungle and I backed the cab down to an inconspicuous 35 mph as we moved through the side streets. In the distance, in the alleyways that separated the buildings all around, I could make out the glow of the sun as it began to rise. It had been another long night and I was anxious for shift change.

In a small corner of my district there is a relatively quiet park that I like to visit when the nights are slow. I made my way to it and found a parking lot to idle in so I could finish up the shift change paperwork. Putting the cab into park I tapped twice on the glove compartment and opened it to find a few documents attached to a clipboard. I've never seen what happens to the paperwork I fill out, but I have a sneaking suspicion that it serves no purpose in the grand scheme of things other than to create work for people who need to fill up an eternity of waiting in limbo. When you think about it, forms have to be designed, proofread, printed, sorted, distributed, filled out (that's where I come in), collected, re-sorted, reviewed, approved, filed, and then probably dumped into a giant pile in an isolated corner of the Gray somewhere and burned. All that combined gives quite a few souls a lot to do as they work away their sin debt; so as much as I hated the tedium of the job, I didn't want to be the squeaky cog in the machine delaying someone's possible salvation.

Just finishing the first page, I began to flip it over when I felt an oddly familiar sensation on the side of my temple. Within a second I somehow knew it was the barrel of a gun, causing me to sit motionless in the driver's seat as it pressed harder. "Ok, how are we going to play this? Since you haven't shot yet I'm assuming you have something you want to say?" I turned my head slightly, moving slowly not to spook the gunman but just enough to see from the rearview mirror a fidgety arm reaching through the window. "This looks like some kind of collector's car," came the shaky voice of the gunman. "I bet there are all kinds of people who'd pay a lot for something like this." His eyes were glazed over, and through the reflection I could make out his stained "Bigger in Texas" t-shirt that had an arrow pointing towards the crotch. It was clear from how tensely he held himself and continually checked over his shoulder that his body was running solely off of a substance he probably shouldn't have been pumping into it. Like a rubber band stretched to its limit, he pushed the gun a little harder into the side of my head. "Get out now and we won't have to clean your brains off of the seats." I raised my arms in surrender. "Woah, threaten me all you want but leave the upholstery out of it." I pointed towards the handle. "I'm going to open the door. The car's all yours."

I climbed from the driver's seat watching as the carjacker kept the gun on me the entire time. Stepping back, I continued to keep my hands raised as he found his way behind the steering wheel. "Listen, just be careful with it ok. It's kind of got a mind of its own" The creep flashed a smile that would make a dentist shit their pants as he shot me the bird before driving off.

I knew what was coming, but I waited, letting him get a few yards away before a moment of concentration and a small familiar tingle behind my eyes did the trick. The car suddenly vanished from existence. I watched in amusement as the disappearance of the cab sent the driver tumbling forward onto the asphalt before he skid to a stop a few rocky feet away. With tweaker reflexes he rolled himself over in a daze, trying to focus on the sky and figure out what the hell had just happened. With a little more concentration I willed the car back into being, only this time it sat idling safely over the splayed-out would-be carjacker.

I took my time walking over, kneeling to see him lying there staring up at an engine that revved only a few inches from his face. "What the shit man," the gunman said in a panicked scream. "What's your name, friend?" I asked as I pulled a new cigar from my jacket. I know it sounds douchey, but this was one of those cowboy moments that are few and far between in a person's life, so maybe it's okay to be a little douchey. "What? Anthony! Who are you?" The strike of my match off of the ground startled him. "Cool, I'm gonna call you Tony. Now, Tony, I told you the car had a mind of its own, but you didn't want to listen." I gave him a moment for the thought to register. "See, if I'm going to be honest, I don't think it likes you much because of what just happened." The cab's engine revved deeper, "however I'm willing to bet that if you were to apologize and ask nicely my partner might just let you out from under there without running over any of your limbs." The car honked its horn in what seemed like agreement. "That's up to you though." Reality set into his face and suddenly turned to anger. "You can kiss my ass! I ain't apologizing to no damn Car!" Through his dry cracked lips, he spat in disgust. The engine revved again but this time the cab jerked forward slightly, nearly pinning one of the gunman's legs under its tire. "Tony, Tony, that wasn't very nice at all. I think you could do much better." He looked over to see the sleeve of his left arm was now held tightly under the wheel, pinning his arm in place. Turning back, he began to shake in fearful frustration "Ok, I get it. I'm sorry. Please let me out. You won't see me again." I smiled with the cigar held between my teeth. "Oh, Tony. Just looking at you right now I have a good feeling we'll be seeing each other again soon." I placed my hand gently on the door of the cab. "There's no reason it needs to be today though, I think we should let him go." The car seemed to disagree and lunged forward again, trapping another inch of sleeve under the tire. "I know," I continued to the cab, "but I think this may just be a turning point for him. Plus, the whole bygones be bygones thing and all that. What do you say?" As I took my hand off of the door, the engine sound smoothed to a low hum and the cab began gently rolling backward.

After what was probably the longest ten seconds of Tony's life, he was once again staring into the dawn sky as the cab cleared him completely. A few feet from where he was laying, I noticed the gun that had been pressed against my head minutes prior. Out of curiosity I picked it up to examine a little closer. "Oh Tony. Are you serious right now?" He sat up, turning to face me. "A pellet gun. For real? You are some kind of loser Tony." He scrambled to stand but just as he found his footing the cab lunged at him, causing him to again land on his ass. "Loser was probably too nice," as I shook my head. Bouncing to his feet, he took off running, finding the courage when he was a little over 20 yards away to turn back towards me. "You better hope I never see you again," he yelled with an attempt at confidence. Not wanting this to go any further I let him bandage his ego by having the last word.

  With that distraction now resolved I climbed back into the driver's seat and tossed the pellet gun into the rear. The sun was almost completely up and I still hadn't finished the damn paperwork. I grabbed the clipboard and picked up where I left off, rushing through any notes I had to include and marking all my transports as successful. Pulling the papers from the clip and shuffling through them one last time to double-check, I gripped them tightly and extended an arm out of the cab window. Licking my lips, I whistled as loudly as I could and began counting. "One Mississippi, two Mississippi, three..." but before I could finish, a rough breeze hit me in the face and emptied my hand of the paperwork. "Mississippi," I pulled my arm back through the window. "Time to call it. Let's go home"

  In a city this size renting an apartment is usually your only option, but when a landlord notices that a tenant hasn't aged a day in the span of a lifetime, it can be a little problematic. Then there was the idea of Jumping from apartment to apartment every few years to avoid the questions but that didn't sound very appealing either. So instead, I took the advice of a co-worker. If a person rents the same apartment for 60 years people take notice, but when a business does the same no one bats an eye. With the help of a cash-only lawyer that doesn't ask questions and some books I found at the library I managed to lease a small warehouse in the city's aging commercial district under the name "Eternity Cab LLC".

  Sure, the building was old and probably dangerous, and I'll be the first to admit that the water was brown, came out of a garden hose, and had an odd smell you couldn't quite put your finger on; but it was somehow comforting. The old saying is "home is where the heart is" but I think it's more realistic to say "home is where you no longer notice the smell." I steered the cab into the warehouse through the large loading dock ramp and climbed out as the automatic door rolled itself down. Inside, the warehouse was exactly as you would imagine. Large and dark with birds that flew in through one of the many broken windows. Aged brick walls surrounded a cracked concrete floor and rusted steel beams that held up a roof whose existence pissed in the face of building codes. A deathtrap storage warehouse that would have been empty had it not been for the large OD green army tent set up in the center, from which hung a small wooden sign painted with the words "home sweet tent." I stretched as I stepped out of the cab. "Same time tomorrow. Get some rest," placing my hand back onto its roof. As its lights dimmed, I focused my thoughts and turned as the car blinked out of existence.

The great thing about living in a tent is never having to unlock a door since one didn't exist. I pulled the flap back and stepped inside of my well-worn home. It took a few years of wear and tear, trial and error, but the place was pretty comfortable. As you walked in there was a small dining area with a simple dinette set on one side. A folding table on the other acted as my makeshift counter which hosted a hotplate, a mini-fridge, and the all-important coffee maker. I stepped over and poured myself a cup of the thick black liquid that had been waiting for me since I had left earlier. It was harsh and bitter but relaxing in an unexplainable way. Beyond what I call my kitchen was the living area. A couch against one wall of the tent, and a basic tube television on the other. It wasn't anything technologically impressive, but since I didn't get around to watching much tv I think "free from the curb" was the right price for me. There were some days when I couldn't sleep though, and for those I had a pretty impressive collection of westerns on VHS. Still sipping on the tar that was once coffee I made my way over to the small record player in the shade of the television and dropped the needle on a spinning 45. Setting down the now empty cup as the well-worn cracks and pops played as Roy Orbison began strumming the first chords of "Crying."

At the back of the tent was what passed for my bedroom. A single twin bed that I don't believe has ever been made, and an ornate wooden wardrobe that seemed slightly out of place. I shrugged off my wool coat and hung it inside. *"I was alright, for a while. I could smile for a while..."* I listened as the record continued and pulled my work boots off, tossing them into an empty corner of the tent. My jeans and white t-shirt came next, landing in a crumpled pile beside the bed where I could find them easily in a few hours. I had only been wearing this set for about two weeks now, and since dead guys don't sweat, I would say I could get at least another month's wear out of the jeans. The shirt would only last me a few more days before I would end up spilling something on it, but I had a whole drawer full of them.

I crawled into bed and listened to Orbison perfectly hit the final high notes as the morning sun reached its full effect. Another sunrise, another chance to grab as much sleep as I could before my next shift. Not out of physical need, but because it was the easiest way to keep myself sane. My routine, how I separated my days even when I couldn't remember which month it was anymore, and how I washed all the unpleasant images of the day from my brain. The suicides, the murders, the dark secrets everyone kept to themselves, and the total solitude of the Gray. I let the silence of the empty space wash over me and released my emotional grip on the thoughts. The kid who was stabbed on the street and my first pickup of the night; the overcooked eggs at the diner; the last moments of Andy's life, the feel of the gun against my head, and the odd excitement it brought with it. I released it all into the peacefulness of the room as I began to doze off when one final thought came as the world around me faded away. "I wonder if Tony pissed himself."

IV

Surprisingly, I ran into Andy again only two days later. It's true that if you exist for long enough you'll eventually run into everybody again at some point. It was also why I had a feeling that the most overused phrase in the afterlife was "Long time no see." This wasn't randomly bumping into him a few centuries later though; this was unexpectedly reconnecting with someone on an entirely different plane of existence after a very short time. That was unlikely to say the least, maybe even suspicious, but let me back up.

It was a new day, and I was making my way back to The Gray. A pretty common thing but this time was one of the odd ones since I was crossing without a passenger. Every year I was called into headquarters for a formal review of my performance and standard practice to bring me face to face with someone representing the powers that be. I would get my formal dressing down for something I screwed up in the previous year and then be sent back to work with an unenthusiastic "better luck next year." It was pointless repetition made worse since I never got a vacation. I may not have much of a social life, but there were other things I'd rather be doing.

I wallowed in annoyance for the entire trip before reaching the curb of the drop-off terminal as I did so often. Stepping out into the mist I gave the cab a pat before willing it away as I checked out the wait. The line of entrants had to be 40 souls deep, and I was not in the mood to piss around any longer than I had to. I sidestepped the group and made my way to the front of the line, the same shaggy-haired worker trying his hardest to ignore my approach as he stared into his tablet beside the turnstile.

"Hey Eddie, I've got one ticket to paradise. Let me pass and I'll leave tonight." I sang as I started to slip past him. "It gets funnier every time," came the voice battered from years of smoking and postnasal cocaine drip. "You know the rules Austin, every soul that enters must be accounted for." His arm stretched to block me. "Yeah, accounted for. I got that. You know, the last 60 some odd times I've come through here. I've been accounted for more times than there are people in line right now. Not to mention the 800+ times a year I drive right up to that curb." I pointed to the spot the car had been sitting moments prior, "each time since you started this job a couple of years back, I get to look over to see your pleasant face standing here *sha-sha-sha-shakin*." I sang the last part again just to get under his skin. "Just give me a break, please. I've got an appointment with Maggie and you're killing me. You know we can't be late to this crap." Eddie's expression never wavered beyond mild irritation. "Stop bustin' my balls man. Every soul must be accounted for in the order in which it arrives. I'm not trying to fail my review like someone else I know. I didn't make the rules, and I don't break the rules." He pointed to the back of the group. "Now if you are in such a hurry I would get in line before anyone else shows up."

15 minutes, if there were minutes in purgatory. That's how long I waited. For someone like Eddie who had a few decades to spend processing new souls into the Gray, fifteen minutes didn't mean much. For me, I was running late, I still had an appointment to keep, and my shift started in less than two hours. I didn't have 15 minutes to spare. I bit my lip as I finally reached the front of the line. "Ah, Mr. Austin. Long time no see. What is your business here today?" "Come on Eddie we just went through this. If I'm late then there's a 100% chance I'll be pulling back up to the curb 5-10 times per day every day for the next year. There's nothing in my job description that says I can't lay on the horn every time I pull up. Just to say *hello* and brighten your day." His expression shifted as he tried to figure out if I was bluffing. "Yeah, that'd be just great. Do you have your ID on you?" "This, this is my ID," I said as I circled my face with my finger a few times. "Since you just called me by my name, and we've been through this same crap way too many times now. That's my ID." Eddie pulled an unlit cigarette from a pocket in his blazer and used it to accentuate his words. "All previously processed souls who enter this area must show proof of identification before being allowed through. You must carry your identification with you during your entire..." before he could finish, I pulled the beat-up wallet from the back pocket of my jeans. It was a small brown leather bifold with a picture of an overall-clad bear posing above the words "Billy Bob" half faded in red ink. I flicked the wallet open federal agent style and showed him the ID card that was inside. "Please remove it so I can look at it closer." I rolled my eyes but didn't want to give him an excuse to waste more time. He inspected my ID closely before running the magnetic strip through a slot on his tablet. After a beep he handed the card back to me. "Look at that, Fairy Man of River City District 3. Driver: Austin" It didn't escape my attention that he made sure to put extra emphasis on mispronouncing

Ferryman. "It says here that you have an appointment scheduled with Maggie" I shoved the wallet back into my jeans. "You don't say." Eddie looked up from his tablet and smiled in a way that invited a punch to the teeth "You know Austin, you may want to quit wasting time. You're going to be late." I brushed past him and through the turnstile "Yeah, thanks Eddie. I'll keep that in mind. Sorry you're stuck here for who knows how long, otherwise I'd let you..." annoyingly singing at him one last time. "...*Take me home tonight*...." As I trailed off, he went back to punching information into his tablet before giving me the finger. It seemed to be a theme when I was around.

Beyond the turnstiles and processing is when the actual town part of The Gray started. Slate sidewalks ran between dense sections of unimaginably tall high-rises obscured by the misty sky. Souls filed quickly through the busy streets determined to get to their assigned jobs. It was otherworldly in the magnitude of cleanliness and devotion to order, an ethereal ant farm for souls. Imagine the busiest day at Disney World but mute the color pallet and take away all rides. It made sense too when you heard the rumor that they pulled in ol' Walt himself to help redesign the whole place a while back. I bounced through the crowds like a pinball until I found a flow of souls moving in the direction I needed to go.

I've heard before that Gray city is limitless. Not infinite, since that's more like a lack of a beginning or an end. No, the city had an end; it was very easy to spot since it was where the buildings stopped and the groundwork for new ones was being laid. Limitless was its true nature. There was no set limit on just how large this place could grow, and it grew at a dizzying rate. For every year that humans exist, the number of souls grows exponentially. Two turns to four, four to eight, and so on; and as the number of souls born into existence increased, as did the number of new tenants. New buildings went up every day and that made it all the more confusing for someone like me who only came through this way once a year. I squinted hard at the number on every building I passed as I was swept along the sidewalk with the crowd.

"11478...11479...11480. This is the one." I pushed my way out of the flow of the sidewalk and into the doorway of the building, pulling open one of the large glass double doors to step into an immaculately clean lobby with the words "Corporeal Services Division" hung in large silver letters on one plain white wall. The empty lobby led to a single silver elevator door and a small red call button that I pushed before hearing the rush of gears turning behind highly polished steel. A simple "ding" signaled the arrival as the doors split to reveal a familiar face. "Well I'll be damned..." slipped out as I saw the figure standing inside. "Don't say that Mr. Austin, you never know if it might happen." Andy smiled the type of genuine smile I don't believe he ever had on earth. He stood towards the side of the elevator in an expertly tailored black and gray bellhop uniform outlined in perfectly polished brass buttons and a matching pillbox hat. "You're running late, we had better hurry," he said as he held the door for me.

I stepped in and watched as he placed his hand on a small lever built into the side nearest him. With his crisp, white-gloved hands he flipped the lever from "Down" to "Up" as the elevator began to move. "So, this is what you were assigned huh? Elevator attendant." He smiled a little wider and more sincere. "I know, it's awesome. Isn't it?" His enthusiasm caught me off guard. "Really, awesome?" "Think about it, it's perfect. I spent my entire life stuck either in a hospital room or holed up in that tiny apartment. Small spaces, it's all I know. So here, in this elevator..." He tapped on the back wall lovingly "I'm safe, I'm in control. I am master of my domain, it's perfect. I also never really got to meet new people in life but with this job, I meet all kinds. I hear all sorts of wild stories. It's the best."

It gave me a little comfort to know that even in a place like the Gray this kid seems to finally be happy. I guess whoever was assigning the jobs around here put a little more effort into it than they used to. He continued, "You know, just the other day I met another Ferryman like you." "Charon." I corrected him. "Oh yeah, another Charon like you. He called himself Hinkley. Have you ever met him? Really neat stuff, instead of having the cool old car like you, he's the engineer of a steam train running through some parts of the Midwest." He laughed to himself for a moment, "I mean can you believe that? An actual Soul Train. Isn't that amazing?" I tried not to kill Andy's excitement. "Yeah, super awesome." I'd heard of Hinkley but never got around to meeting the guy. In fact, I hadn't had a chance to meet most of the other Charons on Earth, but I've heard rumors. Each one with their own transport like the train Andy described. I've heard of other cabs, boats, trucks, and helicopters. Someone even told me about a rickshaw one guy was assigned to. Made me wonder who the hell that poor bastard pissed off.

"So, shouldn't I tell you where I'm going?" realizing he never bothered to ask. His smile curled with a tinge of mischief. "I know you got some cool tricks, but you aren't the only one you know." With his free hand he placed two fingers against his temple like a cheap Vegas mentalist "You have an appointment with your caseworker, Maggie. Floor 214, office 2153." He dropped his hand and stared, waiting for applause. Admittedly It was a pretty cool trick, but I wasn't going to tell him that. "Anytime someone steps into the elevator I somehow just know where they're going and why. I guess that way everyone gets to their destination, and it keeps me from taking souls somewhere probably shouldn't be."

The elevator made a sudden chime and as Andy cranked the lever to its halfway point we slowed to a stop. The doors sliding gracefully apart he again reached one hand out to hold them for me. "Don't worry about pushing the button when you're ready to leave. I'll know and I'll come to grab you. Good luck while you're there, I have a feeling you're going to need it," and with another mechanical ding the doors sealed shut.

Floor 214 was less minimalist than the downstairs lobby. Beginning with a small entryway and a few uncomfortable-looking plastic chairs it led to a small receptionist's desk that controlled all entry into the maze of beige cubicles encircled by small offices each with a shiny brass nameplate. It was an organized chaos of incessant phone conversations as junior caseworkers rushed between desks and mail workers weaved through the aisles dropping off large stacks of envelopes. I made my way up to the receptionist desk and stood for a few moments waiting to be acknowledged by the mountain-sized man sitting behind it, intently focused on a cheap romance novel. Not wanting to be outright rude I coughed slightly, hoping to get his attention but got nothing in return. After another moment of the large pile of a man refusing to acknowledge me, I reached towards the small brass bell that sat at the corner of the desk. With a press of the shiny metal button, a loud ding echoed through the mass of cubicles. The entire floor fell silent before a hand the size of a catcher's mitt reached out and muted the bell. "What the hell do you want?" came the outrageously deep voice. The giant looked up from his book finally admitting to himself that I was standing in front of him. He dwarfed the chair he sat in, his overwhelming bulk held into place by a pair of ill-fitting khakis and blue oxford shirt as a small portion of tie could be seen peeking out from under his chin. I guess tailors were in short supply in the Gray.

The din of the office resumed. "The name is Austin; I have a meeting scheduled with Maggie." My explanation must not have meant much since he stared at me like a fly that had interrupted his picnic. After a few beats, he broke and pulled a clipboard from a drawer in the desk. "Sign here," his massive finger pointing to the next open line on the sheet. I scrawled my name onto the paper, leaving a streak down the front as he yanked the clipboard back. "You're late" he barked as he stuffed the sign-in sheet back into the open drawer. "You know, people keep saying that to me like it's going to help. Well, guess what, it's not." He stared expressionless, "Get your ass moving then," as he hooked a thumb towards the commotion behind us before burying his face back into the book. I moved a few feet to the side and strolled past him, waiting until I was within earshot but out of striking distance. "Thanks for your help. Sorry for interrupting your smut time."

To the left of the desk was the first office, a large contrasting white 2100 printed above the door with the numbers increasing in succession as I made my way down the line. After continually dodging determined workers, I finally arrived at 2153. It was a door like any other, with a small nameplate imprinted with the words "Ms. Margaret, Senior Corporeal Services Liaison."

I wasn't looking forward to this, reaching out to knock as a voice pierced through the door before my knuckles ever touched wood. "Don't bother, just come in." The office was basic, to say the least. One wall stood empty, while the other was lined with a series of metal filing cabinets. I stepped over towards one that held a simple drip coffee maker and a stack of Styrofoam cups. In the center of the office sat a wooden desk buried under stacks of manilla file folders. The files almost threatened to take up the entire surface except for a small, very old, well-worn typewriter positioned in the center. It was a machine that looked almost cartoonishly outdated, with the only thing in the room that looked any older being the thin fingers that pecked away at its keys. The fingers belonged to the unpleasant-looking schoolmarm caricature who sat with perfect posture behind the desk. I grabbed a Styrofoam cup from the stack and pulled the carafe from the coffee maker. Pouring myself a cup, I gestured the pot towards Maggie, "top you off?" trying to sound helpful. Without looking up she took one hand from the keys and extended a floral-patterned bone China cup towards me. I filled the cup to the brown-stained ring that encircled the inner wall and stared at Maggie as she continued to otherwise ignore my presence. Her face, wrinkled and aged with years of clerical work, held only two things worth noting. The rounded pair of Victorian spectacles she stared through with determination, and her all too familiar scowl. She was buttoned from neck to floor in an itchy wool dress that would make most nuns feel frumpy, her gray and white streaked hair stretched back in a bun so tight it defied physics.

Putting the pot back I took a sip of the bitter brew and sat in one of the small wooden chairs in front of her desk. I knew I was late so my goal wasn't to piss her off any further, but after a few minutes of feeling invisible I started to get annoyed. I decided maybe some gentle teasing would get her attention. I grabbed one of the folders and pretended to read through it. "Do any of these files have anything spicy we can look at? Maybe a few *lusts of the flesh* incidents worth reading? I may be dead but some parts of me still work if you know what I mean."

"You truly are an insufferable child," she yelled, slamming her hands down on each side of the typewriter. I mocked the sound of the carriage return with a loud "Ding!" as she pulled the paper from the typewriter and tossed it into the wastebasket beside her desk. "I'm assuming Mr. Roussimoff informed you that you are late," she said as her face settled back into its resting state. I looked over my shoulder at the closed door behind me. "You mean the patron Saint of Customer Service you have out there. Yeah, I think the eighth wonder of the world mentioned something about that during our delightful conversation." She pulled a file from one of the stacks on her desk and placed it in front of her. "Mr. Roussimoff is our current temp. The prior receptionist received her ascension a few days ago. Although that is excellent news for her, it left us with a vacancy. He will be filling in until we find a suitable replacement." The file that sat in front of her was larger than any of the others and rivaled the thickness of a dictionary. "If you do not mind, let us please begin so you don't cost me any further lost time."

She flipped open the cover of the folder and through her small round glasses began inspecting the top page. "This is your 63rd year assigned as the night ferryman for River City, district 3. Is that correct?" I sipped the coffee before answering. "Well, based on the 62 previous times we've had this conversation I would say that sounds accurate." She pulled loose one of the pencils she kept skewered into her tightly wound bun and made a mark on the page. "We see that you are always successful in your assignments, you have not had any absences since your appointment to this position, you are always careful in ensuring that your charges are transported to their assigned location. In summary, your performance is satisfactory." I sat forward in the chair trying not to get my hopes up for what could come next. "And as such, The Metatron Council has convened on your case. It has been decided that in this 63rd year of assigned responsibility, your Ascension to the light has been..." For the first time during our conversation Maggie met my eyes as a look of satisfaction crept across her face, "Denied."

I slumped back in the chair and took another sip to mask my disappointment. "You know," I began, trying to act indifferent. "You would think that after the 50th denial we could forgo all this formal nonsense. What about a nice postcard once a year? I mean you could get a whole team of limbo'ed graphic designers to spend years picking out just the right shade of off-white to soften the rejection. That right there is a great assignment for new arrivals, and fewer times you would have to see me. Talk about a win-win."

She continued to stare, but her smile faded. "Yes. I could see where that sounds appealing. Unfortunately, it has been mandated that all souls assigned to the corporeal plane must have a face-to-face formal review once a year. Besides," She slid open a drawer from the desk and reached inside. "If you didn't come in for these yearly reviews, I wouldn't be able to do this in front of you." She pulled out a large rubber stamp and red ink pad. Flipping the pad open she slowly inked up the stamp with great amusement before slamming it down on the paper with childlike enjoyment. "Please sign here," she said as she pushed the paper towards me, the fresh ink of the "Denied" stamp drying across the top. I signed the page before pushing it back to her. "Now," she began again as she looked over the papers, "Let's move on to updates."

Apparently finding that everything in my file was in order she placed it onto a new pile, and with no file to focus on she steepled her fingers to stare at me. "As you are currently assigned to district 3 of your city you should be aware that Mr. Ford has been granted his Ascension. His date for processing is in two weeks. When that occurs, it will leave his position vacant." I felt a tinge of hope. Ford was the other driver for the same district as me and essentially my partner. I covered the crossing of souls who expired during the night hours, and he did the same for the day. He was a good guy, so I was glad to hear that he had earned his access into Heaven. It gave me some encouragement that my time would eventually come, but it also meant that after sixty plus years of working nights and sleeping days I might finally get to move over to a normal schedule. I nodded as she finished. "You will not be taking over for Mr. Ford." I could see her hiding a sadistic satisfaction as if she could hear my thoughts. "Instead, Mr. Peugeot is transferring from another division so he may take over the vacancy." I finally broke, "what the hell Maggie? I've been doing this longer than Ford, and don't get me wrong, he deserves to move on, but why the hell am I still stuck on nights?" She pulled my folder back from the pile and flicked it open again. "You're not exactly a people person, are you Mr. Austin?" She licked her fingers and began flipping through pages. "We have noticed that although you are technically good at your work from a broad perspective you haven't done much in the way of earning your ascension, now have you?" Wanting to argue I kept my mouth shut to consider what she was saying. "In 63 years of your assigned duties it has come down to you begrudgingly ferrying souls between realms for 12 hours a day and frittering away the other 12. You have done nothing, and I repeat nothing, to show that you have earned your ticket to the Kingdom." I always hated it when they used sanctimonious terms. "What exactly am I supposed to be doing then? I mean this is the first I'm hearing about this. Do you want me out there during my off hours selling war bonds and helping old ladies carry to cross the street?" "What do *I* want you to do?" She asked "*I* don't want you to do anything. I honestly don't care about one single thing you do Mr. Austin. Do you know why? Because in the grand scheme of eternity you are a very minute piece of my time. What you do to earn your way means almost nothing to me. I will say that *they*, however... " She extended her thin finger upwards, pointing towards the ceiling "obviously *they* want you to do something to prove that you are worthy. What that may be is not my concern." I set the coffee cup on the corner of her desk between a few folders. It may have been a little presumptuous, but I didn't bother asking for permission at this point. "So let me get this straight." I reached into the pocket of my jacket and pulled out the flask. "63 years ago I died, somehow, and because of whatever it was that I did during my life I end up here." I could see her eyes move from the silver flask I held in my hands to the Styrofoam cup. "And when I get here, I have no memory of whatever it is I did, not to mention who I am, where I'm from, or anything about my former life; what I do know though is that you..." I pointed the flask towards her, "you tell me that to balance out the scales I have to, on the daily, drag these obnoxious bastards to Heaven or Hell; and I have to keep doing it until someone finally decides that it's enough." I pulled the flask back and held it up to my ear, shaking it to hear how much was inside. "And now, after all this time, I'm being told that just doing the job I was assigned isn't enough to earn my way into the party?" She gently closed the folder again and rested back against her chair. "Your assignment will, in some time, earn your passage. That is the nature of this place, but paying a debt takes time and you're paying in pennies."

I unscrewed the cap from the flask and poured half of the whiskey into the coffee. "I hear about this debt a lot. The scale I have to balance to earn my way through, but what's beyond me is that you and all the others around here insist that I pay off some debt I have no memory of. Now I don't know what it is I did during my time on earth, but I'm assuming that it's well documented in that file there." I pointed at the folder that sat below her hands, "I have to assume that whatever it was it must have been pretty bad. At least that's what I'm gathering considering the amount of shit you give me every time we have one of these." I twisted the cap back on the flask and returned it to my pocket. "So please give me an idea what I'm working against here. What did I do that was so bad that you have to give me the 3rd degree every time we meet?"

She smiled, but this time it was a smile that seemed to be more *about* me than *at* me. "Mr. Austin. In my time here as a liasson I have worked with many, many souls that have done some profoundly unspeakable acts. I pride myself on not judging an individual by the actions they committed while in their mortal state." She picked up my file and shook it for emphasis. "Any information that is within this file would have no bearing on our interactions. To me, who you were means nothing compared to who you are." She placed the folder back in the filing cabinet "So, with that understanding, have you ever stopped to consider that perhaps I don't care about what you've done previously. Perhaps..." She repeated to emphasize her words, "Perhaps you are just an asshole."

I picked the cup up from the corner of her desk and raised it to her in a salute. "For the first time, I think you may have said something that I just can't argue with. Here's to 64." I said as I gave her a sarcastic wink and I tossed back everything left in the cup.

V

Over the last 60 years with no social life and a moratorium on aging I've had just about every hobby I could carry with me. I started in the city library one day with the idea of reading all the literary classics I could get my hands on, maturing my mind even if my body didn't. Every famous book I had ever heard of, I challenged myself to read them all. I worked my way through shelf after shelf of plays, poetry, novels, and epics before I finally came to realize I just didn't give a shit about any of them. I felt disconnected from the world and working as a chauffeur for the dead revealed the biggest secret in life, what comes next. I saw behind the current and how the gears of mortality turned, and because of that knowledge all the action and suspense in life; the thrills and intrigue of what might happen, all of it was sucked straight out of everything I read. all the drama and adventures felt meaningless in the grand scheme since I knew in the end it didn't matter if the hero got the girl or gave their life to protect the innocent, they would all die like everyone else. Not to be too cynical, but none of it mattered. The greatest books ever written boiled down to a bunch of old stories with extravagant words about future dead people. Good guys go to Heaven, bad guys go to Hell, and the spectators on the sidelines would be stuck right here in my position. So, I marked that endeavor as the first of many I would give up on.

After that, I tried a lot of different things. I got good at crosswords and word searches for a while, but that began to feel like I was just wasting time when I could be doing something constructive. Then I talked myself into learning the guitar until I found out that trying to practice from the front seat of a cab was too cramped. Sticking with music, I decided to scale things down a bit and replaced the guitar with a ukulele. I'm not trying to brag but I did get damn good at it. That's until one night when strumming out a tune, a person passed by the corner I was parked on and openly laughed. I couldn't make out his words exactly, but I understood enough of the joke about how I must have had practice playing with small instruments. That was the end of that venture. Moving on to whittling seemed like the next step. I had seen so many old westerns where the retired sheriff would spend his final days on his front porch whittling small figures. All I would need was a chunk of wood and a small knife, which ended with a few blood stains on the upholstery, an impressive collection of splinters, and a nightly routine of vacuuming wood shavings from the floorboard. Things progressed from there. Speed solving Rubik's Cubes, building little sailboats inside of glass bottles, origami, sleight of hand magic, card tricks, hand polishing rocks. I'm not even joking about that last one. I seriously spent almost a year picking up rocks and polishing them with different grades of sandpaper until they shined. I heard that the Japanese have a similar hobby with highly polished balls of mud. Maybe that's something to look into if things stay this way for another few decades.

Tonight, I was flipping through a manual on chess theory that I picked up a few years back. I had always heard that chess was a game you could practice for a lifetime and still never master. With time being the one thing I was never in short supply of, it sounded appealing. I skimmed through a few more pages of opening gambits as the words entered through my eyes, slid past my brain, and settled somewhere in my stomach before they were trampled by a loud growling. It was almost 4 AM and even though I crossed three souls earlier in the evening, this was turning out to be a pretty slow night. Without anyone officially left on the night's schedule, times like these are what we call standby. It's when anything could happen since that's the nature of free will. Suicide, murder, anything unexpected since sometimes the motto of the universe can be summed up as "Shit happens." Hoping the night would stay quiet I decided to let my stomach, or my mind pretending to be my stomach, make the decisions for me. "Alright, screw this." I said to the cab "There's a stack of pancakes with my name on them so if anything comes up we'll just circle back."

The diner was only about 4 miles from the side street I had been parked on, and at this time of the night that meant only a 10-minute drive depending on the lights. Yes, I could probably just run any of the reds but getting pulled over by the police would have violated one of the main rules of the job, remain as low key as possible. Admittedly it was sometimes hard to look inconspicuous in a nearly 80-year-old English taxi cruising through the silent street at night but as long as I didn't break any laws, I went generally unnoticed. We made it about halfway before the cab began to decelerate on its own. "Ugh, what's going on?" I asked as the car came to a stop, turning its wheel to park along an open curb. "Are you feeling alright?" A small dome light in the ceiling blinked once. "Ok, then what's the issue?" A perfectly timed "thud" could be heard from the glove box. "Great, I guess they'll have to keep the syrup warm for a little longer." Reaching over I popped open the glove box door and pulled the envelope from inside. "Surprise time, I hope it's a good one."

Inside was what looked like a normal requisition that I had handled an obscene number of times prior, only this one felt strange. It was the same printed form as ever, the two sheets of paperwork with individual sections for "Name, Age, Date of Expiration" and so forth. Yet this one, unlike any I had seen before, was filled with thick black bars where the important information should have been printed. It reminded me of classified government files I had seen reprinted a few years back in a UFO magazine. Whoever had leaked the documents made sure large chunks of information were redacted with the same style of thick black bars. (Yes, UFO research was a hobby for a while also). So why the hell was someone redacting information for a soul? I skimmed along the pages and saw that there were only two lines that hadn't been blocked out. One was an address; The Grand Park, 1600 Burr Avenue, Suite 1. An elite and exceptionally expensive hotel famous not only for its deep history but also for an extravagance that made most people's definition of luxury look cheap. I flipped the paper over to see the only other word left uncensored. There, nestled between two large portions of blacked-out data, was the single word "Damnation."

I sat for a moment, perplexed. When you're faced with a job that you can't stand, and you know there's no way around it, most of the time you find that settling into a routine is the easiest way to cope. You force yourself to go through the motions and do what you have to while your brain is on autopilot. I was successful at sinking into such a routine a while ago but now faced with something unusual it was taking some time to comprehend. I settled on a pretty weak plan of action. "I guess we're going to the Grand Park and looking for the dead person," I told myself without much confidence. In agreement, the interior light blinked as the cab rumbled back to life.

After a short drive and a lack of a better plan, I pulled the car into the circular loading zone of the Hotel and parked in front of the valet stand. I know I've mentioned that Grand Park was a high-class hotel, but I don't think I quite emphasized enough just how over the top it was. As I stepped out, I looked down to see myself standing on what I could only guess was imported marble running along the entire loading zone. An apparent necessity for those guests who didn't want their few steps from the car to the front entrance to be soiled by anything like cement. As I stepped around to the hotel side of the car a night valet anxiously popped out from behind his podium. "I wasn't aware of anyone calling for a pickup," he insisted as I turned to face him. "That's because no one did." Screwing with the living has always been one of the few pleasures I get out of this job, so I tried to enjoy it whenever I had the chance. "You can't pick up fares here. We have a no idling policy," he informed me with false confidence from behind his bowtie. "You're going to have to move this thing. If someone needs a ride they'll call down and we'll request one of our executive vehicles." He pulled a brick-sized walkie-talkie from behind the podium, eager to use it. I withdrew a small stub of a cigar I had been saving from my pocket and stuck it in the corner of my mouth. "No worries, I'll just get rid of it then."

Before he could fully register what I had said, the car blinked out of existence. The valet's eyes widened as he stared past me trying to comprehend if the cab that had been there only a moment prior had actually vanished. "Where did it go?" He stammered, finally able to push the words from his head. I walked past him, stepping over to his podium. "Where did what go?" dismissing his question as I poked around through the drawer of his stand. I sifted through the loose keys, pens, and business cards until I finally found what I was looking for. "You don't mind, do you?" I pulled a small book of matches from the podium and lit the cigar stub as he continued to stare in a stupor. I exhaled and blew the rich smoke in his direction, snapping him back into reality as it tickled his nostrils. "Hey, you can't smoke here. This entire facility is non-smoking." I pulled the short stub from my lips and motioned it towards him. "Come on man. There's barely any left. Just let me enjoy the last little bit." I took another deep puff and blew it towards him. He pointed the tip of his walkie-talkie towards me as if it were a taser he wasn't afraid to use. "There is no smoking anywhere at this hotel! Now if you are not a patron, I am going to have to ask you to please leave this area or I will call security." I had pushed the kid far enough and since I wasn't interested in making a big deal out of this situation I conceded. I put my hands up, palms facing him. "Woah, relax tiger. I get it. You're the boss." I pulled the cigar from my lip and flicked it over his shoulder. He followed it as it sailed through the air "Hey! No littering. You have to pick that up," he demanded; turning back in confusion as he now stood in the parking circle alone.

VI

The truth is the puzzled valet only thought he was alone. I was still standing in the same spot, only now I had shifted into my incorporeal form. It was probably the most important trick of the trade that I guess I forgot to mention. It was all due to what I said earlier. I'm not exactly dead or alive; and to be more precise I didn't have a body. Where a body is usually a physical vessel used to contain a soul until that soul is released, I was more like a soul given physical form when it was convenient. That also meant when needed I was able to drop my physical body and instead exist as just a soul. How else would you expect me to interact with the newly dead? I know it can be confusing, so I usually explain it to people like Jell-O. You heat Jell-O and it's a liquid, when you cool it, it becomes a quivering solid, heat it once more and it's back to being a liquid. That's pretty much what I was, 200 pounds of ethereal Jell-O. Right now, I was in the liquid form of that analogy, existentially the same but in a way, it was almost like being a ghost. Notice how I said *almost*. In the afterlife "ghost" is a derogatory term for a soul that refuses to cross over. They're the souls that just hang around on earth wearing out their welcome and watching the living as they shower and shit. I'm not joking about that either. I mean really, some of them are just that creepy. They're the untouchables of the metaphysical world, like a soldier who abandons their post for fear of war. Everyone is going to die at some point and everyone needs to cross over, but these "ghosts" are just selfish assholes who seem to think the rules of the universe don't apply to them. They're the ones who throw a tantrum and stay behind.

I stood as the valet cautiously returned to his podium, reaching through my immaterial chest to place the walkie-talkie back into its base. As we stood face to faceless, I could see the confusion in his eyes as he began to question his sanity. "Good luck explaining that to anyone, dickhead" I thought to myself. Finally feeling pleased with what I had accomplished I maintained my nonexistent form and made my way a few yards to the front entrance of the hotel. Like a hand through a waterfall, I passed through the thick glass doors and found myself staring at the opulence of the hotel. *Opulence* was the most refined word I could think of since the actual words to come out of my mouth were "Holy shit! This must have cost a fortune."

The ceiling was littered with crystal light fixtures that hung throughout the entirety of the first floor. Their main purpose seemed to be to project painfully bright light that bounced back up from the overly polished marble mosaic floor. I looked around at the decor trying to figure out the designer's theme before realizing the only direction they must have been given was to find the most expensive of everything and buy a dozen. At the center of the lobby sat a registration desk made entirely of thick glass slabs that gave it the appearance of being both unbelievably heavy and entirely weightless due to its perfect transparency. I made my way through the minefield of uncomfortable-looking designer furniture and towards the sharply dressed night clerks that stood waiting behind the crystalline desk. My form allowed me to remain unnoticed as I scanned the length of their workspace for a map of the hotel rooms. Usually, these pickups were much easier, but the pages of blacked-out lines only told me "Suite 1" without a clue of how to get to it.

At one end of the large desk, I heard the soft ringing of a phone as an older clerk picked up the receiver stationed in front of him. "Hello," he answered in a perfect customer service tone. "Front lobby, how may we help? Yes sir. Currently our cleaning staff is unavailable, but I will personally bring you a few extra complements of towels." He nodded as he responded to the voice on the other end of the call "Yes sir, room 413. I will bring those to you now," and with a gentle click placed the receiver back on its cradle. His tone changed as he turned toward the second clerk who stood only a few feet away. "I don't know what the hell they're doing up there but room 413 said they need trash bags and as many towels as we can spare," his voice and cadence now lightyears from his phone manner. The second clerk continued to type away at the computer in front of him, "413 is registered to *you know whose* account and billed under Suite 1. If they call down and say they needed a crate of stray cats delivered to their room, your only response should be *what color*?" The older clerk shook his head in disgust as he turned to walk away, muttering to himself. "Rich assholes."

Call it divine intervention or just lucky coincidence, but either way the clerks were talking about the suite I was trying to find. Unfortunately, it didn't sound like they were going there so I still needed to find the way. I passed through the desk and searched around where the older clerk had been standing. His work area was immaculate. Papers stacked neatly in an inbox with an overly designed telephone placed beside it and positioned directly in front was a tablet computer thinner than a picture frame. I inspected the image on the screen and must have been struck with more dumb luck. Displayed on the tablet was a tool the clerks used to place reservations and included a full layout of each floor broken into individual rooms that were color-coded for "occupied" and "vacant." I placed my nonexistent finger on the screen and traced along each floor trying to locate Suite 1. After searching each floor and every room trying to figure out where I was supposed to be going, I kept coming up short. It took a few more moments of stupidity before I finally realized the reason I couldn't find the floor with Suite 1 was because the entire top floor of the hotel *was* Suite 1. all the top level was dedicated to just that single permanently reserved suite.

Now that I knew where I was going the next obstacle was how to get there. In my current form I could easily pass through any object like a person passing through smoke. It made things like a locked door no challenge and set me up as the king of horizontal travel. Unfortunately, I couldn't say the same for vertical distances and I still had to find a way up. I passed through the desk again and circled through the lobby finding a bank of elevators lined along the back wall. I focused intently on my index finger and flexed a series of nonexistent muscles to give solid form to just the tip of my finger. Not the easiest trick but it can be done with a little practice, like raising one of your middle toes while the others stay flat. With that small aspect of solid form, I pressed the call button on the elevator panel until the "up" arrow illuminated. It took a few seconds of patient waiting before the doors of the center elevator parted revealing the plush padded walls within. I slipped into the cabin of the elevator and began looking over the comically oversized panel of buttons.

It seemed like nothing during this assignment would be easy. As I scanned over the wall of unlit buttons, I noticed one separated from the group and located beside a small credit card sized slot. It didn't take a genius to decipher which one would get me to the top floor, but I had to assume the slot was meant for a security key. Hoping I still had some luck left I pushed the button a few times with my solid fingertip and confirmed that without whatever went into that slot I wasn't going anywhere. I relaxed my fingertip to a matching state of immaterial and passed through the elevator doors into the lobby. "Well," I whispered to myself. "I guess I need to find a key." I scanned the quiet lobby and checked out the few nighttime employees. They wore matching gray blazers with perfectly pressed slacks and their hairstyles were expertly maintained as if they were inspected each shift. They gave off an unnatural Stepford feeling with no visible tattoos or piercing, jewelry or distinct makeup, not even facial hair. That is except for one bearded outsider that stood rigidly by the front entrance. He was dressed in the same uniform as the others except for the pigtailed Secret Service earpiece that hung from the left side of his head. His posture was the fingerprint of military training and from the chest pocket of his blazer hung a badge printed with his same emotionless face. That badge was my key upstairs which only left figuring out how the hell I was going to get my hands on it.

I studied the man for another minute. His calm demeanor was a facade given away by the tense look in his eyes. From what I could tell he was the only security member around but in a hotel like this, where the free coffee in the lobby was worth more than most people's weekly grocery bill, it was safe to bet that they had a private army ready to move. Without fear of being seen I crossed through the lobby and took up a position in front of the guard, aligning myself with his left side and hovering my intangible hand over the badge. From over his shoulder, I could see a small decorative table against the wall where he stood. It held a marble bust of what looked like a Roman soldier along with an oversized energy drink that must have been aiding the guard's concentration.

With the same intangible muscle flex, I solidified my index finger and thumb and gently released the clasp of the badge from its position on his blazer. The guard continued to stare straight through me as I lowered the card to waist level and floated it to the table behind him. That was the easy part. Now I just had to get it to the elevator without being noticed. I thought for a moment about saying fuck it and bolting straight for the elevator with the badge in my fingers, but it was too risky since something like that can raise a few eyebrows. That only left one option from what I could figure, one that was louder but certainly more entertaining. I solidified the remaining fingers on my right hand and with my full grip lifted the bust and from behind his back tossed it across the lobby. The statue sailed through the air before crashing down and smashing a mirrored end table into bite-sized chunks. The intense sound of exploding glass rang through the room and sent employees into panic mode. I watched as the formerly low-key guard sprang into action with the intensity that had been simmering in his eyes. He lifted his wrist to his mouth and began barking orders into the sleeve of his jacket. "Wow, this jackass really thinks he's a secret agent," I thought as I waited for the group to gather around the remnants of the table to investigate. Picking up the badge with my still solid fingers, I made my way towards the elevator and repeatedly pressed the call button convinced it would hurry the process along. It took only a second for an elevator to arrive. but it still felt way too long. As the doors finished sliding open, I crammed the card into the slot and pushed the now illuminated button with relief as I sank back away from the panel.

I forget sometimes that I'm stupid. I looked up from where I was standing and could see the guard as he knelt in front of the smashed table, picking up the bust. He realized it was the one that had been on the table behind him, but who threw it? He whispered a few more words into his sleeve before the elevator closing *ding* echoed in the lobby. The unexpected sound caught his attention as his face shot up from the bust to where I now stood. His eyes squinted before turning to shock, a feeling I joined him in as I realized I forgot my hand was still in material form. As the doors closed, I did the only thing that came to mind and with a disembodied floating hand gave him a half-hearted thumbs up.

VII

The express elevator shot past each floor at a speed fast enough to cause waves in my nonexistent stomach. As the discomfort grew it made me wonder if spirits could still vomit. I did still eat, mostly as a hobby, and without going into too much detail I also did *other things* that came along with that. It stood to reason then that if there were such things as soul farts then maybe heavenly heaving also existed. It would have to be an experiment for another time and, with nervous energy, brought myself back into physical being as the car began to slow. A small shift rocked it to a halt as another muted ding signaled the doors. I stepped out into the top floor and a dimly lit foyer designed more like the entrance to a museum than a hotel suite. Two small spotlights hung from the ceiling as they strategically lit a series of four paintings attached to the otherwise bare walls.

As I leaned in to get a better look at the first painting, I could see the subject was a semi-nude woman undressing. She was stylized in a way that was blurry at first but detailed deeper emotions the longer you stared. I peered over at the other three paintings and was impressed. Renoir, Manet, Caillebotte,

Degas; someone put a lot of thought into this collection. All examples of master impressionists, all them featuring nude subjects, and as hard as it was to believe they were all authentic. I studied the brushstrokes of the Manet and had little doubt that they were genuine. Don't judge me here. I'm not trying to be one of those art snob asshats who go on long-winded explanations as they attempt to show off their *understanding* of art. From everything I've experienced, most art critics were a collection of trendy shitheads who were all too afraid to tell the Emperor that his balls were hanging out. I didn't have any desire to join in on that party, but I did know what I was looking at. A few years back I spent some of that free time I mentioned studying art history. Struggling for things to occupy my time I would visit museums and galleries. I even toyed with the possibility of taking up painting so I tried to learn as much as I could about styles and techniques. Who to emulate and who to avoid. Then the whole idea went bust when I realized that having to pack an easel and canvas in the trunk of the cab would be annoying, then the thought of spilling paint on the upholstery put the final nail in the coffin. I did manage to learn a lot in that time though, like how to spot a shitty fake, and for what it's worth, these bad boys were the real thing.

What surprised me as I continued to study the paintings wasn't just that they were originals. Instead, it was how they were hung in a hallway so carelessly, as if they were any other piece of cheap hotel art. They weren't positioned behind safety glass or thick velvet ropes, no sensors or lasers. Hell, for priceless artwork I didn't even see a security camera on any of the walls. It's as if all four pieces almost dared someone to try and take them. I made my way through the foyer and into the main suite as the haphazard display of the paintings continued to nag at me. Who would put such little effort into securing that much value? An uncomfortable thought came to mind. What if it wasn't a risk? What if the owner knew no one would be willing to take them?

Through an ornate archway sat a darkened lounge positioned as the center point of the suite. The dim lights from the foyer bounced off of a few reflective surfaces in the room but left little to be seen. To my left, I could barely make out a well-stocked bar that called my name. I moved through the dark before being reminded of my solid form as I smashed my knee into the sidewall of the bar. "Son of a bitch," escaped through my teeth. I gripped the bar top for leverage and as the pain began to subside ,I ran my hands along the cool surface. It was too dark to see but I could feel the stone top and judging from the paintings, decided it was probably disgustingly overpriced and imported from somewhere exotic. I continued to feel my way down the length of the bar before gently colliding with a glass bottle. "What do we have here?" I said in a tone too loud for a room this silent.

Feeling along the length of the bottle I gripped it by the neck, lifting it above my head so the small amount of light that spilled in from the foyer lit just enough of the label to read. I'll take it as another small streak of luck since I found myself holding a half-filled bottle of 70-year single malt scotch. An expensive whiskey that just like the paintings sat exposed and unguarded. Most of the time I stuck to the cheap shit since alcohol didn't affect me. My thought was why waste money on the good stuff? In this case, when someone else was buying, I could certainly make an exception. Still gripping the bottle by the neck, I swiped my free hand gently over the counter until I heard the sound I was hoping for. I lifted a small rocks glass that had been sitting near the bottle as it *tinged* with the sound of a few half-melted ice cubes.

I raised the rock's glass with my free hand and tossed whatever was left into the darkness of the room before setting it back onto the counter. Since I couldn't see what I was doing I hooked a finger inside the rim and began filling it until I could feel the liquid crest my first knuckle. It wasn't the most elegant way to fill a glass, but it got the job done. I took a small sip of the fragrant liquid and let the complex flavors tickle my throat. Satisfied that I gave the booze the initial respect it deserved then I tossed what was left over down the hatch. At least I pretended to be eloquent for a moment. As I started to pour myself another a slight noise in the darkness startled me. It wasn't the sound of movement or the tapping of footsteps, but a gentle whisper that bounced through the room. "Who are you?" was the question in a reserved feminine voice. I placed my hands back on the countertop as I was reminded that despite the expensive liquor this was what I actually came for. The second shot would have to wait for another time. "I was sent here to pick you up. There's somewhere you need to be, and I've got to get you there." Without hesitation, the gentle voice spoke again. "Where?"

"It's a long story," I reassured the darkness, "but I'll tell you all about it once we get moving. We have a schedule to stick to so it's best for us both if we move this along." I picked up the bottle of scotch, unable to help myself, and took a long uncivilized swig directly from the source. "My eyes aren't working so great in the dark, so I'll tell you what. You see that hallway over there, the only one with the light and the paintings in it?" I gave the hidden voice a moment. "Yes," it broke. "Meet me over there. We'll grab the elevator and I have a car downstairs that will take us where we need to go." The meek voice whispered a weary "Ok" as I could hear us both move.

I remained solid, only occasionally knocking things over in the dark as I made my way without any serious accidents. It was there as I stood just outside the edge of the shadow that I felt a sudden sensation catch me entirely off guard. It was the odd impression of a small incorporeal hand pressing itself into mine as it gave my hand a gentle squeeze. In shock, I looked down to find the last thing I had expected to see tonight. A sight I would never have guessed had I not been there to witness it myself. Standing beside me gently gripping my hand was a child.

VIII

It may not surprise you if I said that I had a general dislike for people. Being in this business I've met more of them than I could count. So trust me when I say most of them turned out to be self-centered, self-aggrandizing, self-righteous assholes. Sure, you may find a decent person here or there but when you step back and look at people as a collective they all have the same insufferable attitude. The narcissistic idea that the moment they die the world suddenly stops spinning because they're no longer in it. The ones heading towards Heaven always have this notion that everyone has been waiting on pins and needles for them to finally show up before the party starts. On the other hand, if they're bound for Hell, they can't seem to comprehend how all those universal rules about not being a shitty person somehow applied to them. People, by and large, are the worst.

Then there are Children. Children are a different story. Where I can confidently say that people will more often than not turn out to be total assholes, I can also say with as much confidence that children are always innocent. Yes, they can be nightmare-inducing snot-nosed little monsters when the mood strikes them but at least they're sincere about it. This isn't just my soft-hearted theory either. It's an actual policy put out by the powers that be ever since the first primate climbed down from the trees and popped out one of those hairless babies you see in the natural history museums. That's why when those on-high in their infinite wisdom make the terrible decision that a child is not long for this world you can at least feel a little comfort in knowing that they will always pass over directly into the light, no exceptions. From the time we are born up until that strange moment when something clicks in your brain and you suddenly snap into adulthood we are all given a first-class ticket to Heaven. No delays and no layovers.

Children, as a matter of fact, don't even need to be shuttled over the same way adults do. Since their transitions are designed to be as comforting as possible, they have their own assigned fleet of "prepubescent post-life transition experts" or *nannies* as we call them. You can think of them as the grandmas of the afterlife. Pleasant motherly types who are especially good at that comforting and consoling nonsense that I prefer to steer clear of.

So hopefully now it makes a little more sense when I tell you what happened next. As I looked down at the sensation and saw the small phantom hand curled inside of mine, I dropped it in panic. Jumping towards the far wall as if that tiny appendage had been a very angry cobra, I let out a startled "What the... *heck*... are you doing here?" It was an odd and unnatural feeling to censor my language, but I was having a difficult time trying to piece together what was taking place. The kid looked at me and laughed as I tried to figure out what was going on. He was about 3 foot something, average kid height I guess; with the same small stumpy hands and round face that every other child seemed to own. He was dressed in dark jeans and a hooded sweatshirt, his shaggy brown hair hung over his eye like one of those sassy teen pop stars the kids love so much these days. I studied him closely in the uncomfortable silence as I tried to convince myself that maybe he was just a little person. The smooth tightness of his young skin and the bright blue backpack slung over his shoulders soon ruined that theory.

I've never been good at guessing ages, but the kid couldn't have been more than 10, and I watched as his amused smile began to fade into concern. "What's your name kid?" I finally managed to get out, trying to break the ice. The kid tossed the hair from his eye and after a moment of contemplation was only able to manage a simple "I don't know." I nodded since I understood all too well. "Ok, well neither do I so we'll move along." I pushed myself off of the wall where I had been doing an outstanding impression of someone cowering and continued with false confidence. "Do you have any idea what's going on? Maybe how you got here, what... happened?" The kid seemed legitimately upset and confused at everything I was saying. He stared at the floor and began shaking his head. "Don't know," he sighed before looking up at me. "What *is* happening? He asked as our eyes met. I broke eye contact first since I didn't want to see the heartbreak. "Well kid I'm not sure yet what happened, and I don't know why. " I knelt beside him and placed my hand on the immaterial spot where his shoulder should be. "But I do know that I'm sorry. For whatever reason, your body has died. Your soul, the real you, has been released and I'm here to take you to where you go next." I stared at the cold stone floor bracing for the soft cries of a child but heard nothing. Puzzled, I looked up to see the kid in thought as he processed the information. "Are you...okay?" I asked, a little confused. He continued to nod and his eyes narrowed slightly, "I'm dead" he said with an understanding that seemed impossible for this age. "I'm dead and I'm scared but there's nothing I can do about it." I found myself in shock but stood up to face the kid. "Wow, I was not expecting that," I gave him my best attempt at comfort. "You know it usually takes people a long time to come to that conclusion. Some never do. You just might be one of the good ones."

It took a moment before I realized that part probably didn't come off as too consoling. Feeling emotionally cornered I rushed to the elevator and pressed the call button more times than necessary "Well, we better get moving. Very busy after all. Schedule, time constraint, appointment." Those last few words were just a panicked jumble, looking for anything to emphasize a sense of urgency. My sentence trailed off facing the elevator door, trying for nonchalance as if crossing kids over was just an everyday part of the job. My best efforts broke as I felt him reaching into my hand again as it hung by my side. My insides sank but I fought the urge to recoil in fear, standing calmly as if we were about to cross a busy street. I'm sure there's some deeper philosophical meaning to that statement that I could try and figure out, but right now I was either too stupid or too confused to wax poetic. After a few more moments within the hushed foyer, the elevator signaled its arrival. I led the kid inside and pressed the button for the lobby. "Alright, so this may get a little strange but here's what's going to happen." I turned to face the kid and settled into my best imitation of someone who wasn't about to shit their pants from anxiety. "When we reach the lobby there are going to be a few people there. Hotel employees mostly. We can see them and we can hear them, but no matter what you do they won't be able to see or hear you. Try not to get hung up on that. Trust me, after a while it's pretty relaxing." The kid tossed more hair out of his eye. "So just follow behind. We'll get you to where you need to be soon enough."

The elevator began to settle into the lobby floor as I dropped my physical being, taking on the same incorporeal form as before. With the kid's hand in mine, I led him through the solid door like mist, and as we passed into the lobby I could see him smile as he realized what we had just done. "Yeah, pretty cool huh?" I asked as he laughed. The guard from earlier was back at his post, except now he was being lectured by an older guy wearing a matching version of the earpiece. My curiosity got the better of me despite the bad timing and I edged in a little closer to hear the low-key conversation.

"I'm telling you it was a hand, just kind of floating in the air. I don't know what the hell it was. It could have been a hologram, or a drone designed to look like a hand. I'm telling you though it was a hand, and it gave me a *thumbs up* when I looked at it." The older man wrinkled the corners of his mouth. "Oh! A hand drone. That makes perfect sense. I was just reading about the military sinking billions of dollars into that research. Now tell me something. Do you think it was a foot drone that kicked the statue across the lobby?" The guard's eyes met the floor as he struggled for an answer. Once it was apparent one wasn't coming the older man continued. "That's not even the biggest issue we have here." He tapped the discouraged guard on the chest where his badge previously hung. "Your card is missing. I don't need to explain to you that a missing all-access card is a major security concern, right? If our Suite guest found out that someone around here had unauthorized access to the top floor, that wouldn't just be your ass, it would be mine too." The younger one scanned the lobby floor impotently. "It's around here somewhere. I had it before the table broke. It must have fallen off, maybe it got kicked under something. I'll find it." The older guard placed a fatherly hand on his back. "You've got 10 minutes to find it and then I have to report it as lost. That means immediate deactivation and termination. Please don't put me in this position." I watched as he pulled his hand back and straightened his tie. "10 minutes. Then come see me whether you find it or not. If you do..." He turned and began walking towards the opposite end of the lobby, "We'll discuss scheduling some off time for you. I think you could use a rest from these night shifts."

The kid and I stood unnoticed as the guard stared at his reflection in the highly polished floor. His sullen face struck me and I couldn't help but feel bad for him. "Alright, give me just a second. I need to take care of this." I dipped around the corner from where the guard was standing and brought myself back into physical existence. "Hey man!" I spoke up to grab his attention. "I couldn't help but overhear that. Sorry for eavesdropping but just a minute ago I saw a card-badge thing hanging out of a slot in that first elevator. Maybe that's yours?" His demeanor became hopeful as he gave me a nod and quickly moved towards the elevator. It took him a few yards before the questions formed in his mind. How did the card get into the elevator, who was I, and how did I overhear his conversation when no one was standing near them? Fully expecting him to ask, I dropped back immaterial as he unsuccessfully looked over his shoulder to find me.

"Why did you do that?" The kid asked as we passed through the thick glass doors. "I take his badge then he gets fired. Soon after, depression sets in and he offs himself. It makes more work for me in the long run. I don't need that shit hanging on my conscience right now." I shook myself, realizing that I was talking to a kid and not another cynical adult. I forced a small, uncomfortably fake laugh. "Ha-ha. What I mean is because it was the right thing to do." The kid rolled his eyes as I changed the subject. "Do you want to see something else pretty neat?" He grinned emphatically in response. With an unnecessary snap of my fingers, I brought the cab back into existence. "Voila. I just made a car magically appear." The rear passenger door of the cab popped open with a creak as I motioned the kid inside. I again cemented myself into physical reality and looked over at the valet once again stationed behind his podium, mouth agape. From his perspective he had just witnessed a car appear from thin air before the driver, me, suddenly poofed into existence as well. I could understand why the situation may have been taking a toll on his sanity. I did the only thing that seemed reasonable in the situation and gave him a playful wink before ducking into the car.

As I started the cab, I turned around to see the kid struggling to find a seatbelt. "You're not going to find one. A buckle or anything. This beauty doesn't need 'em," trying to keep things light. "I should probably just install some at some point. It might calm people down a little." I turned back towards the road and pulled out into the empty street. "Let's roll out," I said into the rearview before an uncomfortable thought struck me like a shovel to the head. It was the jolt of a thought I had somehow repressed, looking down into the passenger seat beside me and the blacked-out requisition form still resting there. It sat folded over to the final page where the single word remained uncensored. The one little word that in all this confusion and excitement I had somehow managed to forget. "Damnation."

The car passed over into the Gray with the interior remaining quiet in stark contradiction to the argument raging in my head. "Kids don't go to Hell! That's one of the rules, there aren't a lot of rules, but that's one of them. There's not a damn thing this kid could have done to set him up for an eternity of whatever goes on down there." My conscience persisted in a jumble of thoughts that were difficult to contain. Then that little voice of self-preservation was quick to reply. "There's a plan for everything and a purpose for everyone. It's beyond us to question why these things happen. Our place is to simply follow orders. These orders say he's going downtown." The battle raged on as I stared through the windshield at the darkened horizon we pushed towards. After some time, the thin mist beyond the car grew darker until we were finally surrounded by a blackness only broken with an occasional series of ever-burning torches illuminating the way. I continued to stare forward, unable to bring myself to look into the back seat, dreading each inch we drew closer.

With no time left, we reached the final stop as I parked the cab along a deep pit glowing red in the light of torches. I killed the engine and sat motionlessly trapped in my thoughts. "Is this it?" He wasn't sure of what to make of the area, but no one ever is. I dropped my hands on the dashboard and rested my forehead against the steering wheel. "Yeah..." was the only word I could push out before popping the door latch and stepping into the darkness. Time moved slowly as I took a few steps towards the passenger door and gripped the squeaking handle. I could see the kid's trusting face look up at me from the back seat with pure innocence in his eyes. It was a look that made this all the more painful. With the rear now open, I turned to rest my back against the driver's door, staring towards the deep pit that resided only a few feet away. The kid crawled out from the backseat and, tightening up his backpack, looked at me to ask "What's next?" Knowing I couldn't explain, I found myself only able to point towards the pit.

The kid acknowledged and with another toss of his hair stepped to the edge of the pit. "How do I get down? Is there a rope?" He asked without fear. I stared at the dark ground and shook my head. With the sensation of being punched in the gut, I forced out a weak "Fall." The kid turned back to the deep abyss beyond. I compelled myself to look up and away. I had seen this happen so many times before, but I couldn't watch this one. That's when I heard one last question I was not prepared for. As he stared forward into the unknown void beyond him the first small crack of fear escaped through his small voice. "Is it going to hurt?"

I wanted to console him, to tell him that nothing would hurt him ever again but I knew that was a lie. Having never seen Hell, I didn't know what went on down there but whatever was in store for him was an eternity of nothing he could have deserved. I wanted to tell him anything that I could that would help. Even if for just a moment, except I couldn't. "I don't know," as I kicked one of the tires in frustration. The kid turned slightly. Giving me a final glance over his shoulder before turning back. It was then with a courage that I had never seen before, courage I don't believe I could ever muster, his heels lifted as his body leaned forward and he braced for the fall.

It caught him by surprise when I grabbed him by the loop on his backpack and yanked him back onto the firm edge of the pit. "This isn't right," I said, finally sure of what to do. While refusing to loosen the grip on his backpack I drug him over to the cab. In total agreement the passenger door popped itself open as I tossed the kid into the back seat. I could see his look of confusion and relief as I slammed the door shut and climbed back behind the wheel. "I don't know what kind of mixed-up bullshit is going on right now, but I know one thing for certain. You're in the wrong place. You taking that fall is not going to hang on my conscience just because some jackass screwed up the paperwork somewhere." I adjusted the mirror so our eyes met. "I'm not going to pretend to understand what's going on but we're going to figure this out. We're going to get answers and this is going to get fixed." I took a deep breath before pressing down on the gas and in a voice that tried to hide how scared I was right now asked, "You like burritos?"

IX

The Burro-Rito. A 24/7 taco stand nested in the center of the city and one of the only places other than the Black Moon Diner where I felt comfortable. Not something that would pass as high-class cuisine by any stretch of the imagination, but it had two important features that warmed my heart. First was the "D-" health code score that hung proudly beside the "order here" window. The yellow grease-stained paper wasn't something many joints in the area would brag about, but it did an excellent job of warding off the trendy foodies that may have been in the mood to slum it with the locals. Second was their famous 2-pound breakfast burrito they called "La Asesina." This masterpiece of gluttony came bathed in green chili and filled with enough eggs that it should have included a replacement heart valve. It was the tortilla-wrapped definition of overconsumption and managed to be the perfect ending to whatever kind of shitty night I was trying to forget. A night just like tonight; and for the first time, I considered ordering two.

I pulled the cab into one of the many free spaces along the side of the stand and locked it into park. The kid and I had just crossed back to Earth a few moments prior, and it struck me that this was the first time I had ever returned with a soul.

The kid sat quietly the entire time, unsure of where we were going but never asked. I on the other hand knew exactly where we were going but was too busy trying to figure out the next step. I had no clue what to do but I tried not to let the kid catch on. "So, burritos. You never did say. You like 'em?" I could see him concentrating too intently for such a mundane question. It was like he was more concerned with trying to remember what a burrito even was rather than if he liked them. "Don't worry about it. Everyone does. Come on, you'll find out in just a moment." I stepped out and began to make my way towards the order window when I noticed the kid still sitting motionless in the back seat. I guess I was so wrapped up in trying to plan our next step that I forgot to tell him how things changed since I crossed him back to Earth. I wet my lips and whistled. Grabbing his attention, I cocked my head towards the stand motioning for him to come along. The kid nodded before reaching down towards the door latch and, with a look of surprise on his face, pulled up as the door swung open. "Yeah, you can touch things again. It's one of the weird side effects of crossing back this way. You need to be a spirit to go over, you need to be solid to come back." I scratched my head for a moment. "Actually, I guess it's not that difficult to understand after all. You're a real boy again, at least until we get you back over. Now come on Pinocchio and I'll explain more after we order." I watched as the kid hopped out of the back seat and slammed the rear door shut. The tinny sound of metal crashing against itself rang through the parking lot. "Woah, relax with the slamming there. The car's got feelings you know. She's an antique." The kid mouthed a silent "sorry" before bounding over to stand beside me.

We eventually made it to the order window and the young guy who ran the place. He wiped his hands on his once-white apron as he picked up the small yellow receipt slip and began jotting down my order from memory. "What's up

Austin? One killer and a large black coffee?" before turning to put everything together. Since I was one of their only repeat customers Chuckie and I usually ignored all pretexts and just got down to business. He knew what I wanted, I knew what I wanted, and the only thing left to do was eat. That's why this time caught him off guard. "Chuckie one second. I think my friend here wants something too." I turned towards the kid "What are you thinking? I think the big boy might be a bit much for you. How about just an egg and cheese?" The kid stared as if I were speaking Klingon and he was too embarrassed to admit he didn't understand. "Trust me on this one. How about a drink too? You'll need one." I turned back towards Chuckie "So, add a regular egg and cheese to that and a small cola." The kid brushed past me and stood on tiptoes to peered through the order window. "Dr. Pepper," he said enthusiastically. "I'd like a Dr. Pepper, please." I smiled down at the kid. "Well then, let's make it a Dr. Pepper." Chuckie pulled the paper hat from his head, clinching it in his hand before making the sign of the cross. "Austin not only changing his order but toting a kid with him? If that isn't a sign that the apocalypse is upon us then I don't know what is." I dropped a twenty inside of the window. "Cute," as I turned to point out the metal picnic tables along the side of the stand. "We'll be sitting out there." With a laugh, Chuckie shifted towards the metal grill as I heard the familiar sizzle.

It was only a few steps away to the closest picnic table. A cold steel mass with a fiberglass top so intricately carved up with graffiti that it could have hung in one of the upscale art galleries downtown. The kid followed and took up a spot across from me, tossing his book bag onto the tabletop. "Let's figure this out, shall we? We need to get you to where you're going and that means we're going to have to answer a few questions." I was speaking to myself more than the kid, but he joined in the conversation anyway. "I thought you said you knew where I was going. You said I was supposed to go to the dark place," with an uncertainty that almost matched mine. "It turns out I was wrong. I know that's where the paperwork said to take you, but it's not where you need to be. To complicate that, where you need to be isn't where I was told to take you."

The kid looked as confused as I felt. "So, we gotta figure out how your paperwork got so royally F...." I caught myself before dropping the big one. Trying to keep in mind that even if this was a monologue the kid was still listening. "Messed up. Why did it get so messed up." The kid snickered knowing what I almost said. "Let's start with the easy stuff. What's your name?" The kid began with a visible concentration in his eyes, trying to force a memory that just wasn't there. "I don't know." "Well then. What do you know? Why were you in the most exclusive suite in the highest-end hotel on this entire coastline? More importantly, why did you die in it?" Sadness crept into his face, and I felt as if I had just sucker-punched him in the soul. His reserves of bravery were beginning to run dry. I sighed, realizing my mistake. "I'm sorry kid. I didn't mean to be so blunt about this. I know it's a hard pill to swallow." Unsure of how to break the tension I placed my hand on his head and tousled his hair gently. "We're going to get this figured out. Let's try a different approach" With another flick he tossed the hair out of his eyes. "Start wherever you can. What is the first thing you can remember?"

It took him a few beats but as he began to piece his few memories together, he finally spoke. "It was dark. It was quiet and very dark." I ran through my memory as well. I pictured myself standing at the bar of the suite and knew what he was referring to. I listened, encouraging him to continue. "I was scared. I didn't know where I was. I heard men talking but I didn't know what they were saying. Then they left and I was alone." I was hopeful that he may have found a memory we could use. "How long were you alone for?" He shrugged while staring at the table as if he were trying to burn a hole through it with his eyes. "It was dark. I tried to feel around but I couldn't touch anything, so I sat down. I sat there in the dark until I finally heard someone else. It was you." I knew everything beyond that point, but we needed to dig a little deeper. "You don't remember anything else? Anything before the dark?" The kid shook his head knowing there wasn't a reason to try for anything else. "Nothing about the men? Just the voices?" He traced his finger over a heart scratched into the tabletop "I heard two voices. I couldn't see anything though. I remember I asked them for help, but I don't think they could hear me." He was right. "Most of the living can't hear spirits. You could have yelled for hours and it wouldn't have done any good."

We sat in the quiet night struggling to piece together something that made sense before the sound of a cheap *order-up* bell snapped us back into existence. Our food sat steaming at the order window while the kid stared into the motionless city streets. He was calm as he gazed into his surroundings. His memories were missing yet something about our situation seemed to give him comfort. I sat the plastic tray down on the table and passed the kid his food along with the tall styrofoam cup. He bent his small head towards the burrito and sniffed at it like a dog inspecting a new toy. With an upturn of his nose, he pushed the plate away slowly, "smells like egg farts." He was right, unfortunately, so I managed the least condescending response I could think of. "Yeah, eggs generally do that," and passed him a straw for his drink. Quickly snapping the paper wrapping off he jabbed the straw through the lid and took a heavy sip of all 23 flavors. As he swallowed, I could see a look of glee pop across his small face. "I love Dr. Pepper," leaked out between sips as he siphoned off the remainder of the liquid. "I think I'm supposed to tell you how caffeine and sugar aren't good for a kid your age but with our current situation it's the least of our worries." I pointed back towards the window, "refills are free here. Knock yourself out." The kid scrambled to his feet and made a beeline for more soda as I listened over my shoulder. "Refill?" Chuckie asked from the window. "That much soda this early in the morning? I feel sorry for your teachers." The sound of ice crackled before the small voice interrupted. "No ice, please. It waters down the taste."

I agreed with the kid. I always hated ice too, but something about what he said struck a chord and I began to think out loud. "You don't like ice." It was a statement of fact, but the kid took it as a question. "Nah, is that weird?" he asked in return before going to work on his drink. "No. Not at all. What is weird is that you managed to remember that you don't like ice." The kid stopped mid-sip to listen. "You couldn't remember what a burrito was, let alone if you like them; but somehow you remembered what eggs smelled like. You remembered that you like Dr. Pepper and you don't like ice. You remember preferences and ideas, but you can't remember your name or anything that happened to you before..." I decided to choose my words carefully. "...before we met," I finished. "all the specifics of your memories are missing. You remember the small things. The things that seem instinctual. The big things though, the *who*, *what* and *where*; those are gone." I was lost in thought trying to make connections. "It's as if the specifics of your life; all the things that would let us know who you were have been taken." A sudden uncomfortable feeling came over me as I remembered the requisition form, "or redacted."

I paused for dramatic effect but with the kid only focused on his soda I was the only one moved by my words. It was becoming clear that the kid wasn't going to be much use when it came to getting this resolved. I stood up from the table and for the first time ever made the regrettable decision to toss the remaining 3 quarters of burrito. "Where are you going?" he asked, suddenly remembering that there were things in this world other than his soda. "I need to make a phone call. There's a friend who might know a little more than we do. You hang tight and I'll be right over there." I pointed towards the back of the building and the small heavily graffitied payphone bolted to the cinderblock wall of the stand. There's a ragged matchbook cover that has spent the last few years in my wallet. It was printed with an outdated logo of the Black Moon Diner on one side and on the other, written in blue pen, was a phone number and a capital "B." I dropped a few quarters into what may have been the only remaining payphone in the city and dialed.

A half dozen unanswered rings turned into a messaging service with a familiar voice. "Hey this is Benny," the voice broke through. "If I know you, I'll call you back. If I don't then feel free to piss off. Or you can leave a message if you think you're so important." A beep punctuated the end of her demure statement. I'll be honest when I say I'm no spring chicken but listening to Benny's message gave me the impression that subtlety is a quality that must wear off over time. "Hey, It's Austin. I've gotten myself into a situation tonight and you're one of the only people I know who would have any clue of what the hell I'm talking about. You know I've never called before but I'm in a tough spot. If you get this message in the next few minutes, call me back. The number is, well, I don't know what the number is." I searched around the phone and, with an extra quarter I found in my pocket, scraped away a sticker of a band called "Assplug" that was covering the digits. "Ok, it looks like 312- 75," but before I could finish a beeping came through the handset. "Do payphones have call waiting?" I asked rhetorically before pressing down on the switch hook. A change in audio tone gave way to a tired-sounding voice. "I don't know who's calling but I just got off work so this better be some life-or-death shit."

The voice was immediately recognizable, which made me feel exceptionally stupid since I forget that those cellular phones everyone uses have some sort of caller ID. "It's Austin. I was just leaving you a message." She interrupted before I could finish, "Austin? Like *dead-guy-taxi* Austin?" she asked quizzically. "Are there any others?" That seemed to perk her up. "Wow! I am seriously amazed. Do you know how many times I've wondered if you even knew how to use a phone? I guess I got my answer. Unless of course this is your first time. Did I take your phone virginity? Tell me, was it difficult, did it take a few attempts to get it to work?" You could hear the smile in her voice. "It's not something I do too often, but you're certainly not my first. Seriously though, I think I need your help." something shifted in the background. "Come on man. After all these years you know I'm here for you. If there's anything you want to talk about I'm more than happy to listen. Especially if it was something gruesome." A high-pitched yawn broke up her speech. "I'll always be here to play therapist. Just let me get a few hours of sleep. You should probably be doing the same." I looked over my shoulder and saw the kid still sitting contently at the table unconcerned with anything going on around him. "It's not like that. I think I may have gotten myself into some trouble and I'm not sure what to do next. I'm not exactly flush with friends. Even less when it comes to people who understand situations like ours." The sound of shoes being kicked off echoed from her end. "Ok. I'm putting you on speaker. You have until the time it takes me to put on my pajamas and get into bed. What's the story?"

I filled her in on all the details of the night. I explained the odd paperwork that was heavily censored. I told her about the dark and extremely overpriced top floor Suite. It was right around the point of mentioning that the pick-up was a kid that she stopped moving. Once I explained how I brought him back over she took me off speaker. "No Shit! You actually crossed him back? I was expecting you to say that you lost a passenger, or the car got broken into. This situation puts you on a whole other level of fucked." Oddly enough her words didn't do much to comfort me. "Yeah, I've come to that conclusion as well, still doesn't answer my questions though. You know, like what do I do from here?" Her usually playful voice took on a serious tone. "I think you have two choices at this point and only you can decide which one is right." I watched the kid sip at his third refill as the first glimpse of dawn broke in the early morning sky. "What are they?" I asked, knowing I wasn't going to like either option. "You could rush him back. Ignore the guilt and just do what you were ordered to do. If you hurry, then there's a good chance that this whole thing will blow over. It's not a fun option but every time you feel guilty about what happened just remind yourself that you were only following orders." The thought left what felt like a rock in the back of my throat. "Or you can tell yourself that it's too late for that and focus now on finding out who he is and more importantly how you're going to get him approved for ascension." She knew my answer before I ever had to speak. "I'm not taking him back," I said. "So, it looks like I need to start finding some answers." I could hear her grinning through her words, "Well then. Let's see, what have you done so far?" The unfinished bulk of my burrito stared back at me from the garbage. "Tried to get something to eat. When that didn't fix anything, I called you."

"No one is going to be confusing you with Elliot Ness any time soon." I ignored the insult and pulled a cigar from the silver case in my jacket pocket. Realizing that I wasn't in the mood to quip she continued. "My suggestion then is to retrace your steps. Find out more about where he was. It's not going to be pleasant, but you'll probably find something related to who he is and what happened." For the second time since making this call, I again felt the weight of my stupidity. "Sure. I was thinking that may help also," in a pointless attempt to save face. "You're a terrible liar. D you still have the paperwork with all the black bars?" I did, since I was supposed to have it submitted by the end of my shift. Now probably wasn't the time to be a stickler for the rules though. "Yeah. I can hold on to it. Why?" "I know a guy. He makes it his business to know answers to strange questions. Let's just say he's always happy to see me. You go check out the Suite again and then get some rest. Meet me tonight at my apartment. 108 Bridgeview terrace, 6th floor, apartment 66."

I didn't say anything because I didn't need to. She could sense my thoughts through the phone. "Shut up. I know it's tacky. Bring the paper and the kid. We'll see if we can get some answers." The basic outline of a plan was beginning to take shape. "Thanks Benny. I owe you for this one." She didn't hesitate "Yeah you do. I want a ride-along sometime and not one of the boring ones. I want to go for one of the really dirty jobs." Hopefully she was joking, at least partially, but I wasn't in the mood for false bravado. "Can I ask you one more thing?" I said as something kept nagging at me. "I've been to the edge of Hell more times than I can count. It's a darkness that you wouldn't think is possible, but I've never seen anything beyond it. When I've pushed souls over, I've heard the screams the whole way down until they just fade out. After all these years... I still never know what happens to them. I need to know. What's it like down there?" Her voice took on the serious tone that felt alien coming from her, but this time it had a tinge of motherly concern. "I've heard stories but it's nothing I would want to repeat. It's also nothing you should know about right now." She took a long pause before finishing her thought. "I will say this. Despite what it may end up costing you, you're making the right decision. I'll see you tonight. We'll get this figured out," and with a click, the call ended.

X

With my best attempt at being playful, I tossed the kid's backpack through the rear passenger window knowing it would be the easiest way of coaxing him back into the cab. I didn't expect him to put up a fight, but with all that was going on I wanted to keep things as light-hearted as possible. We made it about halfway back to the hotel before the kid finally spoke again. "Are you taking me back?" You could hear the apprehension in his voice. "Not entirely. We're just taking a short trip to where I found you. The dark room we were just talking about. We're going back there." Hoping to get ahead of any fear, "but I'm not leaving you. I promise. Until we figure this thing out, you and I are stuck together." Reminding myself that I was talking to a child I did what I could to remain upbeat. "We're going to go investigate. See if we can find anything that might tell us a little more about what happened." Reaching over my head, I extended my hand into the seat behind me. "So, as long as we're working on this thing; Partners?" The small soft hand gripped mine and wrench it up and down. "Fine," came the excited voice from the back, "You're my Watson."

I tried not to let my concern appear too obvious. It wasn't exactly an obscure reference since Sherlock Holmes was almost universally known. When the kid didn't even know his name but could still somehow reference Watson, it raised a lot more questions. Then I thought about seeing Andy in the elevator. It struck me that he didn't just remember who I was, but he also remembered everything about his own life. So why couldn't I? More importantly right now, why couldn't the kid? We pulled through the last few blocks to the hotel when I heard the soft sound of a zipper coming from the back seat. The sudden too common feeling of idiocy hit me again. The damn backpack. "You know, you've had that thing on since I picked you up." Playing it off like the idea had been bouncing around in my head for a while and I was waiting for the kid to catch up. "Why don't we start there?" I parked along a side street near the hotel before turning around to see the kid already rummaging through the bag. From inside he pulled out a small pencil box that rattled with something inside. He popped the lid to reveal a bundle of colored pencils and a few well-worn erasers. "Come on! You're getting pencil shavings all over the seat. Close it up. See what else is in there." A spiral notebook came out next. Half of the pages must have been missing from the collection of perforated strips nested in the center of the wire binding. The kid flipped through what remained of the book but found only blank pages. "Ok. Nothing much helped there. Anything else inside?" He shook his head apologetically and as he pushed the notebook back into the bag a slight metal ping could be heard as its spine scraped against something. The kid reached elbow deep within the bookbag, pulling out a spark of hope. "A cell phone? Aren't you a little young to have a device like that? I don't even carry one" I managed to sound even older than I was. "May I see it?" The kid handed it over as my brief hope washed away. I held the phone up to the emerging morning sun to see a beam of light running through a knitting needle-sized hole pierced directly through the center. "I've seen these things accidentally smashed up before. It's pretty common. In fact, I have a suspicion that they're designed to break easily so you have to keep buying new ones." I held the phone up to my face so the kid could see my eye through the hole. "But call me crazy; I don't think this was an accident." To demonstrate I fit my pinky finger through the center. "I may be going out on a limb here but I'm going to assume someone didn't want anyone seeing whatever was on here." I gently tossed the phone back to the kid. "Better hold on to it anyways. You never know about these sorts of things."

The bag zipped shut before he slipped it over his shoulders. "Alright, we're close enough. Let's keep this discrete and just hoof it over from here." I stepped out of the cab and opened the back door for him. As we walked, I used the time to clear my mind and explain a few things. "Before we go in there's some stuff you need to understand. First and foremost is the idea of what you are now. That's a pretty important distinction when it comes to how we interact with people." I paused and corrected myself. "Living people." The kid's short legs pumped harder than mine as he tried to match my strides. "I'm dead," he said confused. "Isn't that what I am?" I pulled the flask from my jacket pocket and shook it against my ear, annoyed as I realized I had forgotten to refill it. "Not anymore. Now you're like me. You're not dead but you're also not alive." His interest was piqued "like a zombie?"

I blame movies for kids' obsession with zombies. Every horror fanatic or imaginative kid has some weird obsession with them now so I couldn't tell if his question was a hopeful one. "You see that guy over there?" Across the intersection was an early morning dog walker intently focused on his text messages. "Look at him. Is your first thought to go over there and crack his head open. Maybe take a few bites of whatever you find inside?" A look of disgust came over the kid as he shook his head. "Then it's safe to say that you're not a zombie. You and I are something different. My old day shift partner used to refer to us as *The Alius*, which I always thought had a cool ring to it. I looked it up and it's just Latin for *Other*." I stopped walking and turned to face him, kneeling to eye level. "The name doesn't matter. What matters is that while you're here back on Earth you can do things that living people can't. Some of the normal laws of nature and science don't apply to you anymore. We'll say you've picked up a few new talents" The kid smiled a deep toothy grin. "Like a mutant?"

I'm not proud that my first response in most situations was to shit on someone's excitement but reminding myself that he was just a kid helped keep my response to just an eye roll. "Don't get too excited. You're not going to be shooting eye lasers anytime soon." I lifted his hand and held up a few of his fingers, drawing his attention to them as we started counting them off. "First. Since you're not alive you won't age. That means until we get this figured out, I hope 10, or however old you are, is a fun age to stay at." With my help his pointer finger curled down. "Second. You don't breathe, you don't bleed, and you can't be hurt. Not permanently at least. Now I haven't gone out of my way to test this but the entire *not being alive* thing should also mean we can't be killed." His middle finger went down next. "Third. I was enlisted into this job and shipped back here, but you on the other hand were smuggled over. Because of that, I don't know the limit of what you can and cannot do. I also don't know what's going to happen if we don't find some answers. Let's assume that it's not going to be good." I pushed down his ring finger emphasizing my next words. "That leaves the last but most important part." I quickly reached over and flicked his earlobe. An immediate "Ow," squeaked out as he cupped his ear to dull the sudden pain. "Sorry, but I needed you to understand. Even though you can't be permanently hurt you can absolutely still feel pain. Do you remember about an hour ago when something like that would have passed straight through you?" He dropped his hand back to his side and gave me an annoyed nod. "Good because now you need to go back to that. At least for a moment. It's something others like us can do but it's going to take a little work." I grabbed both of his hands and held them out in front of him inside of mine. "I need you to listen to me. I wouldn't do this unless it was necessary, but I have no other choice. In three seconds I'm going to punch you in the chest as hard as I can, and you know what? It's going to really *really* hurt."

I pulled back my fist in an exaggerated motion. I'm sure a lot of parenting experts would say that throwing your kid into the deep end of the pool and challenging them to sink or swim isn't the right way to teach them. Then again, those same experts have the luxury of time and patience on their side. They've never been cornered and forced to teach a kid to swim for their lives when they're only minutes away from a flash flood, and that's exactly where we were. We were standing on the banks before a tidal wave of metaphysical shit, and I needed the kid to start doggy paddling. "Here we go. One!" I tightened my knuckles so they audibly popped under the pressure. "Two. I'm sorry kid." I could see his jaw tighten in fear as he panicked not knowing if I was serious. "Three!" With an exhale I swung my fist forward burying it as hard as I could in his chest.

"You can open your eyes," I said calmly. His tight grimace softened as he peeled open clenched eyelids to see my fist floating in the haze of his chest. "I thought it would be cooler to show you rather than try to explain." The kid stepped back and watched as my forearm and hand emerged from his torso. "That's awesome!" he said as he took an open-handed swing at my face, laughing as it passed through my head unimpeded. He was never in any real danger. I knew from experience that fear and excitement would instinctively shift his form as a means of protection, like blinking right before a sneeze so the pressure doesn't catapult your eyes from your head. At least that's what I was hoping was going to happen. Devil's advocate let's say I was wrong. Yeah, it would have hurt him, probably even knocked him back a few feet, but the only permanent damage would be psychological. Remember, I never claimed to be good with kids.

We stood on the quiet street as I dropped my physical form to match his and placed my hand on his head. The kid pushed it off and shook the hair from his eyes. "You need to remember that when you're like this it's just like before. It's as if you don't exist to any living person around you. You're nothing more than a spirit." I turned and began to make my way back towards the Grand Park with the kid quickly in tow. "If we find some free time I'll show you how to solidify individual parts of your body. Wait until you see people's reaction when you manifest a body with no head."

Judging from the morning sun I had to guess it was around 7 am, and for the first time in over 60 years I missed the deadline for turning in my forms. It gave me a queasy feeling, but I knew we couldn't stop now. We needed to keep pushing forward and get this fixed since I could only assume that every second mattered. Sure, screwing with the valet was fun, but we had to get to the suite quickly while remaining inconspicuous. That meant stairs, and knowing there had to be an employee entrance somewhere around the back we cut through an alley towards the rear of the building hoping to find a way in.

A soft "cool!" came from the kid before I turned to see him further behind than I expected. He stood in the entry to the alley as his spirit arm went elbow deep within a brick wall. I gave him a moment, waiting for him to get it out of his system, but it only seemed to encourage him to explore further. He pushed his head through the wall, curious to see what was on the other side. "It's just a boring old closet full of brooms and stuff," disappointed as he withdrew himself. "Isn't that amazing, though? I bet we could do all kinds of cool stuff. We could get into any R-rated movie we want, or sneak into Six Flags after it closes. I could be like a bank robber!" I pulled him back by the strap of his book bag before he could push himself any further through the wall. "Alright, babyface. I don't think planning the next great crime spree will improve your chances of getting into heaven any sooner." Taking this as a learning opportunity, I pulled us both halfway through the wall, leaning into the darkened broom closet beyond. "Besides. Yeah, you can get in, but did you ever consider how you would get something solid back out?" I solidified my hand and grabbed a mop before leaning back through the wall. The solid handle popped against the interior wall and crashed to the floor as the kid leaned back out with a look of embarrassment. "If you ever figure out how that whole *pulling a solid object through a solid object* thing would work, just let me know. Until then, let's stick to one plan."

I turned to keep moving towards the rear of the hotel, checking more often that the kid was following. "We should be able to find a way back in. You need to stay incorporeal until I say otherwise." The kid looked at me not understanding, "In a what?" We were dangerously close to getting stuck in an Abbott and Costello routine. "Incorporeal," then repeating it a little slower "In-Cap-Or-E-ul. It means not made of anything, hollow," still walking as I turned and passed my hand through another wall to demonstrate. "Invisible just like you are now. You need to stay like this. If anything goes wrong or if I tell you to switch for some reason, all you need to do is use your fear just like you did to get this way. If your body thinks you have to be solid, to prevent something bad from happening, guess what? You'll be solid again." The kid gave me another confirming nod. I was beginning to worry if all these nods meant he understood what I was saying or was he just trying to shut me up. As we rounded the back of the building several morning delivery trucks were parked along a loading bay leading into the hotel. "Bingo," I whispered to the kid as I pointed out the handleless door with the red plastic "Fire Exit" sign bolted to it. "Are you ready for some exercise? Be thankful your lungs don't work anymore."

XI

Climbing Sixty-two floors without breaking a sweat is something most people would brag about, except the kid and I couldn't perspire even if we wanted to so the accomplishment lost a lot of its magic. It was kind of like bragging about spending an hour on a treadmill when you were wearing roller skates. All you've accomplished is wasting time. In this case, it was time we didn't have. Still, we endured the monotony of the climb rather than risk stealing another access card for the elevator.

"We're almost there. Now when we go in, please stay behind me. You have to trust me and do exactly what I say when I say. If I tell you to stay still, be a statue, and if I tell you to look at your feet, then stare at them like someone is about to steal your shoes the moment you blink. Is this understood?" The kid bounded up a few stairs to grab a position in front of me. "Why? I thought no one could see us." I kept pushing forward and climbed past him. "I'm not worried about anyone seeing you. I'm worried about what you might see." The thought of what we were about to walk into struck the kid hard as I stopped a few steps above his head. "I've got your back, and you have to have mine. Just listen to what I tell you and I promise this will all be over soon. Keep your ears open. If you hear anyone coming, let me know. You're my lookout" It was the best I could do to give the kid the false sense that I knew what the hell I was doing.

The final steps of the stairwell wound around to a cement landing and solid steel slab of a door that hung imposingly to protect the suite. It was in stark contrast to the sixty-plus others we had passed on the way up. The generic hotel doors are designed to blend into their surroundings and allow guests to escape in emergencies. Then there was the steel door of the suite, with a design that would make most bank vaults feel inadequate and placed here to keep assholes like me away from whatever was on the other side. Luckily, I had a few more skills than your average art thief. "Remember what I said," I reminded the kid as I took his hand in mine and passed effortlessly through the heavy steel.

As we pulled our immaterial selves to the other side, we passed through a tacky set of velvet drapes strategically hung to hide the door from view. The kid turned to take in the room as I continued to stare at the drapery. "Well, good. God knows whoever stays here would hate for something like a fire exit to interrupt the general design flow of this place." My words trailed off as I turned to see the entirety of the room surrounding us. Sure, I had been here before, but the memories of my last experience could be summed up with the words "dark" and "whiskey." In the light of day, I would also add "holy shit" and the cash register "cha-ching" sound you hear in cartoons. It was decorated in a way that exuded wealth by definition. Not "rich" or "expensive" since the hotel's lobby oozed those qualities and proved money didn't also buy taste. Instead, this room radiated the idea that money was low on the list of importance.

I stepped away from the door and into the great room that stretched in front of us. Towards the center sat the bar I stumbled my way up to only hours before with the glass still sitting where I had left it. Beyond the bar, the room was laid out in a way that felt like a perfect blend of library, entertaining space, and personal museum. The handmade furniture throughout looked simultaneously comfortable and too expensive to consider touching. I crossed over to a small seating area only a few feet away. Chairs older than most of this city were arranged near a cart that held a delicate tea set. I picked up the pot and glanced over the design. There was a small banner with "White Star Line " painted into the glazing. "White Star Line. Why does that sound familiar?" I looked down at the kid standing beside me as he shrugged with complete indifference. While turning the pot over in my hands I felt my knees almost buckle as I read the small black inscription printed neatly below. "RMS Titanic."

  The kid, still immaterial, extended himself on nonexistent toes trying to peer over my arm at what I was reading. "What is it?" with an annoyed curiosity, "Just some kind of teapot?" I shook my head and turned the pot right side up. "No. I'm pretty sure what we have here is the definition of history." I placed the pot back on the serving cart and looked across the room towards the foyer that so brashly displayed the priceless paintings. "Almost priceless and sitting around like any other cheap knick-knack." An unintentional laugh of disbelief came as I lifted the lid to peek inside. "And of course, someone used it recently without even thinking about cleaning it afterward." All of this was lost on the kid as he just stared at me. "So, what does that mean?" Attempting to comprehend. "It's like finding Excalibur and using it to cut up sandwiches." I waited for a moment to see if I would have to cliff notes King Arthur to the kid, surprised that the simile seemed to work. "It means whoever has the money to own this place isn't weighed down by something as silly as sentimentality."

  It was probably still going over the kid's head since I haven't had much practice with anyone under 15 for more than

half a century. "Ignore it. Let's see if we can find anything else."
I took a moment to glance around the suite while trying to
form a plan of where to begin. The suite was set up with most
of the space used as a grand lobby subdivided into quarters. On
one side were the dining area and lounge, while I stood in what
must have been the library and entertainment area. At the end
of each section were hallways that must have led to bedrooms
and more. With the suite's open floor plan, I could see there
wasn't much for us in the main area unless our goal was to
browse through poorly secured antiques. Taking my best guess
the far hallway seemed as good of a place as any to start.

The kid followed behind as we began peeking into each
room that splintered off. There was a sterile kitchen that must
have been a private chef's dream, a bathroom larger than most
of the city's apartments, and a few ornate bedrooms full of
unused antique furniture. As we finished up the last bedroom
on this end, I looked down at the kid who was scanning the
room along with me. "Anything jumping out at you yet? I
know it was dark, but what about smells, sounds, anything feel
familiar?" The kid must have been confident in his answer since
he didn't bother to look around before telling me "No."
"You're not even looking. How can you be so sure?" With a
devious grin he pointed to the opposite end of the suite. "I was
over there somewhere." I repressed the growing frustration
with the time we had wasted. "Well, let's move over there then."
Across the great room we found another bathroom, a personal
gym that contained the most technologically advanced
equipment on the entire floor, and another series of bedrooms
also unused. As we reached the end of the hallway, I could see
the kid tense up as we neared the final door. "You hold off back
here. Let me see what's inside."

Beyond the door was a bedroom like the others within
the suite, tastefully decorated but carried a sense of disuse. At
least that's how the room would have felt had it not been for

the meticulously laid out plastic sheets that stretched from floor to ceiling. Each was heavily painted with large black symbols unlike anything I had seen before and covered nearly every aspect of the room. Everything except the prominent four-post bed that sat at the center with its canopy curtains drawn closed. On the spooky shit meter, someone had dialed this room up to 11.

I bit my lip and knew I wouldn't like what I was about to find. I pushed myself towards the bed instinctively, knowing that this was what we had come to find. I moved forward, hearing plastic crunch under my feet and seeing dried painted symbols flake away with each step. It was only a few feet before I reached the bedside, delaying what I had to do for as long as I could. Knowing that we had no time left to spare, I placed my hand on the curtain, preparing for what was within. I took a deep breath and pulled back the veil.

I have been doing this job for a long time. In all my experiences, I have seen a lot of difficult things to take in. Murders, accidents, suicides, and with all them I've found a way to move past them quickly. This was different. I'll spare you the details of what I saw and instead tell you that some things burn themselves into your soul and, no matter how hard you try to forget them, you carry them with you forever. Inside of the curtained-off walls of the bed was the kid, or at least what was once the kid, and it was something I will never be able to forget. I quickly jerked my attention down to the floor and tried to remind myself that anything within that room, no matter what had happened, was no longer the kid. It was simply an empty shell. The discarded wrapper of what he once was, with his true self now standing right outside that door.

I took another deep breath and with willpower I hoped never to use again, peered up at the bed looking for answers. I repressed the gut-wrenching repulsion within me and scanned from base to headboard, spotting something that the shock had previously overshadowed. Laying to the kid's right was a small ornate silver dagger, blade painted over with slowly drying blood. I pulled it from the bed and wiped the blade clean with a corner of the sheet as I turned it over in my hand. A deep red uncut gemstone was recessed into the base of the handle and surrounded by a series of carved symbols. Symbols that matched the ones painted on the sheeting throughout the room. I looked over what remained of the body one last time and noticed a deep cut the exact size and shape of the dagger blade on his forehead. It was a wound that seemed unnecessary compared to everything else that had occurred, but it must have served some purpose. I ripped a small section of the sheet and used it to wrap the dagger before placing it within the breast pocket of my coat. Then with a sense of sentimentality, I held the kid's hand within mine and looked towards the door that his spirit stood behind before quietly whispering, "I'm sorry."

"Should I come in now?" I could hear the apprehension in the small, timid voice as he hid. "Nah, nothing much to see here. I'm coming out now," was the best I could come up with as I pulled the canopy drapes closed once again. I wanted to do more since it felt obscene leaving everything for some poor maid to find. Still, I reminded myself that I was walking away from nothing more than a husk and the best thing I could do for him now was focus on the soul that stood outside. I could feel the blade shift in my breast pocket as I walked from the room. Each tap of it against my chest counted out another question with no answer. Who was the kid, and why him? Who could have done this? Why did they choose here? Most importantly, how could the result of something this unjust be final damnation to Hell? Back in the hallway, I pulled the door closed tightly. "Did you find anything?" The kid looked up at me with a hopeful expression. but I was unable to look him in the eye. "I found...something. Mostly more questions, none of which I can seem to answer. We're going to have to call in more help."

We made our way back towards the fire exit, pulling back the drapery as it occurred to me that I wouldn't be unable to pass through the steel with the knife I now had in my pocket. I hoped there wouldn't be an alarm connected to the door, but as I pushed slowly on the latch bar, a loud buzz rang through the suite. "Ok, time for a backup plan that I haven't come up with yet. For now, start running." We made our way into the stairwell and began descending the steps as quickly as possible. As we rounded our tenth floor down, a door slammed open above as a series of footsteps pounded down after us. It wouldn't take long for them to catch up to us and I wasn't about to hand over the knife. "Listen kid, stay incorporeal just as you are. They can't see you, which means you aren't on whatever security cameras they have hidden around here. I can't say the same for myself. Remember that no matter what happens, hold onto that feeling of being invisible. They may catch up with us, but they won't see you. Keep moving and head back towards where we parked. I'll be waiting for you." He seemed to understand but couldn't help to ask, "where are you going?" I peered over the edge of the railing in the stairwell.

"We have to lose them. If those men catch up to us, I can't go incorporeal. If I do, we'll lose the one clue we have so far. I also know we can't outrun them, so I have an idea." Each floor wound around the wall of the square fire escape leaving an open center that led to the ground floor. I stopped running and climbed over the rail, standing on the ledge that led to the drop. "You're going to have to trust me on this one. Remember how I said we couldn't get hurt?" and with that, I let go of the railing and finished the thought in my head as I fell past each floor. "But we sure as hell can feel pain."

XII

I don't know how many people have lived to describe the sensation of falling almost 50 stories onto a concrete floor. Speaking as someone who has experienced it, I can tell you that it's interesting to say the least. The best way I can describe it would be the feeling of time slowing to a crawl while simultaneously speeding up. Every moment you're clutched by gravity as the world goes silent and you prepare for the inevitable messy conclusion. In a way it was very peaceful, or it was until my ankles shattered and my shins were pushed up through my midsection, puncturing a few extra assholes. It's the kind of extreme pain that only the non-living like myself can genuinely enjoy without being interrupted by that annoying thing called death.

I lay crumpled in the center of the ground floor, giving my best impression of a well-loved ragdoll while mentally struggling to come to grips with my senses. With far more effort than I wanted to exert, I pushed myself into an incorporeal state, wondering why the hell I didn't do this before hitting the ground? I laid there and made a mental note for next time before returning to a solid form now fully healed. A couple years back, I stumbled onto this little trick when I was patching a hole in the warehouse's roof and slipped. Shifting between forms allowed me to quickly recover from whatever injuries I may have stooge'ed upon myself. Unfortunately, as I mentioned a few times, the wounds don't last long, but I'll be damned if the pain doesn't.

Fully healed but still reeling from the trauma, I stood on shaky feet before shuffling into the street. It would take a little while for the pain to subside so out of necessity I focused on remembering how the hell humans were supposed to walk. *Right, left, left*, no, that's wrong. *Right* again, then *left*. Keep switching back and forth. I settled into the pattern and continued along hoping I didn't do all this for nothing. Closing the gap, I was able to move in a way that almost resembled a natural person as I reached the cab. I fell into the driver's seat and, hoping to avoid any pursuers, reclined to the furthest position possible. It was also an excellent excuse to shut my eyes for a moment and take in everything that had just happened. I placed my hand over my chest pocket and felt the knife was secure. It was a relief knowing I still had it, but what would I do with it?

For a moment, while sitting alone in the silent cab, I couldn't help but worry about the kind of trouble I was about to bring down on myself. More so, why was I even doing it? I've kept my head down and did as I was told all these years. I accepted that there are beings whose entire existence was predicated on pulling just the right levers and putting things together to fit in with that famous *Master Plan*. Why did I let some stupid emotions screw over my winning streak? The second-guessing quickly subsided when the images of what someone had done to the kid pushed themselves back into my thoughts. Something more was going on here. Some sinister slipping of the gears that spin the world, and with the unjust way the kid was forced to exit, I'd throw myself off of as many buildings as I had to before I let him suffer down south because of some bullshit clerical error.

"Are you still alive?" surprising me from the back seat. Startled and flinging the reclined seat forward; I smashed my forehead against the rearview mirror. "No, and neither are you." I rubbed at the spot where a lump would have formed on anyone else and repressed my urge to curse. "We're still moving, though, and that's the important thing. Are they still looking for us?" The kid shook his head, expecting me to ask the question. "They ran past me down the stairs, and just like you said, they couldn't see me. When I got outside, they were already going back in. It looked like they were giving up." Building security must have been too focused on jogging down the stairway to appreciate my swan dive to the ground floor. They didn't have much to work with since no blood or body was left behind on the cement. They'll probably chalk it up to a malfunctioning door sensor or something. "Good. One less complication to an already jumbled mess is a welcomed relief."

I fixed the mirror back into a position I could use and started the cab. It was time to find some answers and not just more questions, which would require reaching out to anyone who might know something. Unfortunately, I needed to figure out who that was. In all the time I've been tied to this job, I've met more people than I could count. There were so many faces and stories that passed through the back seat day in and day out. When it came to knowing people though, and I mean truly knowing them, my pool was sadly shallow. There was Benny, and God bless her I'm sure she was trying to find out anything she could for me just from the short call we had earlier. Yet I couldn't put all my dependence on her alone, so it was time to expand. I knew a few others out there, but most were acquaintances limited to the familiar faces of the diner regulars and a small number of other Charons I knew that worked the city. Neither of those groups had anyone that I could depend on, at least not in a way where I could call someone up with a "Hey, someone killed this kid and I stole him back from Hell. Any idea why?" Knowing I had to start somewhere and not wanting to risk wearing out my welcome at the Diner, the other drivers might be my best bet. Considering the weird shit we see day in day out, there was a chance someone might have picked up on some info.

"We're going to head back to my place. I need to make a few more phone calls and figure out where we go from here. You should probably get some sleep too." The kid crossed his arms and slumped back against the seat. "I'm dead. Why does a dead person need sleep?" He pushed back with a childish demeanor that did well to remind me that he was, in fact, a child. I held the urge to laugh directly in his face and tried out my best *father knows best* voice. "Because you do and because I said. Remember that deal where you do as I say, when I say?" I looked through the mirrors and pulled onto the street. "But if the question is what is the functional purpose of sleeping for those like us, then I'll happily tell you." The kid must have been getting cranky since he dug his heels into the pouting act. "When you're alive, sleep is important to help rest the body. It's like a reset button we press in preparation for another day. When you're like us, sleep does the same thing for your mind and the soul." I tapped the side of my temple with my finger for emphasis. "You can only fill a glass up so much before things start to spill out. Without sleep, all thoughts and memories can just start to run over each other. Before you know it, you've been going nonstop for a month and can't seem to figure out if you ate that hamburger two hours or two weeks ago." The kid uncrossed his arms as a subtle sign of submission.

I turned the car into an empty alleyway to avoid commuter traffic. "Sleep helps keep you sane. It's the period you put on the end of the day's sentence and how you empty that glass so it doesn't run over." I could see that his act had almost completely faded. "Trust me, after a while; sleep is the part of the day you look forward to the most." Morning fog was setting in heavily in the back-alley streets as I slowed to a cautious pace. Most of these passages were one way and rarely used. Driving these streets for so long earned me the benefit of getting acquainted with every back alleyway and side street, it was how I moved through the city as quickly as possible while remaining relatively unnoticed. Not an easy thing to do in an antique foreign taxi with a personality of its own. We pushed forward through the thick white fog, twisting through the narrow side streets towards the warehouse.

It finally started to strike me as strange when I noticed the fog getting thicker with each passing moment. An immediate case of deja vu struck as the streets began to look more like... The Gray. I clenched the wheel tighter and leaned heavier on the gas pedal, trying not to show concern so I wouldn't scare the kid. Was the fog just a precursor to a nasty autumn downpour, or were we driving headlong into an ethereal shitstorm? I tried checking to see if the sun was still visible in the sky when a new and unexpected thought struck me out of nowhere. *Asphalt hurts like hell.*

Physics was never my science of choice. From my ignorant perspective it feels like a concentration devoted to questions I either already had answers for or didn't care about. So, after acknowledging that I'm a moron, I'll admit that I don't know much about speed theories and how it affects the world around us. I can tell you, though, that I am fully aware that the term "fast" is relative. For example, a person walking 4 MPH might consider themselves to be moving "fast." Put that same person on a bicycle, and 4 MPH becomes "slow." In an example more closely related to my current situation, cautiously driving through a thick bank of fog at 35 MPH doesn't seem fast. That is until you find yourself sliding ass first across the asphalt of a back alley. At that moment, 35 MPH meets every requirement to become "Holy shit, that's fast!" That was the position I found myself in now.

Through no action of mine, the cab suddenly vanished. Not wrecked or locked up, not lifted into the heavens by an unseen crane. No, it was simply gone. That left me skidding snow sled style along the asphalt before switching to a less comfortable end-over-end tumble. I did my best to tuck and roll through the alley taking in the swirling world around me. I managed to get a glimpse of the kid moving behind me at a slower pace. Somehow, he twisted himself into a slightly more comfortable-looking rolling pin spin, and there was a chance he was even enjoying this. With minor relief, I also noticed an odd metallic scraping coming from somewhere behind me but the rhythmic bouncing of my head off of the pavement was too distracting to figure out what it was.

After a few more feet the world settled itself into a single position. I caught sight of the kid rolling to a safe halt a few yards to my left behind a large green dumpster. Lying on my side and trying to decide exactly which part of my body hurt the worst, I pushed onto my stomach and raised onto all fours, taking inventory with each movement. Two feet, check; glad I wouldn't need to go track those down. Two arms; always a good sign. I moved my neck with a series of ungodly sounding pops, but the motion still worked. all the significant bits and pieces seemed to be there still. Not bad, considering I started this adventure off inside of a moving car.

Oh yeah, the cab. Where the hell did that thing go? I raised to my knees, and with a chorus of cracks that would make a bowl of Rice Krispies jealous, I turned towards the far end of the alley. The heavy fog was too thick to make out much beyond a few yards, but I could tell that the cab was nowhere around us. I scratched my head in a stupefied gesture that only a person with no clue about what was going on could pull off and turned towards the kid to see him sit up. He was resting his back against the dumpster and had no apparent wounds. The sound of something splashing through a puddle bounced between the buildings as the noise began to take shape.

A tall thin figure emerged from the mist. Clad in a brilliant white cloak that radiated purity in such a way that made the fog surrounding it seem dingy. The figure made a beeline straight for me as the small cracking voice of the kid whispered, "What is that?" I tried to move my bruised jaw out of its stuck position but failed to get any cooperation from my body. If I could have answered the kid, I would have told him the words that echoed in my head and seemed to freeze on the tip of my tongue.

"It's a Fucking Angel..."

XIII

Angels. It's difficult to say much about them since I'm not sure where the line between fact and fiction begins. Yes, they're talked about by souls in The Gray, but what they say never amounts to much more than rumors passed around by people who probably know even less than you and I. Despite that, most of the stories include a few basic facts that seem to persist.

First is where they came from, and everything I've heard pegs Angels as the firstborn creation of God. That is, whoever of whatever God is. (*That's a question far beyond my paygrade.*) They were the rough draft. The early sketch that appeared in almost all aspects to be utter perfection but still disappointed their creator. So instead, God (*He? It?*) moved on to their final masterpiece, us. I know that sounds a little backward. How could you create something perfect just to toss it away in favor of something so broken? That was easy because perfection is boring. Any artist will tell you that beauty exists in flaws. So as God worked the seven-day magic piecing us together, the angels were sidelined and forced to watch. I could only imagine that led to some uncomfortable jealousy.

Next is what they do. That's something I still can't put my finger on yet. Where demons will possess any available body they can get their hands on, causing trouble, perpetrating sins, and just generally being assholes; angels keep it low-key. They act like heaven's KGB from the best I can tell. Staying in the shadows and only making their presence known when necessary. Those times when you know you've taken a running dive headfirst into the turbulent waters of shit creek. Unfortunately, it looked like that's where I was right now, no paddle in sight.

The angel moved with frightening confidence as it approached. White boots gliding over the pavement with a precision that barely made a sound. I watched as its cloak split open along the center, unfurling over bare shoulders. From beneath the cape was brilliant white leather armor unlike anything I had ever seen. The angel reached up with a graceful hand and pulled back the hood revealing her smooth snow-white head absent of any hair. A head that, when caught from just the right angle, seemed to radiate a light of its own. She was both breathtaking and terrifying. Perfection of a kind I had never seen. As if she was carved from a single piece of otherworldly ivory. I kneeled in awe of her, slack jawed as I took in the wholeness of her virtue, and that's when the bitch kicked me right in the chin.

Have you ever been clocked hard in the jaw? It's a magical experience. The closest thing to time travel you'll probably ever experience. One moment you're standing there (or, in my case, kneeling) and the next you're clawing your way back out of some very dark corner of your mind trying to figure out where you are and how you got there. I was struggling with those very odd concepts right now when I put my finger back on one thought. "She kicked me!"

That wasn't exactly true. Sure, I got punted right in the kisser, that couldn't have been truer had I painted a target on my cheek and installed a homing device inside her boot. No. The wrong part was where I kept saying "her." *She* wasn't a *she* at all. Instead, *she* was more of a *they*. You see, angels don't have genders. There are no boy angels or girl angels. No separate angel dressing rooms. No arguments over which angels should hold the doors for the others. There are only angels. It goes back to that earlier analogy of God's first draft at sentience. Suppose you know that you are only working on a rough sketch. Why bother putting effort into the overly complicated genitalia portion? Nope, not needed, and although the angel gave off a very feminine physical impression, it was unfair to call them *her*.

I crawled back to all fours, a position that was becoming too familiar as of late. My neck popped again as I craned my head upwards to see the angel standing over me. The disgust on their face was so intense that I almost felt as if I could taste it. I was still trying to decide if I had the strength to stand when a voice broke through the silence. Feminine and stern, militant in every sense of the term. "Ferryman Austin." My vision became a little more focused. "Charon," I thought to correct the angel, but the clicking sounds my jaw made reminded me to shut the hell up. "You have been accused of failing to complete your entrusted duties. Unauthorized usage of your transportation, willfully disobeying your given assignment, and the un-sanctioned return of a human soul across the divide. How do you respond to these charges?

Never being comfortable in a vulnerable position, I struggled back to my feet and faced the angel head-on. Yes, they stood a good foot taller than I was. Perhaps they had more musculature in just their legs than I did throughout my entire body. I can also admit that they could break every bone in my body without making a sound, but did they know that I knew that? Probably not, and besides, you may have noticed that I'm not a big fan of anyone trying to intimidate me. "Yeah" I reached into my jacket and pulled the flask out. Taking a sip of the aged scotch I snuck into it from our return to the suite. After swallowing, I offered it out. "What was the question?"

With a single remarkable motion, the angel backhanded the flask from my grip before bringing their palm back across my jaw with a thunderous clap. I don't think I need to explain how emasculating it can be getting knocked from your feet by a smack to the face. Instead, I'll say that physically it tossed me a few yards to the right so that I could again become acquainted with my old friend, the ground. I laid there for a moment listening to the clinking metal of the flask as it bounced along the alley street and tried to place my finger on why that sound suddenly felt so familiar. A memory tried pushing its way to the front of my thoughts before it was muted by the angel's voice. "Allowing you to explain yourself was merely a formality. You have been judged guilty." Through my blurred vision I could see the angel move in closer towards me. "As such, you have been stripped of your assigned equipment. Your contract with Hamistagan is subsequently terminated. I am to take possession of both you and your charge to ensure you are both delivered to eternal damnation.

Words pierced their way into my ear but muddled as my thoughts wandered to the clicking sound and why it was so familiar. From the position on my back, I turned my head to both sides, looking around the damp street for something that might bring my thoughts into a cohesive picture. The kid was still cowering in the corner beside the dumpster nervously chewing on the sleeve of his hoodie. It was an effort to put a shaking finger to my lips, hoping he understood to stay quietly hidden. I couldn't give up on him. I didn't know who he was, nor did I know why this was happening to the both of us. Hell, I didn't even know why I suddenly kept getting my ass kicked; but I knew he deserved more. I rolled back to my side, planning just far enough ahead to get back to my feet. The rest I would have to play by ear. That's when I saw something that brought new clarity to the clinking sounds that haunted me. It was the sound I heard closing in behind me when the cab was pulled out from underneath us. The pellet gun, the one I pulled off of the would-be carjacker in the park the other evening. It must have slid somewhere underneath my seat after I tossed it in the back. It only made sense when the cab popped out of existence; anything not actually part of it was ejected the same way we had been. Objects in motion remain in motion and all of that.

The world froze in place as everything the angel said snapped into a clear and frightening reality. I was a man marked for Hell, and despite having only seen the doormat of damnation, I knew there was no chance I would just roll over and let them flush us both down death's toilet. I reached out and grabbed the pellet gun drawing it close to my chest. I had a thought that was probably insane, but I knew one thing. When faced with Hell as your only alternative, even the most bat-shit ideas seem somehow viable. As the angel stepped closer, I jerked myself upright and knelt on one knee, snapping the gun forward and holding it directly at the angel's chest. For the first time since making themselves known, I saw uncertainty in their face as they became motionless. We both remained there, unmoving for far longer than I would have liked. One of us would need to make the first move. Why shouldn't it be me?

"You know what this is, don't you? I'm sure you do. Quick question. Your kind don't gamble much, do they?" The angel made no response other than the narrowing eyes of deep contempt. "Yeah, I didn't think so. Down here, we have a saying when it comes to gambling. *Always play the odds.*" I knew I was rambling, but maybe a better plan would present itself if I stalled long enough. "You see, on this rock we don't know much about your kind. A few myths here and there but nothing concrete, and you know what? I think you like it that way. God's muscle. The ones we're supposed to be looking for over our shoulders. I have heard quite a few rumors though. Many of them repeated from different mouths." I stood up on both feet and continued, "Those are the odds. If you hear something enough there's bound to be some truth in it, even if it's only a half-truth. Like how I kept hearing that your kind is barred from waltzing down here any time you want." I took a small step backward, hoping to put as much space between us as possible. "A pact you have with the demons. They can only manifest themselves on earth through possession. You, on the other hand, can only come around here if your boss grants you mortal form. I didn't know if that was true, but you gave yourself away. Judging from your reaction to this guy," I tilted the gun slightly as they glanced down at it. "I'd say the mortal part is particularly true."

The angel's face twisted into anger as I called their bluff. I lifted the gun higher, leveling it at the center of their head. "Relax. I'm trying to work this out like two reasonable people." It took me a moment to realize what I had said, "or a reasonable dead guy and a sexless bald angel. Reasonable though, that's the key part." The angel spoke for the first time since the gun entered the picture. "I will make no deal with a blasphemer, and" I cut them off since I was not really in the mood for name-calling. "And the guy holding a gun to your head," I finished for them. "Then there's a second idea that I'd be willing to put money on as well. Seeing as how you're in a current state of uncomfortable mortality, I'd bet that if I put a new peephole through the center of your face, you'd find your soul-state standing around in this same alley waiting for a return ride to the pearly gates." The angel grit their teeth like a rabid animal about to pounce. "Now that seems embarrassing. A proud whatever you like to be called, being driven back across the divide to explain to your bosses how a lowly Charon got the better of you." I emphasized the "Charon" for a little extra sting. "So let me propose an arrangement. We call this little event a stalemate. No one wins, no one loses. That means besides us, no one will ever need to know that a pathetic soul like mine got the better of a mighty angel." They relaxed, as if the idea of no one knowing about this situation sounded like a decent compromise. "In return, you give me 24 hours. Give me a chance to finish up what I've started, after 60 years of service I think I deserve that. You walk away and agree not to seek us out again until that time is up." I could see the consideration before they spoke. "Why would I agree to such terms?" Son of a bitch, this just might work in my favor. "You give me 24 hours' passage, and I agree that when you do find me again, I will not put up any resistance. There will be no fight on my behalf." The angel took a half step towards me as we now stood less than a few feet apart. Not within reach but with the gun close enough to the center of their head that even the worst marksman would only need one shot (*had it been a real gun*). "I do not trust you. What can you give to ensure you maintain your end of this arrangement?" My arm was getting tired, but I fought the urge to shake, thinking for a moment. "Everything can be taken from me except for my dignity. Your kind must understand that. It is all I have left so I will maintain it no matter what. That is what I promise. My word and my dignity that I will honor our agreement."

I know it sounded dramatic, but I was dealing with an angel for fucks sake. I had a hunch that the theatrics wouldn't be lost on them. The angel bowed their head to seal the deal, and with that we were finished. The cloak wrapped itself around them before lifting the hood to obscure their head. They spun silently and with an air of dignity left the alley, taking the enveloping fog with them. It was a sight to behold. The type of creature a poet could dedicate their lives describing, but I was no poet and as I dropped the pellet gun back to my side, simply managed a dumbfounded "Well, I'll be damned."

XIV

There's a bit of advice I would give to anyone considering signing a contract with the afterlife. Always read the fine print. It's something I wish I had done. Unless I did, I can't remember; and that's the point. One of the final stipulations of making my deal with the hereafter was the total forfeiture of all earthly memories. Not the basics like language and culture but all the important personal ones were gone. They took them all, and other than the bare minimum, like my affinity for greasy foods, I couldn't remember any of the actual details about who I was.

I've been told that the memories aren't gone forever. Instead, they're just locked away for safekeeping, waiting for when you finally finish your contract and earn your ascension. With the way things are going lately, I'm not sure if I'll ever find out if that's bullshit. I do know this, though. Out there somewhere I left behind a body. That meant I more than likely had a grave and a headstone. Now, for the first time in a very long time, I sincerely wish I knew where that headstone was. I would pay any amount to have it removed and replaced with a new one of my design. "Here lies Austin. He Stared down an Angel and won. We had to dig the grave a little wider because of his giant balls."

A sense of relief finally hit once I realized that the angel was gone. I bluffed an angel and not only did I live, but I won. How many people can say that? I tapped the pellet gun against the side of my leg and laughed. An honest to God belly chuckle, unlike anything I had felt in a long time. It must have sounded a little crazy because it was interrupted by a concerned quivering voice peeking from the side of the dumpster. "Are you okay?" as a small section of his hood edged around the corner of the green metal container. I straightened myself out, reigning in the hysteria. Not a difficult thing to do once I remembered we were still wandering around with no answers, no ride, and a severe time limit. Nevertheless, thank heavens for little victories I suppose.

"Yeah, I'm fine. We're fine. You hurt?" The kid cautiously crawled out from his hiding spot and scanned himself. "My hands have scratches, but they don't hurt too bad. I ripped the knee in my jeans too." I looked the kid over, trying to find anything he might not be aware of. His clothes were a little worse for wear, but I didn't see any physical damage. "True, but they look cool like that. Trust me. Get them a little dirtier and you can sell them to a tiny trendsetter for a stupid amount of money." The kid pulled his hood back up before tightening the straps on his backpack. "We're only a couple blocks from my place. You may have noticed that fun little spill we took back there, but just to reconfirm, we don't have a car anymore. Since we don't have much else in the way of plans, I say we just stick to our old one and head there so we can start asking around." The kid approved, but we both knew he didn't have much choice.

We made it a few yards through the alley before realizing something. I turned towards the kid, putting my hand to his chest to stop him in his tracks. "Hold up here for a second. I need to grab something." With a quick jog that produced more popping from my joints than I would have heard a few days ago, I found the silver flask lying amid a pile of restaurant trash. It was a little dirtier and had plenty of pavement scratches that gave it some unique character, but I only cared that it was still usable. I wiped it off and held it up so the perplexed kid could see what was so important. "These things aren't as easy to find as they used to be. Not the good ones anyway."

He had no idea what I was talking about, but it didn't matter. I slipped the flask into my coat pocket and walked towards the dumpster against the opposite wall. It was the same one the kid had been hiding behind when all the action went down. With one arm I lifted the lid and held the pellet gun up with the other. "Want to learn some more gambling advice? Never bluff the same way twice. Eventually, someone will call." No longer seeing a use for it, the gun went into the dumpster as the lid snapped shut.

Considering the last few days, I was pleasantly surprised to make the three blocks to the warehouse without completely blowing out my still clicking knee joints. Something a little less surprising was the look of disappointment on the kid's face when we arrived at my place. He stood at the front entrance, too young and innocent for false compliments. "This is where you live? Gross." "Out of the mouths of babes," as I unlocked a rarely used side door and held it open for his highness. "Gross was what I was going for. No one is going to bother stealing any of my stuff." As he moved a little closer, I put my hand on his backpack and nudged him inside.

I watched the kids' face as the door shut, latching it from the inside. He scanned the open warehouse. Taking in the pigeons that sat cooing in the rafters, the series of broken windows that met the ceiling, and finally the OD Army tent that sat in the center of the nothingness. "Have you ever been camping? Well, this is kind of like camping year-round, only with fewer bugs and more television." I walked ahead of him and opened the flap to the large tent, holding it there to direct him in.

Inside, I turned on a small electric heater to help knock some of the chill out of the morning air. The thick canvas of the tent worked as a decent insulator and was much easier than trying to control the temperature of a few thousand square feet of open warehouse space. "Let me give you the 5-cent tour," as I helped him toss his backpack onto the couch. "This is the kitchen," pointing to the small card table and essential utilities. "It's where our five-star meals are prepared by the private chef. Sorry but I gave him the week off. Next, we have the lounge." I waved my arm over the well-worn couch that sat opposite the television. "Featuring an endless variety of westerns and silent comedies on cutting edge videocassette. Do you like Harold Llyod? Yeah, all kids love Harold Llyod." I stepped into the small section I used as my bedroom. "This is my master suite. It's where I enjoy my favorite pastime, sleeping. Today it will double as my office while I try to figure some of this out. The suite is off-limits to guests." I crossed back over to the couch with him. "Luckily for you, I designed the lounge to also double as the guest bedroom." I smacked the dust off of one of the couch cushions and tilted it into a more pillow-like position. "Feel free to make yourself comfortable. A nap would do you good." The kid accepted that he wasn't about to win in this situation and crawled onto the sofa, stretching out as I thumbed through some VHS tapes near the television. I finally settled on one and popped it into the player. "You'll love this one. The Mask of Zorro, 1940. It's easily one of my favorites." The kid laid there, not quite sure how to respond. "I'm going to start tracking down some answers while you get some rest." "Austin?" I only made it a few feet since I was expecting him to say something eventually. "Yeah kid?" "You didn't say anything about a bathroom." I guess I had forgotten that minor detail. "Back corner of the warehouse, look for the blue port-a-john.

The honey truck just cleared it out last week, so the smell should be bearable." I left him to zone out on the movie.

Spending the better part of a century by yourself means never worrying about privacy. Now stuck in a position where I needed to find a few minutes alone, I was struggling to come up with an idea. I settled on stringing an old wool blanket across the room to divide the sleeping area from where the kid sat. It wouldn't last as a long-term solution, but I don't think *long term* is a concern right now. I took a moment to myself to stretch my aching back. The usual popping sounds were now replaced with almost comical crunches, but I was still moving. I should count my blessings.

The messenger spirits were probably banned from helping a fugitive from death, so I turned to the old standby, the phone. Yes, I have a phone. Ever since they introduced the novel concepts of pizza delivery and Chinese takeout, I decided I wanted to make a few calls from time to time. That's when I went out and bought the most advanced technology available.

Beside the bed, on a small round nightstand sat a cream-colored cordless phone charging on its base. The receiver was roughly the size of a brick and only worked if you fully extended the 10-inch silver antenna. I know that today with kids and their e-phones it might be seen as a dinosaur, but if it got me an extra-large cheese craver pizza delivered in under 30 minutes, I'd use a set of tin cans and string if I had to. I pulled the antenna out and sat on the corner of the bed, flipping through the few ratty business cards that stayed in my wallet for the rare instances I needed to jot down a number.

I skimmed through the few contacts trying to find one that might be useful. Ford was still on shift, so I knew I wouldn't be able to call him until he was off duty. Same for any of the other day drivers in the area. I scanned over the next card and found someone who might have a chance at helping. Propping the handset against my shoulder, it took a few rings before a groggy voice finally answered with a nasal whine, "Whaaaaaat?"

"Hey Chubby, it's Austin. You got a minute?" Chubby was the night driver from the next district over. He was an okay guy, I suppose. Sometimes on slow nights we would meet at a pancake place that sat on the border of our two areas and grab a late-night coffee while bitching about who's had the worst pick-up. The name Chubby stuck after the second time we met. He drove a yellow checkered cab, and since there was already a Mr. Ford, he was given the name Checker. Hence the nickname "Chubby." It was a joke that made a little more sense when The Twist was still a dance craze but now felt ironic since his lanky frame barely weighed in at 120 pounds.

The tapping on the other end of the phone meant the half-conscious Chubby was blindly feeling around, trying to find his impressively thick glasses. "Yeah," came the voice filtered through his thin nose, "I was just wasting time sleeping, but who needs that. The real story here is that someone explained phones to Austin. Tell me, who did it?" It was the second time this morning I've heard that joke, making it even less funny now. "You're a riot. I need to ask you some questions. I don't have a lot of time to waste." "Well then, by all means, please continue. I would hate to waste any more time while you're trying to sleep." I liked Chubby. Not so much personally since he was an insufferable jackass, but I appreciated how his personality made me look like a gold star people-person. His sarcasm probably developed as a defense mechanism. The ideal spokesmodel for pocket protectors who decided it was easier to reject everyone before they rejected you.

"Sorry, I get it. I'll hurry. I just need to know if you've heard anything lately about a kid being crossing over without a nanny." There was a pause of confusion on the other end before his matter of fact response. "Kids don't cross without nannies. That's not how this works." "I know how it works, which is why I'm asking. I'm in a bit of a situation..." It took me a few minutes to explain what had happened as I ran through everything as quickly as possible. "We just walked into my place, and you're the first call I've made. I was hoping..." He cut me off before I could finish. "Bullshit! You're not going to get me caught up in this. If your contract was pulled, that's bad enough, but you've got a halo coming for your ass. No. I've got nothing to do with this. Do me a favor and don't let anyone know you called me." I tried to convince him to help, but it was of little use. "Stop, just stop. If anyone found out I was even talking to you right now, there's a chance I'd be heading downtown right next to you. No thanks. Take this advice. Turn yourself in. If you give a shit about anyone besides yourself, don't get anyone else involved. Not all of us want to keep you company in Hell." The chance I gave him to change his mind was only met with a click as he hung up. It was frustrating, I was still at square one and some part of me knew he was right. I was in over my head, and there was no point in dragging anyone else down with me. All I could do was keep kicking and try not to drown.

I put the phone back on the charger and laid back on the bed, resigned to enjoy what could be my last chance to relax. Behind closed eyes I tried to picture what would come next. Would there be fire? I knew the cliche image of Hell with the brimstone, the eternal torment and pain. Was that the next step? It didn't seem to make sense. After a few lifetimes of anguish, wouldn't you just get used to it? Could it be something worse, or were those just the fables we told to scare children away from lying? Hell didn't seem like something that would limit itself to anything as simple as physical pain. It had to be something else. It was despair. It's standing behind the velvet rope of Heaven and seeing everyone inside having the time of their lives while you're stuck outside in the cold without a coat. The loneliness and isolation, a torment worse than a few hundred years of demons shoving splinters under your nails.

I was deep into my philosophical breakdown of damnation when a sound brought me back. I sprang up as it caught me off guard and caused me to roll out of bed, smacking my head against the floor. The phone was ringing, a completely new experience considering I didn't even know that this phone had a ringer. I bounced to my knees and lifted the phone from its cradle, pulling the antenna out before answering with an incredulous "hello?"

"Austin. That you?" It was only a few words, but that was all it took for me to recognize Benny. "Yeah. How'd you get my number?" "You've called in to-go orders, and the diner has caller ID. About a year ago I plugged your info into my phone. You never know when it might come in handy to have a Charon in your contacts list." Ah, Benny, she used the C-word. "I have to admit I'm glad you called, but after a new development I can't get you involved any further. It's too risky." I explained the angel and the weird murder room with all the symbols. I hoped it would deter her from pushing this further, but it did the opposite. "Holy Shit, A real angel? When it comes to fucking up, you've just pushed yourself to an award-winning level. I'm impressed." I chose silence, not knowing what to say. "Austin. You're a good guy, and from what I can tell I'm the closest thing to a friend you've got. No matter what you say or how badly you've fucked this up, I'm in." Secretly relieved to have her help, my conscience wouldn't let me roll over so quickly. "I can't get you mixed with what's going on. It's not like we're talking about a slap on the wrist and a few nights in jail. We're dealing with the big one, full-on damnation. It's not going to be any easier for me down there if I know you're stuck." Before I could finish, she cut me off with the one thing that would shut me up. "I'm damned anyway," as a statement of fact. "I'm half-demon. My place in Hell was registered before I was even born. Nothing we do up here is going to change that." I knew her lineage. It was something we discussed on a pretty casual basis, but I guess I never put much thought into what it meant. "Aren't you the one that's always going on about not believing in fate? Spitting in the face of destiny and all that?" She brushed it off in her usual manner that often accompanied a slightly red face of embarrassment. "Not believing in something doesn't mean that thing doesn't exist. It just means you disagree with it. I was born with a job waiting for me. Even if I don't want to do it, that's not going to stop the fabric of the hereafter."

The moment froze to sink in. "It's easy to understand. Just because I'm supposed to take a shitty job one day doesn't mean I need to spend my time on earth screwing over poor schmucks to an eternity of damnation because I shake my ass a little." She sighed with acceptance, "We're getting sidetracked. None of this matters right now. What matters is that you need to shut up and accept that I'm helping. Understood?"

Understood and appreciated. I agreed to let Benny help me but only until things got too intense. I was desperate to hear anything she may have dug up. "I couldn't find much," she said with a shift in tone, "and by that, I mean I couldn't find anything, but I know someone who does." Since she was part demon, a lot of unsavory characters out there were desperate to make themselves known to her. "This guy is the biggest scumbag of them all. He's also our best bet." I'd be lying if I said this whole idea wasn't making me uneasy, but I could feel my back against the wall, and this sounded like our only option. I listened in agreement as we planned next steps. "Get some sleep Austin. You're starting to sound like shit. Remember. My place tonight, 9ish. Oh, one more thing. What size pants do you wear?

XV

Turning off your mind. Dropping away into deep darkness as it wraps itself around your unconscious being. It's the sensation that accompanies the heaviest sleep a soul can experience. It can be frightening until you learn to let yourself go and trust that you'll find your way back. It was Zen, if you believe in that sort of thing, and something I looked forward to every day.

Today I decided to forgo those few hours of sleep, instead focusing on what had to be done. I paced the floor, gripping the phone tightly with fingers turning blue and numb but too deep in thought to care. The same questions were rolling through my head over and over. Where did he come from? Who would do that to a child? How could they and why? That was the hardest question to comprehend; the why. From all that I've seen, I knew that the darkness in people could be unfathomably deep. This was different. There was too much involved, too many coincidences to think this could be random cruelty and stupid mistakes. There was a bigger picture here. A puzzle I was trying to solve with only a few pieces available.

I placed the phone back on the dock and unclipped the blanket separating the rooms. Folding it as I saw the kid now stretched across the couch deep in that peaceful dark sleep, his tiny body only taking up half of the sofa. I knew I had to relax to keep from driving myself insane. I made a pot of coffee, took some before the carafe had filled halfway, and grabbed a seat on the open end of the couch. I sipped at the steaming cup and stared at the television as the movie played, focusing beyond with nowhere else to look. As the credits rolled the screen went dark and static took its place. A small whirl sounded from the player as the tape rewound before ejecting itself. I used my toe to push it back in as the movie played from the start. It was the sound that was important. I ignored what was happening on the screen, but the sound of anything helped mute the thoughts. We sat with the kid in his silent slumber and me slowly downing cup after cup of cheap black coffee while the movie played another 2 times.

I waited until it had rewound itself once more before deciding it was time for us to go. I rinsed the cup and placed it back with the small, mismatched collection of others before gently shaking the kid awake. "Hey, sleeping beauty. I think you've successfully reset. Time to get moving." Have you ever seen a kid wake up? It's insane. The kid shot up with a sense of purpose, his eyes wide and ready to go. "I'm starving," he said as he wiped the last remnants of sleep from his eyes. "Same, we'll grab something on the way."

I recognized the address Benny gave me earlier. An art deco apartment complex in the historic district that stood unchanged since the mid-twenties, presumably around the same time she had moved in. It was only a couple of miles from my place, but we would need to hoof it over on foot since our ride options were severely limited. I didn't mind. After spending the last few hours feeling like a caged animal, the exercise was a welcome distraction. Along the way we stopped at a hotdog vendor preparing to call it a night. I grabbed a couple of dogs and quietly motioned for a few cans of soda, slipping them into my jacket pockets while the kid was distracted. Handing the vendor a $100 bill from my wallet, I let him keep the change. He looked at us suspiciously before accepting it as unusual generosity. Money never meant much to me on a typical day; when you knew you probably only had a few hours left in this world it meant even less.

The kid took one of the dogs and I peeled back the foil on one for myself. As I eagerly chomped down, the kid inspected his with mild confusion. "It's a hotdog," I pushed through a mouthful as he considered what to do. There was the possibility he may never have had a hotdog before, or it was another memory he no longer had? "What's it made out of?" He asked as I pushed his hand gently up to his mouth, motioning for him to eat. "That's the first rule of hotdogs; never ask. Just eat." Moving to my second dog, the kid took a cautious bite.

He must have liked it since the next time I looked down the kid was rolling the now spent foil into a ball and tossing it into a garbage can. I followed suit and pulled the cans from each side of my jacket. His eyes lit up as I cracked one open, passing it to his little hands. We quietly walked through the night streets as the city began to change shifts. It was that odd time of night where the ordinary folk, the 9-5'ers, called it an evening as they packed themselves away in the suburbs to catch a few sitcoms before bed. That only left the oddballs on the streets. The night owls, the partiers, and the predators, all out to clock in for their nightly shifts. I kept the kid close, knowing he wasn't in any real danger but feeling a sense of protection I couldn't overcome. It didn't take him long to empty his can before I handed him mine to finish also.

"We're here," pointing up at the ornately decorated exterior of the building as we arrived. "My friend lives here. She promised to help us find some answers. She's a little *different*, but I promise she's good people. You still trust me, right?" The kid gave me his hand and it was all I needed. We pushed our way through the revolving brass doors into the warmth of the lobby before catching an elevator to her floor. It was a beautifully maintained complex, like a museum to classic modernism with deep rich jewel tone walls and well-shined decorative sconces. I took in the surroundings as we moved through the hall, the contrast between such a classic style and Benny's stripped-down grunge nature wasn't lost on me.

"Apartment 66. This is the one." The kid and I stopped short of her door as I lifted the scrolling brass door knocker, letting it fall with a reverberating ting. I could hear the shifting of footsteps from inside the apartment, a complex series of mechanisms unlocking before the creek of the door swung open with a smiling Benny just inside. She stood partially hidden behind the door, covered in a white terry cloth robe, her hair wrapped in a towel. "You're a little early, but no harm. We just won't be as rushed." As she opened the door wider, I took a step forward, slamming my face full force against an invisible barrier with an audible crunch. "What the Shit was that!" leaked from my hands as I grabbed my broken nose. Apparently amused, she reached out, grabbing both the kid and me by the shoulder. With a stern voice, she began. "You are both welcome guests. I grant you sanctuary." It was a strange statement that seemed directed more towards the empty hallway than at either of us. As she pulled us into her apartment, I felt obligated to respond despite my throbbing face. "Thanks, I guess." Instead of acknowledging me, she bounced away, disappearing into another room. "Seriously, what the hell was that?" I asked loud enough to be heard a few rooms over. She popped her toweled head around the corner, trying to suppress laughter. "Sorry." She ducked back in as I heard drawers opening and closing. "It's not like I've ever hidden who I am over the years. Err, or what I am." She returned from what I assume was the kitchen, carrying a set of chopsticks. "Every few years, a new generation of assholes fancy themselves demon hunters. They'll come along trying to earn some street cred by taking my head off. I admit it sounds badass, but since it's *my* head, I'm just not cool with it." She pointed to the door, "a few years ago I found a decent warlock who agreed to put a hex on this place. It was a good deal. Didn't take long to set up and keeps out anyone I haven't formally welcomed." She turned towards me and slid one of the sticks into each of my nostrils. "Only cost me a lock of hair, a few drops of blood, and five grand cash, but if it keeps some basement-dwelling paladin from charging into my home to kill me, then it was worth every penny." Before I could ask anything else, she gripped both chopsticks and popped my crooked nose back into place. A quick action that allowed me to enjoy an entirely new type of pain. It took a moment to catch my breath before I could speak again. "Well, thanks for letting me test it out. I appreciate the first-hand demonstration." My words were obscured from my hand still holding the bridge of my nose. Benny smiled and punched me in the shoulder a little harder than necessary. "Toughen up soldier. Remember, pain reminds us that we're still here." She took a break from teasing to bend down and look the kid in the eyes. "Hey there. I'm Benny. I'm a friend of this guy," she said as she pushed me hard enough to knock me off balance. "And do you know what that means? I'm your friend too, if you want me to be." She had a great way with kids, a gentle demeanor that came naturally. He gave her a sincere look of agreement before continuing with caution. "Aren't you afraid the white lady is going to hurt you too?" Benny looked back at me, knowing exactly who the kid was referring to but trying to get a little support. He had already seen me get the shit kicked out of myself before we barely bluffed our way out, so I wasn't in much of a position to play the tough guy right now. I watched as she leaned in close to the kids' ear, whispering just loud enough for us both to hear. "I promise you if anyone, even the white lady, tries to hurt any of my friends...I'll make them eat their own butts!" Her pink barbed tail snaked its way from under her robe, lowering itself in front of his face. "So, are we friends?" she asked, still leaning in close as the tip of her tail hung in the air, pointing at his face. The kid nervously agreed as the tail snapped forward, flicking him gently on the nose as Benny let out a clownish "Bonk!"

The kid laughed for the first time since I'd met him. Yes, he'd giggled a few times watching me get hurt, but this was an honest to God belly laugh that almost brought me to tears. I turned for a moment and heard Benny bounce to her feet. "Ok boys. Make yourselves at home. There's junk food in the fridge and plenty of channels on the TV. Austin, there's a suit inside that gray bag next to the couch. Put it on. Where we're going, you need to look a little better than the dumpster-couture you usually wrap yourself in." With those orders, she zipped away to finish getting ready.

It didn't take the kid long to get comfortable. He rummaged through her food and found a few bags of chips, along with a few more sodas. Tossing all of it into this backpack, he plopped himself down on her oversized leather sofa and began flipping through stations on the television. I, on the other hand, was a little more cautious. I picked up the large gray bag beside the couch and peered inside to see a series of smaller white boxes. I pulled each out and spread them on the counter. A well-made black suit. Not quite a tuxedo, but still very formal. A crisp white collared shirt, a pair of mirror shined loafers, and a small box containing a thick leather belt, a deep red tie, and the largest pair of ruby cufflinks I had ever seen. It was a very nice outfit that came with some hefty prices from the tags that still hung from the items. It was also completely out of my comfort zone, but I would have to trust that she knew what she was doing. I stripped down to my boxers and began untagging and pulling on the clothes. I had the basics on when I decided that some of the pieces just wouldn't work. The blazer was too stiff and restrictive. I had no idea where I was going or what would happen, but after the run-in with the angel I needed to be prepared for anything. I opted to stick with my wool peacoat. Over a dress shirt and tie, I didn't think it looked too bad. Also, in the category of "you never know," I left the loafers and went with my leather work boots. Steel toe sounded like a good option right now, all things considered.

I put my old clothes and the unused items back into the bag and set them beside the front door. "Hey kid," I said to grab his attention as I stepped in front of the TV. "How do I look?" I did a small twirl to show off the partially new duds as the kid cocked his head to see around me. "Lame," was the only response he managed between a mouthful of chips. "Well, that's a good thing. I always like to make sure I look the same as I feel." I adjusted the shirt to ensure the back was tucked in evenly when a clicking sound preceded a figure emerging from the hallway. My mouth leaked a very faint "Good lord..."

Benny, or maybe Bernice was more appropriate in this situation, stood in the light as she radiated an unearthly amount of beauty, sexuality, and confidence unlike anything I had seen in a woman before. She wore a sapphire blue cocktail dress that somehow formed itself around every generous curve I never knew she had. Large jeweled bracelets decorated her wrists, and her deep black hair was put up in a perfect bun, allowing tiny ringlets to frame her face. "Yep, take it in because I don't do this shit that often. Now, if you wouldn't mind closing your mouth, we should get moving." It took her saying something for me to realize my jaw had been hanging open as she stood here. I snapped it shut and went back to fixing my shirt as she walked, her black patent leather heels clicking along the floor with each step. "Your tie is crooked." She said as she reached up to refine it. I could smell her as she stood closer and it was otherworldly. She smelled in a way that I could only describe as how flowers would want flowers to smell, mixed with the feeling of a perfect spring day and a relaxing night at the beach. It was a scent that transcended smell and somehow triggered emotion and feelings. I didn't know it was possible to bottle the concept of desire into a single fragrance, but the bastards managed to do it somehow. I'll give them that.

She took a step back as she finished straightening my tie and looked me up and down. "Urban Chic, not too formal but not too sloppy. Very *New Wave*. I love it." she said as she lightly slapped me on the cheek. "Now, let's get going. The car is waiting for us downstairs." She grabbed a small black clutch that perfectly matched her shoes on her way to the door. I took a step to follow her but couldn't help thinking that I had forgotten something. I checked my pockets while giving myself a once over, then glanced around the room before realizing what I had left.

"What do we do with him?" Quietly motioning toward the kid, "Is he going?" Benny looked at me like a stupid child. "Manuel's place is not somewhere we would want to take a kid. He'll be safe here. No one, or better yet, no *thing* on Heaven or Earth, can get into this apartment unless I explicitly grant them entry. My place might be the safest spot in the entire city for him." "I get that, but do you think he'll be alright by himself?" He sat stuffing his face, entranced by colorful cartoons as she conceded.

"Hey hun, Austin and I need to go out and ask some not nice people a few questions. We need you to be safe, and my home is the safest place you could ever be. So, is it alright with you if we go out for a while?" The kid took a break from shoveling chips into his mouth and looked at her. "Are you going to get hurt?" he asked with honest concern. "No baby. We aren't going to do anything that would get us hurt. Plus, we have to come back for you, right?" The kid agreed. "Good. While we're gone you need to hang out here, ok? Don't leave this apartment no matter what you hear, and I promise we'll be back very soon." She leaned down and gave the kid a soft kiss on the top of his head that did more to comfort him than anything I had been able to say up to that point. It was time to go, and as I held the door open for her, she smacked me in the stomach with her clutch before walking out.

I followed behind as she made her way down the hallway towards the elevators. It was an unexpectedly pleasant view, but I tried to keep my eyes on the floor. As I did, I could see the bright red bottoms of her heels occasionally flashing as she walked, winking to the world. It was too perfect to be a coincidence, and I understood that her entire act was intentional. I had no idea where we were going, but I knew she was prepared. Suited up for battle in her evening wear armor using every trick she knew —the devil in the deadly blue dress.

We rode the elevator to the bottom floor, and I tried to limit how much of her scent I took in. It was intoxicating, but I had to play it cool. I mean, this was Benny for God's sake. The same tough little girl that served up some of the worst food in town almost every night. I wondered if she knew what I was thinking, realizing it was safe to assume that she did. She knew what tricks she was playing and how to get what she wanted. It was in her nature. As we reached the lobby of her complex, I could see an antique limousine parked in front of the building. "Is that for us?" A stupid question to ask, but at this point I was lucky I wasn't stammering incoherently as she stood next to me. "This isn't the kind of place you just walk up to and get in. You either make a grand entrance, or you don't make an entrance at all." We stepped outside into the cool night air through the revolving brass doors. "This has to be expensive. Are you sure you can afford it?" She stepped to the back of the limo and gave me a disapproving look as if I had completely forgotten my manners. I realized the faux pas before reaching down to open the limo door for her.

"No, it's not cheap, but money's never been a problem. I only work at the dinner to keep myself occupied" She gave me a coy wink, "and I like the company." I could feel my face turn red. "You're not the only one who can squirrel away a few lifetimes' worth of savings, you know. Besides, this place has been rent-controlled for decades. I've got the rent paid up for the next 15 years. Why not spend a little extra here and there." She lowered herself gracefully as she entered the back seat. "Might as well have a little fun, right?" I agreed with a gruff snort and ducked in behind her. "Let me know when the fun begins. I'll be waiting."

XVI

The Old Town Waterfront. It doesn't matter which city you're in; you'll always find one area that feels the same. The discarded carcass of what was once the high-end side of town, built by the wealthy elite before they decided to move on to greener and more exclusive pastures. It was the same again and again. The leftover framework of a once plush area, it devolved into a home for those who met life as a struggle rather than a soiree. I sat on edge, uncomfortable at the mercy of another driver with anxiety made worse as we left my district and drove deeper into the darkest part of this depressed area. I stared out of the side window, taking in the once upscale boutiques that had since transformed into a series of repeating pawn shops and payday loans.

My unease was noticeable as Benny reached down and grabbed my hand as it rested on the limo's seat, squeezing it gently. "Relax. The kid is as safe as he could be. We're going to get some answers and you know you can't get hurt, not permanently anyway." She smiled wolfishly, baring her canines. "I thrive in this kind of darkness. We're fine." I returned her smile, unconvincing as I rested my head against the glass, enjoying a few quiet moments. The rhythmic bumps of the limo as we traveled the well-worn streets did all it could to rock me to sleep, but I resisted as Benny squeezed my hand again, bringing me back into now. No rest for the wicked.

"We're almost there," softly pointing through the window on her side. The limo made a cautious turn down a side street, slowly approaching a tall building that could have been a department store in a previous life. It was dark, faded paint chipping in large chunks as it gave off the vibe of danger and disrepair. A feeling that matched the surrounding area with one glaring exception. As we pulled closer, you could see a large group of out-of-place fashionable socialites hovering along the building, corralled into a line by a red velvet rope. "Driver," Benny directed towards the front, "Go ahead and pull up to the head of the line. That's where the front door is. After we get out, find somewhere to park but stay close. I have a feeling that when we're done, we're not going to want to wait around." Understood, the driver slowed the limo to a stop. I waited, swallowing anxiety before popping the door open and sliding out. It was the Hollywood experience as all eyes of the waiting crowd focused on my exit from the limo. The wave of whispers was soon silenced as Benny's delicate hand extended from the shadow of the backseat and held itself out. I gripped it with care as she emerged into the street, taking everyone's breath as she moved.

I relaxed into her "plus one" role that I seemed suited for tonight. She smirked at the staring crowd before moving towards the doorman blocking the entrance. Benny looked up at him, a sideshow giant in a custom-sized white dinner jacket, and with all the confidence of someone who wasn't dwarfed by their opponent, chastised him loudly. "I am a personal guest of Manuel's, and I can't help but notice that you are in my way." I stood behind her waiting for what may come next as the Man-Giant produced a small pair of glasses from his jacket pocket, making a show of checking the clipboard he held in his beefy hands. "That's funny," in a deep grumble, "Because I can't help but notice that you ain't on the list." It was a game of elitist chess, and the doorman had just put Benny in check. Butterflies began whirling in my stomach, but I held my tongue and trusted her ability.

The two of them looked each other over for a quiet moment, the silence extending into the crowd as we waited for the next move. She stared him in the eyes and began to giggle slyly as her tail danced from its hiding spot under her skirt. With a flick, she knocked the glasses back from his nose and onto his head. "Perhaps it's time to get a new prescription," She quipped as the arrowhead-shaped barb of her tail struck down at a name on his list. "It looks to me like my name is right there. Don't you agree?"

The Doorman stood dumbfounded as the chorus of awe came seeping from the crowd. Knowing she won, Benny locked her arm inside of mine, her tail curling itself around her neck like a flesh boa. I felt the nudge of her elbow and stepped forward, brushing past the apologetic brute who ushered us through the front door. She was still laughing as the door slammed shut, leaving us alone in a dimly lit hall. "You realize what you just did, don't you?" I asked in a low voice, unsure if the need to whisper was warranted. She held my arm tightly as she confidently pulled me along. "I know. Wasn't it awesome? Nothing feels better than knocking a big dumb asshole like that down a few pegs." I agreed with the sentiment but still found myself very confused. "That's cool and all, but I'm talking about the whole tail thing. Aren't you concerned? All those people out there saw…" She stopped me before I could finish. "What they saw was exactly what they spent their entire night hoping to see. They saw a demonic something-or-other and her date getting into a club too exclusive for any of them. That's all they saw." We arrived at a set of tall red leather doors, taking a moment to process what just happened. "They saw your face.

They saw your tail. They saw my face. I know you don't put much effort into hiding who you are, but that's a lot different from intentionally making a spectacle yourself. I'm in enough shit as it is. I can't have it on my conscience if something happens to you also." She dropped her arm from mine and turned to face me, pointing back the way we came. "Those people out there. They define us by what we are, not who. They will stare directly at us and still see nothing more than the stations we were born into and how they can use us. They think their money and status mean they have all the answers, but they don't. They don't know that we're real people beyond the roles we were forced into, and the moment we leave their sight, they'll remember nothing about who we are, only a few details that make up another good story to tell at a party." I could see the sincerity in her face and had to accept that she knew what she was doing. "All of the people that come here," she said as she grabbed my arm again, "They come to live dangerously. To dip their toes into a giant pool of evil and act like it's no big deal. So, let's give them what they've come to see. If we play our parts right, we'll get the answers we need." Her tail lifted off of her neck and arched into a deep S shape, waving gently behind her. "Now, a succubus and undead taxi driver walk into a bar...let's find out what the punch-line is."

      I pushed the red doors open and led Benny through as we stepped into a smokey scene of unquestioned excess and sin packaged tightly under a bow of nostalgia. I was immediately taken with the neon sign that encompassed the wall directly to our left as it brightly lit the area around us. The giant glowing red tubes twisted to form the words "Hotter Than Hell Lounge" as a caricature of a demon girl rocked back and forth, bathing herself inside an oversized martini glass. "Classy," I managed as Benny pulled me along, pressing us further into the club. What lay inside could only be described as Hell's best interpretation of The Peppermint Lounge. A 60's go-go paradise that seemed plucked out of time. We made our way through the crowd of swinging sweaty dancers as I looked around, taking in the sites.

To our right was a well-tended bar where young women draped in fringe and mod-suited men sat sipping multicolored martinis. Just beyond were rows of tables and booths, all decked in rich red suede and blonde wood tones. Every table was packed beyond capacity, with more vintage-clad patrons laughing and drinking from overly garnished tiki ware. Behind us was the dance floor steamy and dense with patrons hiding heavily dilated eyes behind their indoor sunglasses. They twisted in time to the brass band busy at work on the stage, pumping away at a lounge rendition of Arthur Brown's "Fire." It was all too much to take in. The retro nature of it all was disarming at first, like a stroll down memory lane. It took a bit of perspective to see that it was just another gimmick used to sell the beast's true nature. Greed, Lust, Gluttony, Envy; the headliners of the seven, sold to anyone looking to buy and wrapped up nicely under the guise of demonic kitsch.

"Hey Mista " came a high-pitched voice as I felt a hand softly grab my shoulder. "You lookin to buy any party favas?" I turned to bring Benny along with me as a petite blond looked up at me with a smile that only comes naturally to someone being paid. She wore an undersized crescent hat with protruding plastic devil horns. It was a theme that extended down her body from the sequenced red corset of her torso to the blood red heels she balanced on, finally accentuated with the novelty felt tail that hung from her frilly shorts. She motioned to the wooden display box that hung suspended from a leather strap around her neck. "We got everything you could need." I peeked down to see her wares and found a healthy assortment that began innocently with gum and cigarettes before progressing rapidly from cigars and joints to an extensive collection of unmarked pills and powders that I could only guess the nature of. "Um, no thanks?" I said, trying not to stand out as too much of a square. Benny leaned forward, plucking one of the unfiltered cigarettes from the tray and popping it into a long onyx holder she produced from her clutch. "Sorry, Sweety," purred Benny in an affected tone, "You ain't got what we're looking for on that tray. We're here to see Manuel. You know where he is?" The young blonde's false smile dropped as she took a more serious tone. "Mr. Sangre doesn't see just anyone. If he wants to talk to you then he'll find you." This wasn't a pissing match I felt the need to join as I knew Benny could play this out on her own. She motioned for me to give her a light. In agreement, I pulled a matchbook from my pocket and struck one, watching as she inhaled.

Benny blew a large cloud of used nicotine in the small girl's direction. Making a production of waving it away with her tail before using it to pluck the spent match from my hand and drop it on her tray. The poor girl's eyes focused on the appendage as she went pale. "Oh... Well..." She stumbled over her words as she pointed behind us. "Yes, Mr. Sangre's personal table is towards the back of the relaxation area. He'll be sitting there." I could see her swallow nervously. "He's got an awful lot of muscle with him though. It ain't gonna be easy getting to him."

Benny smiled and blew the girl a kiss before looking back at me. "Well, Mr. Austin, it looks like we've got another challenge ahead of us. Give this sweet girl something for the cigarette, will you?" I nodded and began to reach for my back pocket when the girl cut in, almost panicking. "No! I mean, Mr. Sangre's personal guests never pay. It's considered an insult. If you need anything else, please let us know." With that, she turned intent on getting herself to anywhere that wasn't near us. I could feel Benny tugging me again in the direction the girl gave us as I leaned in close to whisper. "Mr. Sangre?" I asked incredulously, trying to refrain from including, "Are you serious?"

I was far from what would pass as bilingual by any stretch of the imagination, but I did know a few useful phrases for those times when I might need to make a pickup with a language barrier. My Spanish was limited primarily to phrases like "You're dead, let's go," and "For real, you're dead, come on." but even with my limited knowledge, I was able to recognize the Spanish word for blood. "Clearly, it's not his real name," Benny whispered back, "But with this crowd, it's all about appearances, and these trust fund Satanists eat that cheesy shit up."

We made our way through the first section of tables as I watched the lights go dark on the stage. Benny was too determined to pay any attention, but I took every chance to gawk at the spectacle around me. As the lights began to slowly rise again, I could see a breathtaking older woman take a position in front of the band as she led them into a slow soulful rendition of "Sympathy for the Devil." So engrossed in the sound I failed to realize that we had just run into our first obstacle. It was another large mountain proportioned man monster tasked with only letting the best of the best into the section beyond him. As we approached, I ran through a series of ideas in my head to find some reason for him to let us pass, not realizing I had the best reason of them all hanging from my arm. As we moved within his range, the guard outstretched the tree trunk he called an arm and stopped me dead in my tracks. Benny jumped in like a snake about to strike, refusing to be slowed. She curled her arm and body around his torso and leaned in close to whisper into his ear. I couldn't make out what she said over the music and the crowd, but apparently it was good. Beads of sweat formed on the guard's forehead as he began to sway loosely with a failing equilibrium. Benny kissed him on the cheek and stepped back. Curling herself under my arm as the guard took a knee and waved us past. "What the hell did you say to him?" I asked, concerned. The concern only grew as she laughed. "I'd tell you, but you wouldn't survive."

The song continued as we found ourselves nearing the far corner of the VIP section. I wasn't sure what this Manuel character looked like, but I knew we were almost there when we were confronted with a circle of well-dressed and overpaid muscle blocking the path to the final table. The leader was a mid-sized bald man in a solid black suit who stepped forward to challenge me directly. "Who the hell do you think you are?" I pulled my arm from over Benny and held both palms up at him in surrender. "Whoa, relax. I'm just here with her." Benny's tail shot up as she waved it at him seductively. Baldy only sneered, refusing to budge. "Yeah, and? Am I supposed to be impressed with that?" Pointing at the barb that hung in the air. "I heard there are some doctors on the lower west side that'll craft those things out of extra ass skin for a few hundred grand. You ain't got shit I haven't seen before lady, which means Mr. Sangre ain't got time for you either."

Benny's confident facade faded for a brief moment, mentally reeling from a century without knowing rejection. I saw her take a step back and with the smile of a predator about to pounce, she decided to step up her game. She slithered in close to the leader and lowered her voice with breathy determination. "Well then, let's find something you've never seen before. Tell me, have you ever seen a set of these?" She slowly looked down towards her impressive cleavage as Baldy's eyes followed. Giving him a moment to enjoy his view, she ran a finger up his chin. "No silly, wrong set." It was a psychological blow that made him blush. Benny closed the short gap between them, and I could see her look upwards toward her forehead as his eyes followed. Without breaking her playful smile, we watched as a small set of off-white peaks began to break through her forehead. No skin was ripped, or any blood drawn as a 2-inch set of perfectly formed horns emerged on either side of her widow's peak. "Now, if you don't mind," she began in full Marilyn Monroe mode now, pouty and playful in a way that attracted the attention of every male in the area. "I'd like to speak with Manuel. I'm sure he would be very interested once you tell him how horny I am."

I sunk low in her shadow, trying to remain visibly unimpressed as internally I fought every urge to cringe and hide from secondhand embarrassment at the horrible pun she just made. She turned from the man who was entirely entranced with every aspect of her, and I could see the pride in her face as she knew she had won. Not one to judge, I traded a look with the guard shortly before he collapsed to the floor.

XVII

Schadenfreude, the idea of finding pleasure in the misfortune of others, and right now was the closest I've felt to it in a long time. It wasn't enjoyment from seeing the bald jerk crumple to the floor like a broken marionette as much as the relief that if someone had to be hurt, I was glad it wasn't me for a change. The grounded guard stirred, signaling that he was still alive while my attention was drawn to the dark figure standing over him. A deeply tanned man who embodied the cliched Latin lover stood smiling at Benny with all the sincerity of a great white. He wore a deep red velvet blazer over solid black, his dark hair pulled into a tight ponytail that matched the thin mustache curled above his lip.

"Señorita Bernice," he began in an indistinguishable accent that poured from his mouth like syrup. "You pay top dollar for good help and too often they forget that they are hired for their muscle, not their brains. Please forgive me for that uncivilized display" The infamous Manuel handed the used leather truncheon to another of his attentive guards. "My security has standing orders that VIPs such as yourself should be treated with absolute respect." Benny reached out and hooked my arm, pulling me close to her. "No need to apologize

Manuel. I enjoy a little challenge once in a while." She leaned down to the guard who was now sitting upright in a daze and kissed him gently on the head, leaving a set of red lips on his bald pate. "I don't think this one meant any harm." Manuel chuckled in agreement. "Perhaps you're right. A little spanking now and again never harmed anyone, I'm sure you would agree?" Personally, I was getting tired of the innuendos, yet Benny remained pleasant. "Please join me for a drink. It's the least I could do since you were kind enough to visit my establishment." Benny pulled me along without a chance to disagree. "Of course, we would love to."

Slick leather benches formed a booth around a black marble table at the most exclusive seats in the house. He escorted us over, prompting us to sit. Benny held her hand out and allowed me to help her scoot into the booth in the most ladylike fashion possible. I followed closely behind as Manuel sat across us, looking into the distance and snapping his fingers. "For you, I suggest we enjoy the house specialty. Only personal guests of mine are given this opportunity." He made a scissor motion before holding up 3 fingers towards the bar in the distance.

"Manuel," Benny began to purr, "We appreciate your generosity, but we would really like to ask you..." before being cut off with a simple shake of his head. "No, no, no, we must drink first. As my guest, let us celebrate. Then we may proceed to whatever business you may have." "Of course," she agreed, knowing she had no other choice. I chose to sit quietly, hoping the house specialty was decent whiskey but willing to settle for anything that burned just right. Naive optimism I was soon to regret.

Owning a club had its advantages and not having to wait for your order was one of them. Within moments a set of identical twins in matching red devil-inspired lingerie arrived tableside. Each carried a shoebox-sized wooden crate with the twin closest to me setting hers down on the table. She popped its latch and removed a set of crystal shot glasses that she arranged around a three-spout silver funnel. "Is this Absinth?" I asked as she set a sizable bottle of honey-colored liquor near us. Manuel said nothing, motioning for me to pay attention. In contrast, Benny took the opportunity to jam a knuckle deep into my ribs which I took as a silent "Shut the hell up."

The first twin removed her crate, finished as the second took her place. Optimistically hoping her box would just be an assortment of mixers, Benny blocked me from running away when she slowly withdrew a live and very pissed-off cobra. She gripped the snake tightly in both hands and twisted it to stare directly into her eyes. I watched with suspense, fully prepared for a sideshow snake-charmer act that never happened. The first twin stepped in and snipped off the head of the cobra with a pair of gold sheers. "Oh shit." An unplanned reaction before my brain had a chance to stop it. Manuel laughed, finding this all very amusing. "Relax my friend, you are about to experience a rare treat." I squirmed in my seat as the decapitated body of the serpent was turned upside down over the funnel, the free-flowing blood distributing itself evenly among the shots. "Count my lucky stars," whispering quietly as the second twin topped off the glasses with the golden liquor.

As smoothly as they had transitioned in for the tableside service, they departed, leaving behind only three glasses of swirling pink liquid. Benny and Manuel reached for a glass, and, refusing to be the odd man out, I followed behind. Manuel and I watched as Benny was the first to knock back her *treat*. Her technique was perfect as she tilted her head slightly and tossed the liquid down her throat before slamming the glass back on the table. She swallowed as a slight shiver ran down her body. "Beauty slays the beast," Manuel quipped, enjoying the show before finishing his drink in a more dignified manner. As he placed his glass upside down, he gave me a concerned look as

I had yet to touch mine. Now was not the time to fail, I lifted the shot towards both of them and, with a less than enthusiastic "Que Sera," dumped the contents into my mouth.

The sensations intermixing suddenly hit me like a light-speed brick. It was thick, a taste of copper that burned my mouth and caused my lips to numb. I tried like Hell to swallow as my cheeks fully inflated, eyes watering like a heartbroken chipmunk. I tapped my foot on the ground to psych myself up, eventually finding the strength to get the repugnant sludge into my stomach. I was pretty sure it was in poor taste to call your host a sadistic asshole, so I did my best to seem grateful. "Very smooth," I managed in a way that was less than convincing. Manuel nodded graciously before turning towards Benny. "Senorita Bernice, I do not believe your companion and I have been properly introduced." It felt odd being talked about as if I wasn't there. "Of course," Benny agreed as she laid a gentle hand on my shoulder. "This is Mr. Austin, a close personal friend. He is in the transportation industry and he is helping me find answers to a situation that I have recently found troubling." "Forgive me, Senor Austin but I have not seen you in my city before," as he stretched his hand across the table towards me. Reminded that it was best to use honey to catch flies, I mirrored his politeness, "No, you would not have. I recently arrived." I lied as I gripped his hand firmly. His eyes iced over as all traces of pupil faded into a crystalline white. "No, you have not," he stated as a matter-of-fact, "you have been in this city longer than most."

His eyes returned to their natural state as he released his grip. "I can respect a man trying to protect his privacy however, so I take no offense." I pulled my arm back trying to figure out what happened. "What the hell are you?" Betraying the relaxed image I was hoping to project. "The question is, what are you?" He replied. "Yet I feel that you are owed an explanation, seeing as how you and Senorita Bernice were treated so disrespectfully." He flicked his wrist to readjust an uncomfortably heavy-looking watch worth more than most cars. "I, like my father and his father and so forth, was born a brujo." I nodded, pretending to know what that meant as Benny leaned over, whispering in my ear, "practitioner of witchcraft." I renewed my false confidence, "Yes, A warlock, of course." His eyes narrowed at the apparent insult. "Witches, Warlocks!" He spat on the ground in disgust, "Children playing doctor. I have no need for spells and cauldrons. We are Brujo. Our abilities are birthright." I backed off and tried to redirect him into a topic I could tell he preferred, himself. "Interesting, and your talent is?" His vicious smile returned. "I can see the truth of a soul from a touch. I can see where one has been and where one desires to go." He turned his attention back towards Benny. "Many years ago I had the privilege of seeing Senorita Bernice here. I could see her as the noble rose among thorns." I suppressed further embarrassment at how thick he was laying on the act. "Well, what did you see when you touched me?" He looked me over, intrigued. "I saw time. Lots of time, both past and future. That is all. You are a mystery, and I will tell you that I am a man who enjoys mysteries." Relieved that he didn't understand who, or what, I was, I pressed further to control the conversation. "Why is such a powerful Brujo spending his nights as a club owner? I'm sure there is much more you can do with a *birthright* like that."

He reached into his pocket and removed a rhinestone-studded phone, holding it as a prop to explain. "The world is so different from how it once was. We have the internet, smartphones, social media; you can research the history of anyone right from your phone. There is no need for someone like me. I have become..." He searched his thoughts for the right word, finally snapping his fingers as he found it. "Redundant. Instead, I have found that two things will always be in demand. Information and Entertainment. I choose to deal in both."

Benny reached out and placed her hand on his cuff, careful to avoid his skin. "Yes, and that is exactly why we came to you. You are the best when it comes to information, and we need you right now." Manuel responded with false modesty. "You flatter me, I wish to help in any way I can." "Excellent," Benny signaled that I should explain. "A child's body was found in the 51st-floor suite of the Park Plaza Hotel. He was surrounded by a room painted in sigils. It appeared to be some sort of sacrifice or ceremony." I used a bar napkin and pen from my jacket to recreate some of the symbols as best I could. As I finished explaining the scene, Manuel looked at me, empathizing. "Yes. A city that burns as brightly as this one will sometimes cast very dark shadows. Any time a child comes to harm it is unfortunate, yet it has happened on occasion. Isn't this a matter for the police to investigate?" Anger set in at his cavalier attitude towards everything I told him. Referring to the murder of a child as *unfortunate* rubbed me the wrong way. "There's more. The child's soul was damned. That is something beyond the jurisdiction of the city's authorities. We need to know who killed him and why."

Manuel eyed us quizzically. "Please forgive me, Senor Austin. It is not that I don't believe you. There are just too many questions when it comes to your story." I slammed my hand down on the table, losing the last bit of control I had over my temper. "What questions? I was there!" Manuel remained calm as his guards stood ready. "Yes, well, I find that rather odd. The hotel you speak of, it is a beloved piece of architecture within this city. Its history is well documented. I have been a guest there many times myself. So forgive my ignorance, but I am not aware of such a suite." My train of thought derailed in disbelief. Was he lying? Could he have been covering for someone? Who could be unaware of the entire top floor? It wasn't like they were going out of their way to hide it. Manuel continued, pulling me out of my question loop.

"Furthermore, there are known universal rules. They are set in stone and unchanging. Some of us," he said as he eyed Benny, "were damned a long time ago. No lifetime of good deeds may ever change that." Looking back at me, "children, however; they cannot be damned. It is an impossibility. I'm sorry to say that your information appears to be wrong." He stood up from the table, buttoning his jacket and smoothing the wrinkles. "I wish I could help you, but unfortunately it is outside of my ability. You come to me asking for answers to questions you do not fully have. Once you find out a little more about this *situation*, please let me know. I would be happy to continue our conversation. Until then..." his guards moved in closer, I knew I had to act. Manuel wasn't our best option right now, but with the limited time I had left, he was our only option. It was time to forgo this bullshit act and grab his attention by the balls. As Benny began to say something I pulled the knife from my inner pocket and plunged its tip into the tabletop.

Silence ensued as Benny, Manuel, and the motionless guards stared in disbelief as the upright knife pierced the solid marble as if it were pine. Manuel motioned the surrounding muscle to stand down as he again took his seat. "This changes things somewhat," with a newly focused demeanor. He unfolded a cloth napkin and used it to grip the knife, pulling it from the tabletop. "This is a very powerful object. One that I assume you found with the child?" I was cautious in confirming his suspicion. "Do you know what it is?" He shook his head, "No, but I can feel its power through the cloth. I am fearful of touching it directly." My hopes sank. "So you don't actually have any answers then." Manuel looked up at me from the knife as his smooth persona shattered, only his accent remaining. "Not directly, no, but I do know something that would help." He set the knife back down directly in front of me. "Information is not free, though. We can work out a trade." Benny jumped in, showing she was as eager for answers as I was. "What are the terms?"

Manuel's vicious smile returned. "Senorita Bernice. From you, I simply ask that you escort me to an event of my choosing. It is of great benefit for my professional reputation to be seen with someone such as yourself on my arm." He paused, punctuating his request. "In your true form, of course." He pointed towards the horns that still protruded from her forehead. Benny agreed without a second thought. "Agreed, but nothing physical." Manuel conceded, acting as if he were insulted. "On my honor. I am a gentleman." Turning his attention towards me, "as for you my friend, I ask for a simple yes or no answer to a question of my choosing. That is all. Do you agree?" I tried to play out any screwed-up monkey paw scenario in my head, looking for a way he could fuck me over with a yes or no question. "Agreed." I said as I placed the knife back into my jacket. "Excellent. The item you possess, I know nothing of it. I have, however, heard rumors of other items similar to it. Rare and dangerous objects, all being gathered together in this city. Are you familiar with Thomas Whitehall?"

I took a moment, racking my memory as I saw Benny nod. Knowing I had no time left to pretend, I confessed, "Never heard of it. Is it somewhere in the city?" Manuel laughed as though I had asked why the sky was blue. "No. You misunderstand," he explained. "Thomas Whitehall is a man. Not a place. He is the heir to the Whitehall fortune. Perhaps the most powerful family this city has ever known." I listened with my own suspicion. "This city has been my home for a long time. If his family is so powerful, then why haven't I heard of him?" It was getting old how he kept looking at me as if I were an amusing moron. "It is of no surprise that you have not. Someone who seeks power will do all they can to achieve notoriety, while those who truly hold power will do all they can to remain unknown. His family has spent a great deal to ensure that they are virtually nonexistent. Yet they own almost every important feature of this city. The most renowned architecture, the infrastructure, business interests, even the fine art. All are owned by organizations operated under the Whitehall portfolio." I had a flash of the priceless paintings that hung with so little care in the suite. "Lately there has been talk that Thomas, the last remaining Whitehall and sole controlling force behind their influence, has taken an interest in the metaphysical. I have heard of many priceless artifacts finding their way into his possession. No one is sure why he has begun amassing such a collection." He pointed towards my chest where the knife rested. "Yet the fact that such an item made its way into this city seems like an improbable coincidence. If anyone had the resources to identify what that is and where it came from, it would be Senor Whitehall." He turned back towards Benny, "I will have my assistant provide you with the information on where the Whitehall compound resides. It will be up to you to find a way to contact him. I would appreciate it if this information was not something you received from me.

"This conversation never occurred as far as we're concerned." Speaking up as I motioned towards Benny since it looked like our chance to leave. "We appreciate your time," but before I could finish, an oversized guard blocked my escape. "I'm sorry my friend," Manuel shook his head, his voice dripping with condescension, "we have a standing arrangement. I have upheld my end. Now it is time for you to uphold yours." I slid back into the seat, attempting to show that I wasn't intimidated. "Well then, ask your question." "My question. Please do not be concerned. It is a very simple question, but it does require some context. Please indulge me in the telling of a quick story." He folded his hands in thought. "Sorry, Hell Heffner. We're in a time crunch here and I agreed to a yes or no question. Not story time." Benny pinched my thigh under the table hard enough that I let out a small yelp that she quickly covered up. "Please, Manuel, go on."

He sneered at my pain before beginning. "When I was a child, my grandfather, another very powerful Brujo, used to tell a story from when he was a young boy." He stared at me with an uncomfortable intensity. "He told me how his father, being a Brujo, was not allowed to live close to the other villagers. Instead, they lived further out than anyone else who lived around them, save for one man." He held up a single finger to accentuate his words. "He was an elderly man who lived alone, but no one knew where. This man would often come into the village riding a dark stallion and pulling an empty coach. No one knew who he was or what he did." Manuel unfolded his hands and placed them flat on the table. "That is until one day, as my grandfather told it, when his mother died. She had been sick for a long time. One evening late into the night, unable to hold on any longer, she let go. My grandfather was heartbroken. Not knowing what to do, he took off into the night, running into the desert to cry upon a large stone. My grandfather sat on that stone, crying and sobbing until he heard the sound of hoofs pounding slowly against the ground." Entranced in Manuel's story, hair stood on the back of my neck as I knew where it was going.

"When he looked up, he could see the old man riding through the quiet night, the same coach in tow. Only this time, it was not empty. As it passed, he could see that inside his mother sat, beautiful and more peaceful than he had seen her in years. As their eyes met, she blew him a single kiss to say goodbye." Manuel sat quietly for a moment to let his story simmer. "When my grandfather spoke of what he saw, he was told of those who did God's will by carrying the dead over to their final resting place. Santa Muerte, La Parca...the reapers. My grandfather knew what he had seen that night." He stood up again, the conscious power move of always being the first to leave. "So now is the time where you keep your end of our agreement. I find you to be a mystery Senor Austin, but every mystery has an answer. Would I be correct in assuming that you are as my grandfather saw that night?" I glanced at Benny who returned the look stoically. Void of answers, my gut instinct took over. Refusing to feed into his false sense of power, I stood and helped Benny from the booth. "I have your answer, but it is more than a yes or no." Manuel bowed his head, conceding as I stepped in close. Leaning towards his ear I quietly spoke. "I'll personally deliver you to Hell."

XVIII

Benny's laughter filled the backseat of the limo when I finally told her what I had said. "Holy Shit!" her red face doubled over in laughter, "I'm almost positive he pissed himself. Priceless. that is without question priceless." I wanted to join Benny's enthusiasm but found myself too wrapped up in other things. I knew the direction, but no idea of what lies ahead; I didn't feel much like celebrating. That didn't mean I should stop her from enjoying herself; I only hoped that this night wouldn't reawaken the parts of her she had spent so long trying to overcome.

She joyfully dabbed at her eyes with a tissue. Her horns had now retracted entirely within her forehead and had it not been for two minor puncture wounds, it was as if they had never existed. "Does that hurt?" I asked, pointing to her forehead. "These?" Regaining her composure and running a finger gently over the two small holes. "Nah. It's actually kinda nice. Like cracking your knuckles. The downside is that it's going to look like two giant zits for the next few days, but they'll heal over." As she settled, I reached over and touched her hand. "I really appreciate everything you did back there. I've spent a long time relying on myself and I'm not going to lie, things aren't looking good. I know where to go next but the clock is ticking down. If I were betting, I would wager everything I owned against me right now. If this all fails, I just wanted you to know that you have my gratitude and there's nothing more we could have done."

I was expecting to see her dab her eyes again, overcome with emotion from my sincere and touching thank you. Instead, I rocked forward as she smacked me on the back of the head. "Don't be an idiot," as if I had said something outlandish, "this isn't over until you've been pulled into the pit kicking and screaming. Until that happens, stop making excuses and start getting shit done." It wasn't the most eloquent pep talk, although it seemed to be what I needed at the moment. She slid open a small minibar built into the upholstery of the limo. "Hold this," passing me a half-filled crystal decanter. Next came a slender can and two rocks glasses. "What's that?" I asked, pointing towards the thin aluminum can she had just popped open. "An Energy drink, grandpa. Coffee is for relaxing and discussing the weather. This is what the kids drink now to kick their asses into gear." She split the yellowish liquid from the can between the two glasses and topped them off with the whiskey from the decanter. She passed me one, and I took a cautious sip. It was tart and medicinal but not totally repulsive. "I just got an email with the directions to the Whitehall estate. It's a decent drive outside of town." I finished off the last of the drink and passed the glass back to Benny. "Good. Once we get back to your place I'll write down the directions. The kid and I will find a way there." Concern set into her face, but she said nothing.

A few miles and another energy drink later, we arrived at Benny's apartment. I made a gentlemanly attempt to excuse myself from the back seat, but she wasn't about to wait for me to open her door this time. Instead, after letting herself out, she quickly made her way upstairs. I appreciated her sense of urgency and followed without complaint. As she turned the doorknob of her apartment, she stated loudly to the room, "Austin, you are my guest, get your ass inside." It was a little less formal than her last invitation, but it did the trick since I could pass through without flattening my nose again. "Thanks. I'm going to throw my old clothes back on." I was about to ask her for directions, when she kicked off her heels and vanished into one of the apartment's back rooms. "Hold up," she yelled with the sound of something being shuffled around.

I took a moment to step into the living room and peered over the couch. The kid had fallen asleep. One of his hands firmly gripped the television remote while the other sat resting on the sofa, cake with orange cheese puff dust. I did my best to silently back out of the room, wanting the kid to rest as much as possible. My clothes were still balled up where I had left them, letting me quickly change into the familiar comfort of denim and cotton. Not the most elegant attire, but it served its purpose. Lacing up my boots, I yelled towards the back of the apartment. "Hey Ben. How's it coming with those directions." The shuffling came to a stop as she responded. "Yeah, about that."

She stepped back into the hallway, a renewed image of the girl I had known for so long. She wore faded ripped jeans tucked into high laced combat boots. A faded gray t-shirt with the words "Getting dirty at thirty" was prominent under a red flannel overshirt, and her meticulous updo had been converted into a ponytail pulled through the back of a dirty trucker's cap. She held up her cellphone so I could see it. "You don't have a ride, you don't know how to work one of these, and I'm not writing the directions down for you. Added all together, it looks like I'm going with you." Her points were valid despite not wanting to put her at any more risk. "Do you know what's coming for us? If She..." I quickly corrected myself. "If they see you with us, then I don't know what could happen to you. I'm no expert on angels but I'm fairly certain they're not known for being fans of your kind." "Well, tough shit. No one tells me what I can and can't do." She slipped her phone into her back pocket knowing there was no way I could get it from her. "Either I go with you, or you pick a direction and start blindly walking until that halo comes for your ass."

She was right, and I didn't have the time to argue. I agreed with a simple sigh and stepped back into the living room. Nudging the kid gently, "Hey, Short Stack. Wake up. We've got to get moving." The kid stirred gently and rubbed at his eyes, remembering where he was. "Did you get everything fixed?" He asked optimistically as he whirled back into action. "Almost," I lied, "We just need to take care of a few more details." The hope in his eyes at the necessary lie eroded a small part of my soul. If I couldn't save the kid from eternity, I could at least give him hope for as long as possible. "The nice lady over there whose pantry you emptied is going to give us a ride to someone else's place. We have a good chance at figuring this stuff out." The kid pushed himself from the couch, eager to lead the way. "Let's go get answers then."

Benny led us back to the elevators, this time choosing the button for the basement. As it came to a squeaking stop, the doors pulled back to reveal a dimly lit parking garage sparsely scattered with luxury vehicles and the occasional weekend warrior's motorcycle. "Far corner," she instructed, guiding us through the damp garage. "I don't come down here too often, don't really need to. The city's gotten so big that traffic is a nonstop suck-fest. It's just easier to take the bus most of the time." We moved in closer to the isolated back corner; home to a single tarp-covered automobile. "Nevertheless, I like to keep him around for special occasions like this." She pulled back the cover to accentuate her statement, beaming with pride at the reveal of a pristine 1955 Ford Thunderbird polished to a rich mirror shine. "It's only a two-seater, but the kid's small enough to ride lucky Pierre."

It's been said that a car is a representation of the owner. An odd idea considering I drove the cliche representation of posh British culture that stood right alongside teatime and terrible teeth. I could never wrap my head around how that represented me since most of the time I felt like 12 pounds of shit jammed into a well-worn bag. Benny's vehicle was different. It was solid and sleek, feminine but with a bite that could tear you a new asshole. It was older than any other in the garage but looked like it had rolled off the production line yesterday. It summed her up perfectly. I watched as she reached beneath the undercarriage and pulled out a set of keys stashed away. "Door should be open. Hop in."

The garage echoed with the classic sound of solid steel doors slamming closed as we fell into place. Benny sat behind the wheel, which left me as uncomfortable as ever riding shotgun with the kid wedged firmly between us. "How far is this place?" I asked, still unsure of exactly which direction we were going. Benny looked slightly dejected, "about an hour if we follow the speed limit. I'll get us there in half." She pulled her phone from her jacket and slipped it into a mount attached to the dash. After a few pushed buttons, the phone began to speak with a robotic female voice giving us turn-by-turn directions. I didn't trust it. How would a machine know how to get there any better than I do?

Rumbling through the night streets, Benny enjoyed herself zipping between cars and taking speed limit signs as minor suggestions. We were moving north, outside the city proper and into the large land tracts reserved for private estates. It was an area I should have guessed. "So," Benny broke the silence, leaning back against the bench seat with one hand on the wheel. "When we do get there, what's the plan? Are you going to just walk up to the front door and start asking questions?" I thought for a minute before ad-libbing, "Through the door, not up to it. I figured the kid and I could cross incorporeal and have a look around. It's late, maybe we'll get lucky and this Whitehall guy will be asleep. If that's the case, I could always pull a Jacob Marley and scare a few answers out of him." She looked away from the road and cocked her eyebrow in my direction, pausing to see if I had anything else to add. "Seriously? You're basing your one chance here off an almost 200-year-old Christmas book? That's the best you could come up with."

Sadly it was, but I shot back. "Well, not all of us can make goo-goo eyes and get him to reveal everything in the off chance he might score." She stuck out her tongue before reaching over with her free hand to pinch my cheek firmly. "Awww, with a cute face like that, you're selling yourself short. Plenty of boys would sell out their mothers for a chance to score with you." I pushed her hand away as the kid spoke up. "What do you mean score?" Benny laughed again, both of us forgetting the kid was even there. "Score points. Like a video game, only It's a game for adults. It'll make more sense when you grow up." Her smiling continued as she enjoyed her explanation. I kept my mouth shut, solemnly thinking; "Sorry Ben, but the kid's not growing up."

The city was fading away slowly as we pushed further out. Freeways became single-lane roads, light poles shifting into trees; it wasn't long before our entire surroundings were dark and wooded. We sped along the winding road as Benny's phone ticked away the miles. "Okay. We're coming up on the turn-off," pointing to a small map on her screen. "There's no reason to announce your presence earlier than you need to. It looks like his driveway is about a half-mile long. I'll pull over just outside of it. You two will have to hike the rest of the way." We were in agreement. "That works. Drop us off, then please head back. I have no idea what we're going to find here or how long it's going to take. It's best for you if no one sees us together." She wasn't happy about it, but I knew she agreed.

A few seconds later Benny began slowing as she pulled to the side of the country road. "This is as close as we can get without it being obvious. Keep heading up this road and make a left; that's the entryway to the Estate. It's the only thing out here, so it shouldn't be difficult to spot." Popping open the heavy door to step out, I could hear the kid shuffle as he followed. It only felt right to thank Benny for everything she had done. "Don't...." She stopped me. "You're going to say thanks, and you're going to say it like it's goodbye. Don't" I was taken back. "I do appreciate everything you've done for us." She placed both hands on the wheel while maintaining her composure. "It's not easy to make friends. When you do, you do what you have to when they need help." It was my turn to say something poignant, but she interrupted before I could speak. "It's not goodbye."

I let her finish, "You don't have much time left and this whole thing is a crapshoot at best." I could hear the sincerity in her voice, "but if anyone could get this shit sorted, it's you Austin. Maybe." I wanted to see where she was going with this. "And if I don't?" She gripped the wheel a little tighter. "A long lifespan, even a really long one like mine, it's still just a blip in eternity. If things go bust and you end up down south, know that I'll be down there beside you before you know it." It wasn't the most pleasant thought, but I respected how she faced the future head-on even when the outlook was grim. "Then let's just say, I'll see you soon. One more thing, if you would." Pulling the knife from the pocket, I placed it down on the passenger seat beside her. "For safekeeping." She was timid in a way I wasn't used to as she finally faced me. "I'll see you soon."

With those words she took off, leaving us alone along the dark road. I kept the kid close and leaned towards him, his face barely lit by the moon. "Where we're going isn't far up this road, but I need you to disappear before we go. Remember what I taught you earlier?" He inspected the empty road, uncomfortable with what was going on. "You're scared. I understand. That's good. It's good to be scared right now. You need to use it. Think about what I taught you; focus on those fears. Think about where we are but imagine I'm not here beside you. It's dark. It's creepy. Think of all the things that could come out of those woods at any moment just to get you. Bears, wolves, things you have never even heard of before. Think of strangers, think of gunshots, think of all those things, and use them. Use them to hide; you need to hide from the entire world. Grab that feeling and pull it around yourself like a blanket." A small tear began to well up in the kid's eyes as another piece of me fell apart. I knew it had to be done. His small fading hand reached up and wiped the tear from his eye as his body dimmed into nothingness.

I followed, dropping away the feeling of my physical form and joining him in the ether. "You did good, kid," still leaning in close. "Just like before, you stick by my side unless I say otherwise and stay hidden. Do not go solid unless I tell you, understand?" "Is it safe?" he asked cautiously. "In the form you're in, you couldn't be safer. I haven't let you down so far." I ran through scenarios in my head as we made our way further, considering every question I could ask and how I could force answers. It did little to help when every chance and every possibility was met with the same question the kid had posed to me. "Was it safe?"

XIX

It was only a few minutes into our wooded trek before reaching an 8-foot brick barrier that snaked its way around the property. Passing through, we now had a much better picture of the mansion in the distance. "I'd say it's safe to assume that's where we're going." We followed through the trees along a blacktop driveway and soon heard the creaking of a security gate as a black SUV quietly rolled past. I wasn't sure exactly what time it was, but this was more than a casual visit. Whoever just passed us must have been here for a specific reason. That threw a wrench into my well-thought-out plan of hoping Whitehall was asleep. Our only option now was to fall back to plan b, improvise. "We need to follow them; you up for a jog?" The kid seemed excited at the suggestion. As I pointed towards the moving vehicle, I reiterated, "Ok, we just need to catch up." The kid took off like a jackrabbit. Not wanting to be left behind like the old man I was, I followed, maintaining an even pace as I told myself that my heart couldn't possibly explode no matter how much it felt like it.

I've always believed that a *runner's high* was a bullshit myth, but this little exercise confirmed that *runner's nausea* was very real. The kid stood near the door, watching me as 2 men climbed out of the SUV parked beside us. They were older, well dressed but hard-edged. Giving off the aura of professionals in a questionable profession, similar to the hired help I just finished dealing with back at the Hotter Than Hell. The only difference was the last jackasses had been store-brand generic muscle heads while these guys were obviously the top-shelf alternatives. The kid and I stood as one of them knocked on the front door before it creaked open, revealing a frail and ungodly tired-looking butler who ushered them inside. I hooked at thumb their way and motioned to follow as the door slammed in our nonexistent faces.

It was clear these men had a purpose, and working under my best assumption, I'd say they were here for the same guy we were. If we were lucky, they would lead us straight to what we were looking for. As we followed closely, the butler led them through the maze-like mansion, curving and winding past what felt like miles of rooms and entertainment areas before arriving at a set of large oak double doors held tightly shut. The apparent leader of the two reached out and gave another quick knock. Shuffling behind the doors revealed another well-dressed man seemingly of the same occupation as the ones we stood behind.

The new guy inside the doorway grunted. "Took your sweet ass time, didn't you?" He stood staring down at the two in front of us before the smaller one finally spoke up. "Nah," he said, pulling back his sleeve to gesture towards his watch, "it says here that it just turned mind-your-God-damn-business O'clock. Seems like we're right on time." The door guard stepped aside as I pulled the kid to follow the others inside.

Inside the double doors was a picturesque study that any well-to-do mansion simply couldn't go without. A room dedicated to sipping brandy and planning the next stock market crash that felt oddly familiar. It took me a moment to realize the study was a direct extension of the penthouse where

I found the kid. Designed with the same motif and, in some places, the same unique furniture. Two of its four walls were lined floor to ceiling with mahogany bookcases arranged with antiquities whose age seemed to defy possibility. Interspersed through the open area were pedestals on which sat objects I could only describe as occult. Ornately decorated skulls, ceremonial jewelry, what appeared to be a candle made from a hand coated in wax; all esoteric and perfect companion pieces for the knife. A large stacked stone fireplace burned at the far end of the room and near it was an impractically oversized desk clearly meant to intimidate. Its swirling burl top sat empty save for a single silver pen resting on a sheet of unused paper. A series of chairs were arranged in a semicircle around the desk as they played host to the asses of other cartoonish henchmen. We followed the two men over to their seats before I spotted an area that seemed like the best place for us to post up. The kid and I took a spot behind a well-stocked bar that sat adjacent to the desk area, a perfect place to listen even if the kid was barely able to see over the countertop.

For the first time I noticed someone was sitting behind the desk, twirled around in a tall leather chair so his back faced the circle of men. A power move that I'm sure wasn't lost on anyone. Beside the desk in a cheap-looking black suit stood a tall sunken faced impossibly thin man who set himself apart as the only person in the room who chose to stand. As the two settled themselves, the thin man leaned into the leather chair and whispered something unintelligible.

"I'm glad everyone has decided to show up finally. It was kind of you to be so considerate." The voice dripped with sarcasm as the high back chair swung around, revealing the man who sat within. "I know we planned to meet tomorrow to discuss the current situation as it pertains to our little experiment; however, I was informed of some rather concerning news so I felt it necessary to push that meeting up to now." This had to be our guy, this had to be Whitehall. I moved further down the bar to get a full view of him as he spoke. He was a delicate-looking man with the type of youthful appearance that could only be purchased from the right plastic surgeon. His skin was expertly bronzed and sat in contrast to the falsely colored blond hair given away by the darker tone of his perfectly shaped eyebrows. He wore a set of monogrammed pajamas and a matching robe as he slumped back in his power seat. Steepled fingers gave him the look of a true cartoon villain. "I think we should begin by first explaining where such a successful endeavor began to fall apart. For that, I'll turn things over to Mr. Mancinni." It was evident from the moment he opened his mouth that Whitehall was a dick; Smug yet business-like, the kind of attitude that came with knowing you could buy anyone in the room. I got the feeling that in some corner of the mansion was a vault with a swimming pool full of gold coins he occasionally tried to swim in.

In one of the chairs to his left a man rose to his feet, addressing the others. "We don't have all the details, but it has been confirmed by some of our resources that the kid never made it over. We're not sure why but it's believed that it has something to do with the entity tasked with crossing him to damnation. We have a $500,000 offer to anyone with more information on what may have occurred. Once we find out, we'll relay the information to you." He then sat down as my heart sank like a lead weight. *Kid. Crossing. Damnation.* They were talking about us and somehow, call it sheer dumb luck, we managed to be in the room. The intense feelings of relief and frustration became almost overwhelming. I paced out from behind the bar, trying to think before leaning up against a section of wall. As the conversation held my attention, I saw Whitehall sit up in his seat, lifting the silver pen from the table. "Well then, I think we can summarize that by saying you have no idea what the hell you're talking about. We'll move on." He extended the pen and pointed to the smaller of the men we followed into the room. "You seemed to have some interesting information to go along with that. Care to share with the rest of us?"

He stood next. "Yes. We were told that the kid was more than likely with the Ferryman for the area." One of the group members closest to me leaned in towards his neighbor, "What exactly is a fairy-man?" "We found out who that was, and we put eyes on him. Turns out he and some little piece of demon ass were asking a bunch of questions at Sangre's place a few hours ago. No sign of the kid but one of my informants who works for Sangre said he saw the knife being flashed around." I looked over at the kid who, even at his young age, knew we were in the middle of some serious shit.

"Thank you Mr. Hoffman," drolled Whitehall. "I appreciate you bringing that to my attention, so please do not be offended when I explain the way I have used you." Hoffman's head tilted like a confused puppy as he tried to process what was said. "I pay you gentleman very well, do I not?" Whitehall asked the group. As he spoke, the weirdest feeling came over me. I couldn't put my finger on it, yet something felt out of place. I brushed it off as he continued. "A majority of the time you all bring me excellent information. I do thank you for that. So please try to look at it from my perspective. Mr. Hoffman here has just given a fantastic example of just how slow and stupid you all really are." My nerves were beginning to get the best of me as the strange feeling grew. "Could you possibly imagine if I relied solely on all of you to get information for me? I would have to be as simpleminded as, well, all of you." The men grit their teeth as they took the abuse. I rested a little heavier against the wall when a startling realization hit me, what had felt so wrong all along. I was incorporeal, bodiless, without a solid form. So how was I leaning against the wall without passing through it?

Whitehall's voice seemed much further away. "Mr. Sangre called me personally the moment they left his establishment. He informed me of everything that had occurred. He was also kind enough to direct both of them to my home, knowing they would make their way here." The thin man that stood to his side leaned in again. Only this time, when he finished, he wasn't staring off into the distance. Instead, it looked like he was staring right at me. "I don't believe I have formally introduced my associate here, have I?" He gestured towards the thin man whose attention seemed fixated in my direction. "You may call him Stallworth, and unlike any of you, he has actual talent. He is a clairvoyant." Whitehall then pantomimed a whisper as if he were speaking to children, "That means he can see spirits." He corrected his posture. "Lots of claims for that type of talent of course, but finding someone who truly has the ability is very rare. Very expensive as well." Pieces fit together as the kid looked to figure out what was going on. I didn't have the heart to tell him I just tap-danced us both straight into a trap.

"Knowing they were on their way here, I had to take advantage of such a great opportunity, and that's why I kept you all waiting. We weren't sitting around waiting for these two to show up." Whitehall pointed towards the two men we followed in. "We were waiting for our other guests. Stallworth, where are they currently?" The thin man kept his gaze locked tightly on where I stood as he raised a fragile arm and outstretched his finger in my direction. "Well then, Mr. Austin I believe it is; you might as well just show yourself so we can discuss this in a civilized manner." My thoughts raced as I was called out. Do I give this asshole the satisfaction of knowing he was right? Or do I slink out of the room with the kid, hoping he would just look like a paranoid schizo? I was still deciding when he turned impatient. "You're really going to make me wait? Ok, fine, then do me a favor. Stallworth informed me that you haven't tried to leave this room yet. Just as an FYI, if you had, you would have noticed that the walls were not something you could simply pass through." A tense sensation ran up my back knowing he was right. "Spirit binding. It's inscribed directly into the framework of this library. It cost a little more to have it constructed, but it seems to have come in handy." He leaned forward, folding his hands on the desk. "You're in here until we let you out, and that's not happening any time soon. Come on, let's talk this through like adults."

Backed into a corner, I held my hand up to the kid hoping he would get my message. It was a gesture that read stay put and stay immaterial. With my back against the real and metaphorical wall, I took a breath and passed back into solid form. "You are a tricky bastard. I'll give you that," I forced a false bravado that startled the circle of men. Some of them slid backward in their chairs while others leapt to their feet as a man materialized before their eyes. Whitehall sat unmoved and flashed a brilliant set of sharp white teeth. "Now that is one hell of a trick Mr. Austin. Truly impressive." I didn't have much time to plan, but I dialed up the confidence determined to lead this dance. "Let's hope it's the only one I have to show you tonight. So, what's the game here? Just so I know how to follow the rules." One of the men from the circle moved in closer. I could tell he was debating between tackling me to the ground or running away in fear. I turned my head towards him, barking a loud "Boo!"

The man fell to his ass as Whitehall laughed loudly, finding it so very amusing. "You," he said, wiping his eyes and pointing towards me. "You are something, I'll give you that." I knew I had the circle of men in check, but Whitehall was different. He regarded me as a plaything, a sideshow attraction he wanted to poke with a stick. "I wanted to speak with you Mr. Austin," he said, regaining his composure. "It seems that I am in a bit of a situation where time is of the essence, and from the best information money can buy, I have gathered that you seemed to be at the root of it all. So please understand that my goal here is to come to some form of arrangement." His demeanor changed and became very intense as he sat forward in his chair, "by any means necessary."

I played off his thinly veiled threat and moved back to the bar, stepping behind it as I devoted my attention to the shelves of bottles. I didn't know where he was going, but the longer I could keep him talking the more it played to my advantage. "I'm open to arrangements," I shot back without turning around. I could hear his sly smile through his words. "Excellent. I had hoped you would be a reasonable man. I can offer you anything you could want. My resources are nearly limitless. Money, fame, a new warehouse with an even larger tent?"

I faltered for a moment, hoping it wouldn't show. How did he know about me? I had spent so many years living as a relative hermit that the idea of someone knowing any details of my life seemed shocking. "Wow, I could just shoot for the moon then, couldn't I?" I pulled a silver-topped bottle of rye from the mix on the shelf and held it up at him. "You mind?" pulling a glass from under the counter. "Please. Be my guest." he waved me off as if I were a peasant asking for scraps. "That one is a little stronger than the scotch you enjoyed so much at my penthouse. Be careful. It'll bite."

I cracked the cap and poured a few fingers into the glass, taking in its harsh aroma. "Let's give it a shot," I felt it sting the entire way down my throat. It took a moment for the pleasant pain to subside. "Well, I certainly have a few things on my Christmas list I wouldn't mind having. The only question is, what's the cost?" I could see Whitehall steeple his fingers again as he looked me over. "It's very simple. I only want you to do exactly what you do every day already. I want you to do your job." A gut feeling told me where this was going before he finished. "The Child Mr. Austin. I want you to finish what you started with the child. I want you to take him to where he was destined to go. I want you to set the world right. That is all." He had a lot of information; that was undeniable. He knew who I was, and he knew the kid in some way. He knew more about the bigger picture here than I could grasp. Yet he didn't know everything. "Well, that's where we have a bit of a problem," I said, recapping the bottle. "It's not going to happen. You make it sound so simple. I just drop the kid off and everyone goes about their business. It's just too bad I can't do that."

Whitehall shifted uncomfortably, arching his eyebrows. "Really..." he purred, "and why would that be?" I knew I could tell him. I could tell him about the Angel and my lack of a vehicle, about how I couldn't cross the divide without my car. I could let him know all about the time limit and how if he kept us occupied here a little longer, we would both end up in eternity's basement soon enough. I could tell him all of it, but I chose not to. Instead, I told him the one universal truth I knew above all else. "Because it's wrong."

The words pierced like a hot poker as he sprung to his feet. I could see in his anger he was not used to being told no. "That's not for you to decide," he shouted, slamming his fist down on his desk. A few of the men from the circle who had regained their composure were again startled by the outburst. "You are no judge, no jury. You're nothing more than a gear in the clockworks and it's men like me who do the winding. The child's path is written. You will not stand in the way of his destiny." His tone shifted to a forced calm, yet his eyes remained locked on me. "Stallworth, is the child in the room with us?" The thin man who still stood silently at his side extended his arm once more, pointing to the kid a few feet down the bar. "Well then. We have him," Whitehall smiled, "it would have been so much easier had you simply completed your task, but

with the right leverage I'm sure we can find another ...
Charon... to do as they are told."

He seemed to spit the words from behind his grin as he wrapped his silk robe tightly around himself. "Gentlemen, as I have said, please forgive me for using you in this manner, but I hope with what you have just seen transpire, you have a better understanding of why it was necessary. So now is an excellent time to renegotiate our business arrangement." He turned from his desk and pressed a recessed button causing flames within the fireplace to die out. "This man is a loose end from our previous endeavor, and as you may have heard, the spirit of the child is in the room with us as well." He stepped away from his desk as all eyes remained on him. The man named Stallworth followed him closely. "As many of you may know, I'm not a man that likes the unexpected. Allow me to put this to you. One million dollars to any individual in this room that finds a way to tie up that loose end." He pointed in my direction as all attention was thrust on me. "Two million for the child."

He continued walking toward the set of double doors in the room. Stallworth opened one for him as one of the thugs spoke up. "I thought you said guys like this one couldn't be killed?" Whitehall turned back towards us, amused. "About that. The honest answer is that no one really knows. I look at you, however, and I see a group of men who are very resourceful." He stepped over to one of the short marble columns. It was topped with a glass case that held a gilded copper femur sharpened into a spear. He lightly nudged the column over, sending the glass shattering to the floor as the spear tumbled. "I have spent a lot of money on these items. I have heard they are very powerful. I'm sure something in this room may work to your advantage." The men eyed the bone weapon as the idea clicked. I could see them scanning the room and the occult arsenal.

Whitehall stepped outside, prepared to leave us to our own devices, but not before popping his head back in momentarily. "Oh, one more thing. These doors are really nice, don't you agree? I paid extra for the hand-carved redwood outer shell. Don't let that fool you, inside they're solid steel. Once I shut them, they will be locked from the outside. Consider it a final bit of motivation. You either come out with these two problems resolved, or you don't come out at all." The door slammed shut behind him, the clink of a deadbolt echoing through the room.

I gave a nervous laugh as the eyes of every man in the room locked with vicious intent. "Hahaha. Oh boy. Let's all just relax and have a drink. We can talk this through. I'm sure we can find a reasonable compromise." It may have been the look in their eyes, but I had the feeling my suggestion was ignored. My fears confirmed, the circle of men produced guns simultaneously. Some were pulled from jackets while others from shoulder holsters, a few of the classier ones lifted from ankle straps. I watched as they moved in unison before a shower of bullets erupted in my direction.

The bottle of whiskey came crashing to the floor as I dropped my material form. The bullets passed through where I had been, destroying the array of liquors displayed on the shelf behind me. I knew I was safe as long as I remained incorporeal, but danger was not unique to this room. If I could get them to waste their limited ammunition, I may have another shot at negotiating an arrangement. Sure it wasn't the best plan, but it was all I had at the moment. I began running around the room, popping back into material form at random as the men shot wildly. I ran behind one of the men as he reloaded his silver revolver and shouted "Bamf!" into his ear as I momentarily appeared. The group continued to shoot in all directions, with some even throwing their guns once they ran out of bullets, hoping to hit me with something. As the shooting finally stopped, I resumed my physical form and addressed them all. "So, that was pointless, wasn't it?" One of the older men in the group began shouting, "It's the shit in the cases. Whitehall said to use the weird shit in the cases." In agreement, the men scattered around the room, knocking over displays and scavenging anything weapon-like they could find.

I pulled myself out of existence again and watched as one man began swinging a shaman's staff emphatically through the air, hoping to connect with some part of my body. A younger guy in the group rolled up his sleeves as he pulled a tribal spear from its wall mount and began stabbing at the nothingness around him. I took it all in with odd amusement, the collection of grown men so concerned with money and their own safety that they were literally fighting the air around them. In a way it made me sad, but as I saw an older balding man using the leg bone spear to fence with his own shadow, I couldn't help but laugh. My amusement broke when I found another guy with a look of determination carrying a flint war club over his shoulder as he made his way towards the bar where the kid still hid.

Was the kid safe from everything happening in the room? My best guess was *probably*, but I didn't want to leave anything to chance. I ran to where Whitehall had been sitting and, putting the large desk between the man and I, resumed solid form. "Hey Captain Caveman. Over here shithead." It was enough to get his attention, and with a flash of anger he began running towards me. I focused as he moved, but another strange sensation nagged at me. It was a smell, almost overwhelming once I resumed material form. Something familiar, something unpleasant. I looked around to find its origin. Over my shoulder, I could see where one of the bullets had punctured through the fireplace's wooden mantle, piercing the gas line as vapor leaked into the room. "Wait!" I yelled as the man continued to charge at me. He lifted the club high above his head as I raised my arms to cover my face. Yeah, it looked cowardly, but have you ever seen a weapon like this coming at you? It's a scary tool of war. Not something built just because it was so effective but also because it was honestly pant-shittingly frightening. The man ignored my cries and leapt to the top of the desk, towering over me as he began to swing the club down at my head.

You'll have to forgive me for being a little cautious, but this was the first time I have ever been in a position to possibly have my skull split in half. As I saw the edge of the ax hurtling towards me, I willed myself back into a nonexistent form, watching what came next from a position of immaterial safety. The man's eyes shot open as I vanished, realizing his mistake as the gas fumes hit him as well. It was too late to catch himself as he put every bit of strength into his blow, and as the club came down so did he. He crashed forward from the top of the desk losing his balance as the head of the ax struck down on the slate landing of the fireplace. Flint striking stone inside of a room filled with gas. It was a simple equation that could only produce one result. The last sound any of these men would hear alive.

...Boom.

XX

Remember that one spark? That's all it took to turn the once posh library brimming with rare objects and overly ambitious men into a smoldering tomb of could-have-beens. I stood at ground zero of the explosion from my unique perspective, watching it all unfold. The chance to admire it all in a way that very few could survive to tell about. Unfortunately, my story would be too short to impress anyone, summed up as "really bright and really loud."

I watched, slightly confused as the flames died down and pieces of ash fell through the air like blackened snowflakes. Even from the safety of nonexistence, the sudden impact of what had just occurred rattled my thoughts as I stood centered in the exposed room. I kept trying to put my finger on something important that I was overlooking. Patting myself down, I had my coat, the flask cradled in the inside pocket. All present and accounted for, so that couldn't have been it. I didn't have the car, which would have been really useful right about now. Almost everything else in the room was reduced to little more than charcoal, so none of it would be of any good to me. What the hell was I forgetting?

I scanned the room again, settling my eyes on the still-smoldering remnants of the once fully stocked bar. Its thick wooden sides now charred and barely supporting the scorched marble top struck me as I finally remembered. "The Kid!" I ran through the few remaining flames, kicking away fragments of chair and shelving that buried the back of the bar. As I pulled the final pieces of debris away, I found the kid staring out at me safely nested inside the well, his eyes wider than golf balls as his tone slowly crescendoed. "That. Was. AWESOME!" He yelled as he jumped out from under the bar, surveying the room excitedly. "Yeah, try telling that to the guys they're going to have to sweep into sandwich bags."

We stepped out and began surveying what was left of the library. It was still hazy from the dust and ash filled air, but the entirety of the room became more visible as it settled. The pressure of the explosion had blown the two locked doors from their hinges as they laid across the soot-filled floor like a bridge to freedom. There would be little left for Whitehall to salvage and in a sadistic way, that made me feel a little better. Then there were the dozen men plodding around the room aimlessly as they tried to figure out what had just happened.

It wasn't really them, of course, at least not as they used to be. Their bodies were gone, blown away to small chunks of human charcoal and the occasional bubbling puddle of goo. It was their souls that remained intact, and as the kid and I resumed incorporeal forms, we could see them wandering the room along with us. There was a sudden tap on my shoulder as I turned to see the previously ax-wielding henchman standing beside us. He looked perplexed before remembering his manners if nothing else. "Hey man," he said softly as I turned to face him, "sorry to bother you, but I'm supposed to be here for a meeting with Mr. Whitehall. Do you know if we're still doing that?" Avoiding a panic, it wasn't the best time to explain the truth to him. "About that. I think it's best if you hold tight and let me see if I can find out what's going on.

It wasn't surprising that he didn't remember what just happened. It was something I called separation shock. In a way, a blessing to the person who just died and something that made my job a little easier. When someone dies in a distressing way, most of the memories leading up to their final end will be lost when their soul separates. Think of it like a newborn baby. If they had to work through the memory of being pulled from their mother and scrubbed like a dirty potato, it would be a shitty way to start life. In the same way, it would really suck to start your first moments of death screaming when your soul splits away from your physical body as it's run over by a tractor-trailer. Right now, it worked in my favor that none of the men scratching their heads in the charred room remembered blowing themselves up while trying to kill me. The downside was how they kept asking if I knew when this meeting would start.

I pulled the kid over to a quiet corner of the room, grasping for a moment of clarity. "See these guys around us? Don't talk to them. If anyone asks why you're here, tell them to come talk to me. Understood?" The kid cinched up his backpack and gave me a look of agreement. "I'll be right back."

I left the kid alone in the security of the isolated corner. With the pathway to the hall now unblocked, I thrust my head out prairie dog fashion, examining the empty corridor. Shifting my scan from one end to the other, I could see the matching carpet and wallpaper combo that led to the decrepit butler who stood at the far end. "I have placed a call to the authorities," he said dryly in a way that was possibly a threat. "If you need assistance, they will be here shortly." I stepped into the hallway so he could see me a little better. "I'm fine. No need to worry. It's the rest of the guys in there that we should be concerned about. I don't think an ambulance is going to help much." I pointed back into the room and pantomimed an explosion with my hands for emphasis. "What's more important is that I make sure your boss Tommy is alright. We're old friends, where could I go about finding him?"

Trying to fake an ounce of concern, I guess my acting worked since he didn't waste any time with his response. "Mr. Whitehall and his associate left the compound a few moments ago. He said he was going to stay at one of his retreats for a few days." I tried to play it cool. "Oh really. Well, that's good to hear. Now, which retreat would that be? I've been to so many with him; did he happen to mention anything else? Maybe something to do with a child?" That must have set off an alarm within the old guy's head. "Mr. Whitehall prefers to keep his residences a private matter. I'm afraid only he knows where most of them are. All he made known was that he would be going away for a while, and he gave explicit instructions not to open the library doors under any circumstances." Changing the subject, I pointed behind me. "I don't think that's going to be an issue anymore, seeing as how there aren't any doors left to open anyways." The old man bent his head trying to see around me from the other end of the hallway. "Yes. That's excellent sir. One less concern, I suppose."

As we found ourselves in agreement, the blaring sirens of emergency responders interrupted our conversation. "If you would please wait here, medical assistance will be available to you soon." He turned toward a control panel set into the floral wallpaper remotely opening the front gates. I left the physical world again since there were more significant issues than being polite to the old man. The kid and I needed to find a way out of the mansion and back into the city, and we needed to do it in the fastest way possible. I rubbed my temples trying to think straight. If we went solid, any police officers or firefighters we passed on our way out might have a few questions about why we didn't match the dozen ash heaps on the floor. That was less than ideal since I had no ID, no vehicle, and they wouldn't like the explanations I had to offer. I did, however, have a child partnered with me that may or may not be on a missing person report somewhere.

Our other option was to remain incorporeal and breeze straight past anyone coming in. It was an excellent way to avoid any uncomfortable questions, but it ended with the kid and me hiking back along the dark wooded road. With the time limit we were working with; I might just yell for the halo to drag us downtown now and get it over with. I kept closing my eyes to focus on some way to get us out of here when one of the newly dead henchmen bumped into me. "Sorry about that," he said as he brushed away nonexistent dust from his coat. "You wouldn't know when we're getting started with all this, do you? I got things I gotta do tonight." "I wouldn't make any plans for the near future," trying to hint at what was about to occur when a plan struck me. It would take some convincing, but it was probably the only shot we had to get back to the city in decent time without anyone seeing us.

"Everyone!" I yelled into the decimated room of dead men, trying on my best mafia impression, and hoping to gain some authority. "I just got word from the boss. The meeting has been moved to another spot. He's sending someone to get us, but we need to get outside quietly. No talking to the uniforms when I turn you loose from here. Understand?" Some of the men agreed without question; others scratched their heads in hopeless confusion, while one took the opportunity to speak up. "Whitehall said to meet here. He didn't say nothing about no alternate location." I gave him my best 1000-yard stare before answering. "That is true, but I bet he didn't mention anything about his office getting blown to shit either, now did he? Shit happens, and we make do." I stepped across the room, pointing to one of the charred chairs balancing on its remaining three legs. "Now, you can either shut up and follow me or take a seat and relax here until the boss sends someone looking for you. Your choice."

The man's face flushed red with anger, which was no easy task for a lifeless spirit, but he held his tongue before falling in line with the others. I motioned for the kid in the back of the room to catch up. "Things went belly up real quick around here. As you can see, we need to get our asses moving." I hated cursing so loudly in front of the kid, but I had to keep the act up. If I lost the loose hold I had over these goons, things would take a tough turn. "We got cops out front, firefighters and meds too. You all just keep quiet and walk straight past them. They know what's going on, and I guarantee they're all going to act like they can't even see you." One of the men at the center of the group spoke up. "The boss probably paid 'em off. Told 'em they didn't see nothing going on here." I snapped my fingers and pointed to the man since going along with it was the most believable explanation. "Exactly. Paid them off. Now follow me and I'll show you where we're going."

I lead the deceased men in kindergarten fashion out of the room and through the halls. I could see some of them looking around as we passed through the Mansion. Inspecting pictures and eyeing first responders as they rushed past us. I picked up the pace trying to make it outside before any of them started to piece together memories of what had happened. We snaked along the mishmash of police cruisers and firetrucks that sat idling along the front entrance and out through the opened gates of the property. "Alright. Everyone hold up here. Our ride should be along any minute." I went down the line of men hoping we hadn't left anyone behind. As I made my way along, one of the men at the front became visibly aggravated. "Why are we standing out by the road like a bunch of schoolboys? I have my own driver that'll take me anywhere I need to go." I stomped over to him, a tall, muscular man with the kind of oily ponytail you wanted to yank.

"You see those black and whites over there?" The police cruisers were actually a few different shades of blue, but I heard the lingo in a detective movie once so I figured it worked. "What do you think is sitting on top of all of those dashboards?" I had to look up to meet his gaze as he thought for a moment. "Cameras," he answered in a meeker tone than I had expected. "Yes, cameras. You all followed me because we walked *around* the cameras so they wouldn't have us on tape. Now you want to go skipping over there and wait around for your driver to pick you up? You plan on smiling for the video too since they'll be showing it in court?" His eyes looked away in embarrassment as he went silent. I was having some fun ridiculing these morons when the kid interrupted, "Someone's coming."

This many souls passing at one time, add that to us being this far out from the city and it meant I had a good idea of which Ferryman would be by soon enough to collect them all. As the lights got closer, I could see the bus passing through the closed gate. It was a blue and silver two-toned antique job, the kind of Ralph Kramden special that shuttled people around the city before television had color. It was perfectly tuned and spotless with an infinity symbol stenciled where most buses were numbered. It let out a loud hiss as it pulled to a stop directly in front of us. As the bus settled itself, the door swung open on its well-greased track while the front message board flipped over to display the words "One Way Crossing."

I grabbed the kid and slid towards the back of the line, motioning for the others to start piling into the waiting vehicle. I could hear a gruff voice reading from a checklist as each of the men climbed in. "Stewart, southbound, check. Martinez, southbound, check. Corbin, Northbound," The driver looked up at the confused man, eyeing him from under the vinyl bill of his hat. "Lucky you. Then again, it says that you were just filling in for someone else who couldn't make it. Take a seat with the rest of them. We'll get you where you need to be after we drop the other off at their extended barbecue." He turned back towards his paper with a sinister grin. "Corbin, northbound, check." He continued through the list until it left only me standing in the doorway of the bus. "Hey there Jim. I think we need to talk." The driver dropped his paper, suddenly surprised since he wasn't used to anyone getting the drop on him. "Austin, is that you? What're you doing here?" I stepped onto the bus to lean in closer to him, the men sitting in the back watching us both. "Something big is going on and I need to talk to you for a minute. Can you step outside?"

The driver followed me out of the bus, and I could see him fully in the light of the front gate. He was short and stocky, with dark hair he kept slicked down under his bus driver's cap. He wore the kind of black tie and dull gray uniform that had been out of fashion for decades and carried a plaid thermos cup filled with something steaming. "Austin, Austin, Austin, I haven't seen you in years. What's going on, you forget which route you're running?" I gave Jim, or officially *GM*, a cordial smile before putting my finger to my lips as a gesture to be quiet. I knew he had no idea what was going on from the way he was asking questions, an opportunity I could use to my advantage. "You see those guys you just let on your bus?" I said, pointing back to the group. "Very bad news. Mixed up in some really dark stuff."

I tried to keep my tone low but sharp as Jim looked around freely. He sipped from his cup as he mused. "Yep, bad stuff I'm sure. That's probably why almost all of them are heading for the pit." I grabbed Jim's arm lightly, turning him away from the bus. "That's just it. Even with them gone, there's still something big going on here. I'm talking black market soul trade, underground demonic sales, possession for hire. The kind of stuff that makes your stomach turn." Of course, I had no idea what I was talking about. I was just stringing together words that seemed scary and mixed in a few things I had seen in cop movies. "Those guys in there are right in the middle of it all. For all we know this could be part of their plan. I'm doing some undercover work for the halo's upstairs. They got me tagging along to see what kind of info I can dig up. You know, listening in, seeing what I can find out." Jim stared with uncertainty, but I could see the thoughts processing in his head. "That does make sense." He said, finishing off what was left in his cup. "I mean, I always figured they had spies down here digging up dirt on people." I shushed him again before moving in close. "Exactly, but we need to keep this real quiet. You help me out here, and maybe I'll throw in a recommendation for you to do some undercover work with me." His eyes looked hopeful. "That would be swell! You know a route like this starts to get really old after a while." He tapped the empty cup against his leg to clear it out. "What do I need to do?"

I explained to Jim how I just needed him to be quiet about everything he saw tonight. "Don't tell anyone you picked me up. We don't know who we can trust." He seemed excited at the idea of keeping a secret. "I'm going to sit in the back and just listen in. Before you make the trip across the divide, I just need you to drop me and the kid here off at the docks by my place. You good with that?" Jim looked over at the kid standing beside us as he just noticed him for the first time. "What's he doing with you?" He asked, a little confused.

I knew I had to come up with something quick to salvage our plan. "He's working with me. Training actually, someone up there thought it would be a good idea to use a kid for information gathering. Think about it. Who's going to be worried about what they say in front of a kid?" The explanation must have been good enough since Jim bought it and turned towards me. "Make sense," he said. "Besides, if the kid was dead then one of the nannies would be crossing him over." I looked at the kid as his statement threw off my confidence. "Yeah. A nanny," I agreed somberly.

Now wasn't the time to lose focus. I turned back towards the bus. "Ok, we need to move. Now just treat me like anyone else on this bus, being undercover and all." He straightened his hat as a look of understanding started creeping across his face. "Oh, I get it," he said, whispering, "I got you covered." Without hesitating, he grabbed me by the collar of my jacket and began dragging me towards the bus. "Get your ass in there." He yelled loud enough for everyone to hear as he pulled me up the steps and tossed me onto the floor of the aisle. "No more lip out of you. You're just like all the rest of these guys, no difference whatsoever." Sure Jim wasn't the sharpest pencil in the pack, but I appreciated his effort even if it meant a nice-sized bruise on my back. "Now get your ass in a seat before I strap you to the roof." He made an obvious gesture of winking as I crawled into an open seat. The kid just laughed as he plopped down next to me. "Have yourself a good chuckle kid," rubbing at a developing crick in my neck.

As Jim released the breaks, the door slid shut, sending the bus zooming at break-neck speed through the dark winding roads and into the city. As I gripped the seat tightly to hold myself steady, I made a mental note that if I ever got back into my old routine, I would take it easy on anyone who asked about seat belts. I looked over at the kid who didn't seem phased by what was happening and then back at the others in their seats. They were looking through windows or at their watches, completely unaware of what was taking place. As we moved further into the city, I tried to run through my mental notes. The penthouse I found the kid at was owned by Whitehall. That meant our boy Tommy had to be the one at the center of this all. He knew too much about the kid and too much about me. I was confident he was the one with all the answers. That only left the challenge of how I could get them from him.

The geriatric butler mentioned him taking off with his weird psychic lapdog to a safe house somewhere. That meant our best bet would be to track him down. Finding someone willing to part with that kind of information was going to take time. That was the one resource I was out of. Time to think outside of the box. I could trade information with a demon. They might know a little more since all this shit seemed right up their alley. Unfortunately, Full-fledged demons weren't always easy to come by. Just part of the treaty between Heaven and Hell.

Angels could only come to earth as mortal beings, and demons were stuck with earthly visitations via possession. That meant I'd have to find someone currently possessed and hope they were playing host to a demon that not only had the information but also wouldn't try to jerk me around. Demons are douchebags and like to play a lot of games, don't act so surprised. Of course, there was one other option. As much as I hated it, I needed to stop thinking of myself as the cat and accept that we may actually be the mouse. I thought back to the deal Whitehall tried to make. How he said he was only interested in the kid and the way he was so cavalier about sacrificing his own men just to "take care" of us. We were two stones I knew he wasn't going to leave unturned, and I might be able to use that to our advantage.

The sun was beginning to rise near the docks as I reached up and pulled the thin rope that ran overhead. The kid was out cold, his head resting on my shoulder as the bus pulled to a slow stop a block away from my warehouse. "Hey, wake up. Let's stop by my place real quick, then we'll find somewhere to crash." The kid rubbed at his tired eyes but agreed as he stood up and made his way off the bus. I followed, but not before turning back to Jim as he poured himself more coffee from his plaid thermos. "I owe you for this one." He took a sip from his cup as he turned towards me, leaning over the wheel with a sad smile. "Well, any small difference in my routine is a welcomed change. If there's even a remote chance I might get off this route at some point, then you know I'll take it." He screwed the cup back onto the top of the thermos and stowed it under his seat. "Now, if you don't mind. I've got a bus full of souls, most of whom are late for a really hot date if you catch my drift." He tilted his driver's hat towards me as he cranked the lever that slid the doors shut.

We made our way through the silent early morning streets. Neither of us felt much like talking as the worry began to settle in full force. I could see the orange morning sun had fully risen and that meant there wouldn't be much time left. Birds cooed in the rafters as I pulled back the flap to the tent and stepped inside. There really was no rest for the wicked and I turned towards the kid as he followed me in. "I know you're tired, trust me, I am too, but I think it's best if we find somewhere else to crash for a little while. Maybe a hotel. Benny's place might be an option; I just don't know if I want to put her in any more danger." When he didn't respond, I looked over the darkened tent and saw him staring at me, his eyes wide with concern before my head crashed through what was once my dining table.

XXI

In the downtime between runs to Hell and the gates of Heaven, I've had time to catch up on philosophy. There's nothing like staring at the doorways of death to make you question what it all means. Through it all, I've found a common consensus. That it is time alone that levels the playing field for all souls. From the highest king to the lowest peasant, time is valued over anything else.

It makes sense, really. We're all born into this world with a stopwatch hanging over us, then it's a race through life to see how much we can get done before the timer finally hits zero. That's why we look for other ways to compensate for our limited time. We find comfort in objects, assigning value to worthless things in the totality of existence. We take pointless materialism and shield ourselves behind it as we kill each other for shiny metals or destroy families for pretty minerals. We do it all as we tell ourselves that if we can't get more time, then we'll at least get more stuff.

I was different. My time was long spent and now I was saddled with an unknown amount as a punishment. Time wasn't something I coveted, because of that I never put much value in things either. I had money, coming from a stipend I was granted to live off of. I spent some of it on meals since food was one of the few things I enjoyed. Almost all of the rest just went into a savings account, and I didn't even know the balance. The limited amount of everything else I owned wasn't worth much. Except for an overpriced mattress I treated myself with from an 800 number I heard on the radio one night. The rest of the furniture around the tent was worthless. Some I found as trash, others I collected from yard sales. So knowing the minimal value for the table was a little comforting as my skull crashed through it, splintering it to pieces.

I laid on the living area floor, dazed as I saw the angel move towards me through the tent. I had no idea how long they had been waiting for us but judging from the anger in their face, it must have been too long. The look in their icy eyes told me how every minute of the last 24 hours was another grain of salt in an open wound. I felt them move past me as I turned towards the tent's front flap and found the kid nowhere to be seen. "Smart," I whispered, hoping he was hiding away safely in the warehouse.

As I sprawled on the cold floor, I had a sudden flashback to a magazine article I read a few weeks earlier at the diner. It was a consumer reviews magazine with a section about the latest advances in curved screen televisions and why you should buy one. It's funny how technology progressed as I remembered seeing a television for the first time. Those early sets whose screens were curved outwards like a black and white glass bubble. They were amazing and, at the time, felt like a kind of magic. Then televisions started to get smaller, and then bigger, then smaller again, and now we're back to bigger, all the while going from the glass dome to as flat as possible. This article said the best televisions now aren't rounded like a bubble or flat like a pancake but curved inward like a horseshoe. I had to wonder if I would still be doing this job when televisions become a perfect circle that you had to sit inside to watch.

I assume this memory seemed so important because of the concussion I was enjoying, combined with the sudden slow-motion of my outdated television flying towards my head. I shook off the sluggish movement of my thoughts and pushed away from my physical form. I was lucky enough to escape into the incorporeal world just as the rounded glass of the set came crashing against what would have been my face. I rolled to my side, scrambling to my feet while looking over my shoulder to see the bone-white dome of the angel track my every movement. They may be mortal, but there was no question they could see me in any form. I dashed to the side of the tent as they continued to stare daggers, the white-hot intensity of blue eyes convincing me that staying incorporeal was pointless.

I re-solidified with my hands up in surrender, looking for anything that might save my ass. It was pointless since my pleas came out as little more than verbal diarrhea. "Something bad! Very bad, but we're so close! Few more hours!" I placed as much furniture between myself and the angel as I could while continuing to plead. "Not just bad for us. This is something big for you too. All of your kind." Their expression never changed from fierce determination as they moved closer, lifting the sofa with one hand and tossing it across the tent. "Damn you're strong," slipped as the airborne couch took out one of the tent's support poles. The roof slumped under its own weight to my left as another poorly thought-out plan began to form.

I ran to the opposite end of the tent to test a theory. The angel followed me intensely but never moved faster than a moderate pace. It was as if they either found the idea of running distasteful, or something was preventing them from doing it. I didn't know which it was, but I didn't care. I positioned myself in front of another support pole and began again. "Maybe we could grab some coffee, sit down and discuss this. I mean, you look like a perfectly reasonable *person?*..." The last part must have done the trick. Their eyes widened in rage before they lifted the wooden entertainment center, tossing it in my direction. I was prepared, rolling to my side before the furniture could hit me but not before it crashed through the second support sending another end of the tent draped against the ground. I proved my theory. They were either too stupid to realize what they were doing or too angry to pay attention. I had one last chance I had to take. I bolted to the other end of the tent and aligned my body with the center pole. The angel turned towards me as I whistled for their attention. "You know what. Never mind actually. You feel free to hang around here and keep redecorating. I'll go out and do your damn job since clearly you're too incompetent to do it."

The angel, enraged, reached for the heaviest thing in the area, the mini-fridge I kept tucked away in the makeshift kitchen. They lifted the fridge with no effort and threw it full force at what would have been my head. Expecting it, I fell as far backward as I could at the last moment. The fridge smashed against the central pole and sent it sweeping out as the tent's center crashed down around the angel while I rolled to the closest edge I could find. Popping my head out to scan the open warehouse, I could see the tent had fallen entirely, catching the angel at its center like a tuna in a net. I slid the rest of the way out from under the canvas and bounded to my feet, spinning in a small circle to find where the kid could have gone.

It wasn't a challenging game of hide-and-seek. With the tent now collapsed, the warehouse was empty save for a heap of office scraps the previous tenants left piled in the far corner. If the kid was anywhere in the building, that was the only place he could still be hiding. The scrap was a mixed pile of broken wooden pallets, old office chairs, and crushed cardboard I hadn't bothered tossing out. As I passed around to its opposite side, I could see the kid, scared and cowering in the shadow of the pile but still in one piece.

The angel was still struggling under the canvas when I saw the movement abruptly stop. A rip echoed through the emptiness of the warehouse as two ivory wings pierced through the thick olive drab cloth with razor precision. They twisted to shred a large hole as the angel rose to their feet in the newly formed opening. Immediately locking eyes on the single pile in the room, there was no question they knew where we were. I had to make a choice. I could run with him and risk the angel catching us both, or I could try to buy him a little more time. You may call it bravery since I chose the latter, but I'll call it stupidity.

I stepped out from behind the pile and stared back at the angel, pulling the broken remains of a cigar from my jacket that I lit with the final match in the book. Knowing it would probably be my last smoke, I enjoyed a deep puff. The angel stepped from the hole in the tent and extended their wings in full glory. The opalescent white shimmered in the morning light that darted through the windows. With a flash, they lifted into the air, targeting straight for me. I made a split-second decision and tossed the cigar, raising a small metal folding chair from the pile of scrap and tossing it directly at their fucking head as they spun through the air. The angel smacked it away moments before it connected with their face and leaned backward, landing a hefty boot directly against my chest. I could feel my sternum crack as my body reconnected with my old friend, the floor. There was no time to recover before the angel was on top of me, wings outstretched and blocking the light. They put their entire weight against my body, pinning me to the ground as a forearm sunk deep against my throat.

"You gave your word!" They grit their teeth in disgust as they spoke. "You would accept the judgment placed against you and your charge. You said you would come with no resistance!" As they finished the last words, they pressed harder against my throat. I struggled to respond but managed only a few words. "You hit first..." came out in gasps. The force eased minimally as if they weren't prepared for a response. I could see their conflicted look before it returned to anger. "It does not matter," pressing firmly against my throat. "Your word was broken. Why would you betray your duties and further disgrace yourself by breaking a vow? All this for a soul judged for damnation?" The lights were beginning to go out as I could feel myself slipping into unconsciousness, the angel blurry within a distant tunnel. They pressed harder against my throat but demanded to know, "Why?"

There were only a few moments left before I blacked out. With the last willpower still in me, I looked over at where the kid sat cowering in the shadow of the pile. My eyes felt like they were about to pop as I forced a final whisper, "He's...a...child..."

The angel followed my eyes as the weight was suddenly lifted from my neck. The angel sat upright on their knees, wings going limp as they tried to make sense of what they were looking at. I watched as my vision began to clear. They stood from where I was lying and moved closer towards the kid, unsure if they should believe their own angelic eyes. Sitting up, I did my best to speak. "Stay the hell away from him," I yelled before my command was met with a disrespectful smack to the face from a wing that sent me sprawling on my back.

The back of my head bounced off of the cement floor as the angel moved within striking distance of the kid. I could see him looking up in frightened disbelief as they lowered to a crouch in front of him. A suddenly delicate hand reached out, moving with a gentle flowing grace that held no trace of previous anger. They touched the kid's face, running soft fingers along his cheek as his fear faded away. I crawled slowly towards where the angel knelt, looking at the kid as he touched the pale hand that gently held his cheek. The angel stood, taking the kids' hand and helping him to his feet. "The little ones," they said in a soft apologetic tone. "Within them, behold the love of Father."

XXII

My ass was painfully bruised but I was too focused on nursing my fractured ego back to health to care. The angel hovered over the kid; their gaze focused on his face like a child hearing music for the first time. An image of indescribable beauty had it been through the eyes of a painter or sculptor. Through my eyes, both swollen and watery, all I saw was some bald bipolar asshole I trusted as much as a feral cat. "That was abrupt," I said, spitting what tasted like blood from the corner of my mouth. I grabbed one of the pallets in the pile of scrap and used it to lift myself back to my aching feet. "I'm just saying. Punch, choke, punch, choke, bible verse. It's kind of an odd pattern, don't you think?" The angel broke their gaze and addressed me as if it were the first time. "The children of this world are innocent. For the kingdom of heaven belongs to such as these."

I patted my jacket pockets, looking for a handkerchief, but coming up empty settled on my sleeve to dab the last of the blood from my mouth. "Yeah, that's all well and good, but I already know that. Plus, it's a pretty shitty time to start playing Sunday school. Now, do you want to explain what the hell is happening, or would you prefer I start?" The angel looked back at the child. "My orders are to take you and your charge to your final damnation. However, forcing any child into an eternity of torment is not an order I am able to fulfill. I do not believe it is an order from our father." A sense of relief came from their words. "Cool, now we're getting somewhere. You understand that you can't take us to Hell. That's a great starting point." The angel looked away, inspecting the empty warehouse. "You misunderstood me," they stated as a matter of fact. "I am unable to take the child. My orders are for you both. Once we resolve this new development, I am still obligated to transport you to your damnation until ordered otherwise" My heart sank with frustration.

"Let me get this straight, and I'm summarizing. I risk my salvation to save this kid because I know kids don't go to Hell. As a result, I not only get the ever-loving shit kicked out of me around every turn; but now, if I can hear you correctly despite the blood in my ears, I'm still damned? Then to top it all off, and this is the real kicker, you're telling me that I was right all along. You can't chuck the kid downtown, but I'm still scheduled for the hot seat? You realize how unimaginably hypocritical that is, right?" The angel looked up at the morning light rays as they passed through the high warehouse windows, watching the dust dance through the air. "Perhaps." they turned back to face me, "It's not my place to say."

I was caught in a moment where anger and exhaustion overruled my usual cowardice. Now firmly on my feet, my index finger jabbed at the angel's shoulder. "No. That's bullshit! It's not my place either, but you know what? I call it like I see it. If it walks like a duck, swims like a duck, and quacks like a duck, you better believe it's a fucking duck; and right now I'm standing ankle deep in duck shit." I went for another ill-advised jab for emphasis. The angel's face remained emotionless while one quick movement intercepted my finger and bent it backward, breaking it. I may have had the second part of my duck analogy lined up in my mind, but as my index finger hung limply, I instead opted to go with a high-pitched scream.

I bit my lip, quickly flashing immaterial before returning solid with a now working finger. The pain shot through my arm, making my eyes water. It might be best to take a calm approach, knowing that next it could be my neck. "As I was saying." I began, trying to casually wipe my eyes. "I find it very unfair that this is just going to end with my damnation. I was right to hold onto the kid. You're damning the wrong guy." The angel crossed their arms before deciding what to say next. "I believe your earlier statement" It was as if the words almost hurt to admit. "There is more going on here than simple disobedience." I pulled one of the chairs from the pile of scrap and set it upright, collapsing into it as I tried to massage the pain away from my aching hand. "I kind of figured that. Would you be ever so kind enough to explain how you suddenly came to that conclusion, though?"

The angel pointed to the kid who was now walking the perimeter of the downed tent. I watched as he peered under the canvas as if he was looking for treasure. "The child is the key. A child cannot be damned." I had to interrupt what felt like a circular argument. "There's one problem with that. You see, I got the paperwork. The paperwork I damned myself by ignoring. He's marked for downtown. So that throws a wrench in your whole *children can't be damned* concept." The angel turned towards me. "You do not grasp the severity of what I am saying," they began. "A child's soul cannot be judged; therefore, it cannot be damned. That is why I cannot allow this child's soul to be handed over to Hell. The results could be devastating." I nodded along, acting like I knew any of what they were talking about. "Devastating, yes. I get that." The angel was quick to correct me. "No! Devastating for the world. Your view is so limited."

The kid was lifting some of the tent poles, trying in vain to set it back up. "From your tiny view of this world you see nothing but chaos, and because of that chaos you can never see beyond yourself. However, this world is not chaotic. Instead, existence is maintained through delicate balances defined by infallible laws." They looked back at me as if explaining nuclear physics to a slug. "Constants, unbreakable rules that keep the Kingdom and the Abyss in a state of equilibrium." They put their hands up to mimic a scale. "Existence in unity entirely because of these rules. All that live shall one day die. All who die shall be judged. Those judged as worthy of the kingdom shall find salvation. Those judged as wicked shall be damned. Those judged unworthy of either will be given a chance to cleanse their souls." The angel shot me a look of disgust after that last statement. "There is but one exception for this, and that is the soul of a child. A child's soul is unquestionably innocent." Nothing in the lecture was striking me as new information, "like we've established a few times now, kids are innocent. Got it. So someone screwed up somewhere." They shook their head. "It is more than that. The innocence of a child's soul is a universal constant. If even one child is allowed to be damned, the delicate balance is shifted." They dropped one hand lower than the other like a tipped scale. "Consider the implications. If the pure soul of a child can be allowed to enter Hell, inversely, a damned soul would be able to enter the Kingdom. The nature of existence would take a dark and truly chaotic shift."

It took a moment for the concept to sink in. I began to realize that this wasn't about the kid at all. He was just the pawn, the linchpin used to blow the doors off of Hell. I couldn't make sense of why Whitehall would be so interested in it. Was there profit to be made from the apocalypse? "I don't know the purpose behind this, but I think I get the gravity." I stood from the chair and tossed it back into the pile. "Which still leaves us in the same place; where do we go from here?" The angel folded their arms in thought. "I was only tasked with delivering you both to your damnation. I received a full briefing on where I could find you from the very unpleasant woman in glasses." An angel referring to anyone as "unpleasant" could only mean one person. "That's Maggie. I'd call her a bitch if she didn't document it in my file somewhere."

The angel continued as if I were talking to myself. "I knew of your district and where you reside. Other than that, my knowledge of this world is limited." I cocked my head back towards the tent, motioning for them to follow me. "Lucky for you, I've had plenty of experience moving through this city. I know almost every inch of it by heart. You tell me where we should go and I'll tell you no problem." A shred of self-confidence returned. After all, this was my city. If the Angel knew something about where we needed to go, I knew I was the one who could get us there. "We need to find the man you said is behind this. The Whitehall man."

I nodded along, expecting more to follow. "Okay..." I paused, realizing nothing else was coming. "You're really of no help then. Great. That's great to hear." The angel looked confused. "We need to find this man. Once we find him you will have the chance to make him confess what he has done. He will explain all that has been done to this child and to this world; then I will personally feed him to the mouth of torment. With your expertise in finding anyone in this city, I'm sure this will be of no concern." My hands hid themselves in the pockets of my jacket, feeling very small. "*Almost*. You forgot the *almost*."

I took a few steps away. "I can find *almost* anyone. This guy seems to be the exception. He's the most powerful person in the entire city and until a few hours ago, I didn't even know he existed." All the confidence I was trying to rebuild was sucked out of me. "He could have hiding places all over this city that I have no idea about; he's apparently that powerful. He isn't just well connected. He is the connection." The angel closed the gap between us. "You have no way of finding him? Even if the natural balance of this world is at risk?" I put my hands up quickly, "Woah, hold up. I said I couldn't find him. That doesn't mean we don't have an option here. Remember, we have something he wants." I pointed cautiously at the kid. "We may not need to spend too much effort trying to find him. We could always just let him find us. Have you ever heard the saying *hiding in plain sight*?" The angel didn't bother to respond. "You'll have to trust me. First thing's first, we need to get the word out about where we're going to be. Right now, I think I know just the sack of shit to help us get the ball rolling."

Making a phone call turned out to be a little more complicated than I had expected. With my only phone now buried under a pile of broken furniture and thick green canvas, I pulled at the edges of the cloth trying to see what was underneath. The angel must have seen me struggling since they took it upon themselves to grab two large handfuls of the tent and rip it away like a magician's reveal. I know I said I didn't put a lot of emphasis on material things, but something about seeing everything I had shattered and in disarray rubbed me the wrong way. I stepped through what was once my living room, the broken glass of my dishes crunching under my boot as I drew closer to the angel.

I did my best to make myself taller but still fell a few inches short of meeting eye-to-eye. "You have the option of booting me to Hell right now, which would leave you alone and trying to figure out this shit by yourself." I made sure to keep my hands at my side after the broken finger experience. "Or you could work with me on this one, in which case we need to establish some ground rules. The first one is don't touch my shit!" I made an exaggerated wave at the balled-up canvas and all the exposed broken scraps. "If I need your help, I'll ask for it. The next rule is that I'm done being your punching bag. From this point forward, hands-off." The angel was amused at how fragile I seemed to be. "Third, we've established that you have no idea what you're doing in this situation, so as far as I'm concerned, you're the unnecessary third wheel. Keep in mind that's coming from a guy who doesn't even want a second wheel." I cocked my thumb towards the kid who was struggling to fit the cushions back onto the old couch. "You're the muscle here, and that's all. You stick to our rules, and you'll be back up there singing Hosanna in no time."

I started to turn back towards where my phone used to be but stopped short. "One last thing. It seems you know an awful lot about me. I'm sure Maggie was more than happy to give you an ear full. The point is I'd be happy to spend our time together calling you Uncle Fester or Kojak Since I refuse to keep calling you "Angel." So, do you want to tell me your name, or should I just make something up?" I gave the angel a chance, only pushing further when I was met with silence. "Fine then. I was thinking of something like "Winged Sphincter or Ass-Halo. Get it? Like Asshole, but Ass-halo." Before I could throw any more ideas out, the angel interrupted. "I am known as Anael, angel of the 5th choir, hand of the father, loyal servant of the kingdom." This time it was my chance to interrupt. Sure I didn't need to, but it just made me feel good. "Well then, Anael, until we get this resolved, I propose a truce." I put my hand out to shake, moving deliberately to seem non-threatening since I'd prefer not to pull back a stump. Anael responded in kind, gripping me by the forearm instead of my outstretched hand. It was startling until I remember seeing similar greetings in old movies about knights. It was becoming clear that this was the first time Anael had been on earth in a very long time. It would have been a cool revelation if the iron grip didn't feel like my wrist was being crushed into a diamond. I heard something in my arm pop before letting go of my end of the shake. "I'm going to assume, based on our newfound understanding, that was an accident." I rubbed at my sore arm and again used my quick healing trick to keep using my wrist.

Feeling a little better about the deadly angel towering over my shoulder, I moved closer to where my bed still stood, kicking junk around until I finally found the phone cable buried underneath. Gripping the line, I traced out where the phone was hidden under a broken stack of records. "I need to make a few phone calls to people you're not going to approve of." "You are referring to the demon whore?" I extended the phone's antenna into a makeshift pointer. "Don't you call her that! She's done more to help this kid than you or your kind have even considered. Who the hell are you to pass judgment on her?" Anael bowed their head in acknowledgment. "It is beyond my place to judge. You are correct. I apologize."

I dialed the number before raising the phone to my ear, turning around so Anael couldn't see my involuntary smile. I couldn't help it. Having had my ass kicked too many times recently, it felt good to win something for a change. The phone rang twice before someone picked up on the other end. "Ben, it's Austin." I began. That little statement was met with an avalanche of excited questions. "What did you find? Is the kid okay? What did Whitehall look like? Did he have a really long beard and tissue boxes for shoes?" I tried to calm her without giving away too much. "We're fine. The kid is still with me. We didn't find out too much, just enough that I need to speak with Manuel again. Is there any way you could set up a call between us?" The question was met with a moment's silence as Benny thought on the other end. "It's really early, or really late depending on how you look at it."

I didn't want to be rude since she had already done so much for us, but the less she knew, the safer she would be. "I get that, but based on some recent developments, I really think he's going to want to help. You don't think he'd have a few minutes for a phone call?" I could hear her laugh on the other end. "The guy's an attention whore and one of Hell's personal groupies. For you, he'd probably kill his own mother. If he hasn't already, of course. That's not the issue Austin." She paused, trying to be delicate with her wording. "I just don't think you can trust him." Although her instincts were great, I couldn't let her in on the plan, not yet at least. The idea of using ourselves as bait may not have sounded like the best idea when said aloud. "I know." I told her, "but I don't need to trust him. I just need to talk to him." Benny reluctantly conceded. "Hold tight and let me see what I can put together. I'll call you right back," and without a goodbye, she hung up.

I sat on the corner of my now cracked bed and held the phone in my lap. My place was never the shining example of cleanliness, but it was mine and at the end of a long night it was always comfy. Right now, it looked more like the aftermath of war in a way that broke my heart. I didn't have much that I held dear but damn it, you don't screw with where a man sleeps. I watched Anael study the kid before a shard of broken plate jabbed me in the ass. I was coming close to losing my cool when the phone finally rang. The serpentine voice on the other end cut me off. "Senor Austin. I wasn't expecting to hear from you again *so soon*." He caught himself, correcting his mistake. "Well, that's the thing about me, Manny." I knew I was irritating him, all part of the plan. "I'm kinda like a case of herpes. Once I've latched on, I'm just going to keep coming back. I'm sure that's something you've experienced." A third voice laughed. "Benny? Is this one of those party lines?" She took a breath to stop laughing. "Party lines went out 30 years ago, old man. This is a conference call. I think it's better for everyone involved if you two didn't have a direct hotline to one another."

I could hear Manuel on the other end. "Yes, perhaps she is correct. With that, I am still happy to assist in any way I can. How may I help you Mr. Austin." Aneal took notice, moving towards me to listen in. "I need answers." I continued, "And I don't think you're going to be able to give them to me. I need your connections. Someone in this city has to know more about this knife." It didn't take long for Manuel to agree. "Indeed. I believe I have someone who can explain what you have come across a little more. I must warn you, however, that he is not an easy man to work with. I will need to set up a meeting." I needed to emphasize the importance of time without coming off as desperate as I genuinely was. "The sooner, the better. This isn't just casual chit-chat. I can pay for your contact's time."

Manuel found something amusing about the offer. "I am sure you can, Senor Austin. I am sure you can; with luck that may not be necessary. Just by virtue of your *career*, I am sure he would be interested in speaking with you. I will contact him now. He has a small store in the west end region. A curiosity shop by the name of "Dark Matters." Senorita Bernice, I am confident you know how to find this place?" "I heard that creep pays by the strand for succubus hair. He's a bottom-feeding pawnbroker for demonic artifacts. I'm sure I can find the place." Manuel chastised her. "Never judge a man by how he makes his living if he is good at it. If you are looking for answers, I suggest showing him a little more respect when we arrive." Benny only groaned in response. "I will make the connections now. Let's meet at the location in, say, 2 hours?" "I'll be there." I agreed before Manuel hung up. "Ben, we'll head over to your place, and just so you know, we have another... uh... friend who will be tagging along. I'll explain more when we get there." Benny tried to hide her excitement as she agreed to get ready. I was the last to leave the call, turning the handset off and pushing the antenna back into the receiver.

It took a moment before Aneal chose to interrupt. "We now have a place to begin. That is good." I looked up as they towered over me, arms folded under a radiant white cloak. "We've got somewhere to go, although I wouldn't say begin. Manuel seemed all too eager to help out. He tipped his hand by not asking for payment or attempting to cut a deal. I think it's safer to say that we now have somewhere to end." The angel accepted. "That is fine. I must ask how you plan to transport us to this next location."

Of all this shit going on, how we would get there was somehow swept from my mind. Now, as Aneal brought it up, I realized our predicament. "I don't suppose you can zap the cab back into my care, could you?" Anael shook their head firmly. "It is not mine to give. My order was to terminate access to your transport. I cannot defy those orders." There was no point in arguing. "That's kind of what I figured." I stood up and began pacing through the cluttered area. I knew we wouldn't have much luck catching a real cab with the big bald one tagging along. We were also working under a limited time frame, so that meant the city bus was out of the question also. Trying to trick another Charon into chauffeuring us around probably wasn't going to work a second time. My stomach growled in the quiet warehouse when an interesting thought came to me. I lifted the phone, dialing a number from memory. As the line rang, I looked at Anael who stood emotionless, "you ever had Chinese food?"

XXIII

I've been up and down every street in this city more times than you'll ever know, and I can tell you I've seen some bizarre shit. In the late sixties I remember watching a nudist parade marching straight through the town center. A group of earth-first hippies shouting "naked is natural" as their long hair flowed freely in the wind, and I'm not just talking about what was on their heads. In the early nineties I once drove past a convention being held for people who were devoted to something called "pony play." Grown men and women that liked to saddle up in leather horse outfits while others took turns riding them. Just last month I stopped in a sandwich shop before one of my shifts and I saw a normal-looking joe on a date with a 5-foot rubber love doll. While I waited for my food I watched from the corner of my eye as he occasionally fed *her* potato chips and pieces of bread from his sandwich. That one stuck with me for a few days. Not because it was so outlandish, but because I just kept wondering how he got the food back out.

No matter what unusual things people managed to throw at this city, it was always met with the same sense of disinterest. As if the city itself organized one giant collective shrug and just minded its own business. Today that was working in our favor since no one seemed to bat an eye as a grown man, a small child, and a bald angel clad in white leather huddled together on a moped seat and raced through the morning streets.

The Peking Wall was my favorite Chinese restaurant. It wasn't anything special food-wise, but they capitalized on the drunk after party crowd as the only place around with 24-hour delivery. Knowing that our travel options were limited, I decided to place an order for my usual with the ulterior motive of offering the delivery guy $2500 cash for his wheels, sight unseen. It was probably a few grand more than anyone would ever pay for a beat-down moped, but I didn't have time to haggle. After pushing the folded hundreds into the delivery boy's hand and tossing him my phone to call a cab, he gladly went with the flow.

It took a little maneuvering to get us all on the scooter. I managed to get it kick-started when the kid wedged between me and Anael, who took up the back half of the saddle. I had to assume he was uncomfortable as he was sandwiched there, but he was secure. Besides, the kid was turning out to be pretty tough and I knew he could hold in there for a few minutes. As we moved along the city street, Anael yelled towards me. "Your mechanical steed is rather slow-moving. Are you sure this is our best option?" For now it was, but I might have been exaggerating a little when I used the term "racing" as we sputtered along below the speed limit, making our way towards Benny's apartment.

We were walking into a trap, only it was a trap we helped set. That just left the question of how we were planning on getting out of it. In nature, it's not uncommon for a trapped animal to chew through its own legs to get away safely. If we were left with no other option, which of us would be the sacrificial lamb? My first thought went to Anael, who sat backward on the saddle. I didn't like them, I didn't trust them, and to top it off, they admitted that when this was all over they were still planning on dragging me to Hell. So why wouldn't I just cut my losses and throw them to the wolves when the time came? It was the obvious choice; nevertheless, sometimes the obvious choices weren't always the right ones. The idea of betraying an angel and letting one of Hell's fanboys kill them, I'm sure there was some bible verse that would frown on that situation. Plus, it wouldn't do much to earn my forgiveness with the team upstairs.

I was so deep in my own thoughts that I stopped paying attention to the road in front of us, a big mistake. It goes back to admittedly being stupid. Not ignorant since I'm proud to say that I've learned a lot, but stupid because I don't always put that knowledge to use. I let my emotions get the best of me and jump into situations without thinking. Like bringing a kid back from the edge of Hell, like telling one of the most powerful angelic creatures in existence to go fuck itself, and like cramming three people onto a shitty moped without bothering to inspect it first. If I was a little smarter I may have remembered that Benny's apartment sat at the bottom of a fairly steep hill. The same one we were currently descending at an increasingly faster rate. I looked down at the speedometer as the needle pushed past the 40 when the scooter's front wheel started to wobble. A whole lot of regrets piled up as I squeezed the brakes, expecting the slow pull of the cable only to get the feeling of the handle clicking back without resistance. "Hey, Anael." I yelled back to the unconcerned angel. "You may want to keep an eye on the kid. I think we bought a moped without working brakes, this is probably going to hurt." The kid's arms squeezed tightly around me as we continued to zoom down the hill towards Benny's place. We could abandon the bike and try rolling to safety. No one would be permanently hurt but it would really suck in the short term. It seemed like our least painful option for the time being as I kept the bike steered towards the open road. We were becoming less stable by the second as I promised myself I would get my money back before I ended up in Hell. I accepted the inevitability of the upcoming pain before the scooter began to slow itself with a booming clap.

I don't want to call it divine intervention. If we're going with the loose definition of the term though, that's precisely what it was. I turned to see Anael still sitting on the back end of the saddle, their large white wings completely outstretched to catch the wind like a makeshift parachute. Any hope we had of being inconspicuous had gone entirely out the window, but who cares; I was just happy to avoid a few extra bruises. Besides, anyone who may have noticed us would probably just write it off as obnoxious performance artists being annoyingly avant-garde. As the bike slowed to a manageable speed, I abandoned the brake lever and used the old tried and true method of skidding both feet along the pavement.

We pulled to a final heart-pounding stop just a few feet from the front entrance of Benny's place. The kid dismounting the overpriced death machine first as he smiled up at me with a grin that seemed too large for his face. He had the look of someone who just walked off of a roller coaster and was ready to go again. Anael folded their wings back under their cloak and stepped off next. That left me alone on the font of the moped, which I let fall to its side. I tossed the key onto the ground, leaving it lying there in the gutter. As far as I was concerned, it was either going to end up in a landfill or in the hands of someone stupider than me.

It had only been a few hours since we left Benny's, but this time we let ourselves in with an angel in our wake. We wedged ourselves into the elevator as I reflexively nudged my elbow into Anael's wing as it took up too much room in the confined space. Seeing as how they were already planning on flushing me away to Hell, I decided it might be in my best interest to stay on their good side. "Sorry about that. It's kind of tight in here." It was a half-hearted apology that only garnered an expressionless nod of acceptance.

The kid jumped out of the elevator as soon as the doors popped open on Benny's floor. I motioned for Anael to be my guest then followed a moment later. The kid knew exactly where he was going as he skipped down the hall, and as he made his way towards the apartment a slightly evil idea came to mind. The door swung open as Benny let the kid in and I followed quickly, passing Anael but trying not to look suspicious in the process. Making my way in unharmed meant our invitation from earlier was still valid, and as I took a few more steps into her place I heard the all too familiar "thwack" that usually preceded pain. "Oh no! Anael, I'm so sorry. I forgot about that silly security system Bernice has set up," turning to feign concern. The angel stepped back with a confused anger. "Blasphemous witchcraft!" They growled, placing their hands against the invisible barrier. "Now Anael," as if I were lecturing a misbehaving toddler. "Judge not. Remember that one?" I gave a side-eyed smile. "I think you of all people should know that a good guest does not go around criticizing the home of their host." I stepped closer to where they stood, lowering my voice as only the thin metaphysical barrier separated us. "If you start disrespecting poor Bernice's home, I may not be able to convince her to grant you passage. Then where do we go from there? I could just hole up in here until the whole world comes crashing down. Now that would be really disappointing, wouldn't it?" The angel dropped their hand as the words rang true. "I do not wish to play these games with you. What are your terms?" It was taking a risk with my hopes set on this working. "It's easy. I want to know that I can trust you. I want your word that the kid will be safe." Anael stared into my eyes without hesitation. "I give you my oath by the Father that this child will be protected." I knew that one wouldn't be an issue. "Good, figured as much. There's just one more thing. Heaven, Hell, Purgatory. It's all we ever talk about, but we both know there's one other option, isn't there?" The angel hung their head at the painful thought. "Dissolution..." They said quietly. "That's right. Neither here nor there. Only a great nothingness. If I'm destined for Hell, I would rather be dissolved. I believe I have at least earned that much." Anael was quick to retort. "Only Father can remove one from eternity. I cannot agree to something beyond my power." The answer I had expected. "No, but you can do what *is* within your power. I want your word that if I help, if I stop whatever is happening, you will make my case to your superiors before I am damned. Agree to that, or you can enjoy watching me get pizza deliveries here until the sun finally burns out." It didn't take much convincing as Anael agreed without protest.

I looked back to see Benny still leaning against the open door, quietly taking in everything that had occurred. "Good. Now that we have that squared aware. Bernice, this is Anael. They are an." Benny was not about to wait for me to finish the introduction. "A fucking angel. Listen," she said as if she were about to invite a younger sibling into her room, "don't touch my shit, and the first time I hear you call me "demon," "devil," "evil," "harlot," "whore," or anything else that irks me I'm rescinding your invitation." She now stood next to me. Close enough to touch Anael had it not been for the barrier. "You know what happens if I do that?" she paused for a moment before imitating an explosion with her mouth and hands.

Anael, again in no position to argue, agreed to it all. "Anael, angel of the Heavenly choir. I grant your passage to my home. Don't piss me off." With that, Benny stepped from the door, eager to move on. "So," she said as her demeanor changed, "Manuel sold you out, didn't he?" It caught me by surprise since I had done my best to keep her in the dark. "Uh, yeah. He did, actually. How did you know?" She shrugged, trying to act unimpressed. "Because he's a weasellyley piece of shit. It only makes sense, but also because when I called and told him that you two needed to speak, he seemed surprised. A person who makes their living dealing in information generally isn't surprised unless something's gone wrong. The question is, how wrong did it go?"

"Three fire trucks, two ambulances, six cruisers, and about a month's worth of trying to ID all the bodies. That's *how wrong*." Benny lost her calm exterior. "No way," she yelled as she pushed me. "This is such bullshit. You see why I wanted to come with you?" She made her way over to where her leather jacket was draped over the couch and tossed it on. "I knew I should have just gone." She continued as she stomped into her bedroom. I could hear her rummaging through something before returning, a shiny aluminum baseball bat slung over her shoulder. She looked over at me, "Prepare yourself. I am totally making up for missing out on the fun."

She stepped closer to the doorway, the only exit now blocked from the inside by Anael. "Wait," walking over to her and tapping the bat. "What do you plan on doing with this?" She moved in close, trying to seem both tougher and taller. "You pay someone enough, and they'll tell you what you want to know. You hurt someone enough, and they'll tell you what you *need* to know. We tried buying information last time and it didn't work. That leaves us with one other option." She had a look in her eyes I hadn't seen before. It told me she was speaking from experience. She was losing her grip on that part of herself she had tried so hard to bury, and I was responsible. I couldn't let her do that.

I brushed the bat gently from her shoulder and replaced it with my hand, squeezing her gently. "I've spent so many years here thinking I was alone. Thinking the only person

I could ever count on was myself. Then this shit happened, and you know what? I found out, for the most part, I was right. Except for you." For the first time since I have known her, she had nothing to say. She stared at the ground, prepared for what was coming. "I know now that I have a friend. I know that no matter how bad this shit is about to get, all I have to do is ask for your help, and you'll do it. No matter what the outcome. So please understand that because I know that, it's the one thing I can't ask you to do." She looked up at me, her eyes almost pleading to help. "You're stronger than all of us, Ben. Physically, since there's no question that you could kick my ass, but mentally as well. For so long, you've shown everyone that you're more than sin. You're more than anger, or lust. You can prove to *them*..." I pointed to Anael, who stood behind us watching. "... that you're better than they are. You can show them, for both of us, that they can shove us into a box and label it whatever they want. It doesn't matter. Only we can define what's inside that box, and only you are strong enough to do that now. As my friend, as my *only* friend, please do not come with us."

Have you ever heard how women suffer the curse of Eve? It's a ridiculous belief that women endure pain as penance for original sin. It's kind of the whole "sins of our fathers" thing, where women pay for what someone before them did. The same idea applies to demons. As she stood silently looking up at me, I could see a small blood-tinged tear form in the corner of her eye. She said nothing, and more importantly, she did nothing. She didn't wipe it away or try to hide her feelings. Instead, she stood, letting that one red teardrop roll down her face leaving a trail of blood streaked across her cheek. Demons also suffered for the sins of their fathers. In their case, it was the pain of sorrow. Crying didn't just hurt demons emotionally; it hurt them physically. Benny didn't try to stop it, and it was that

209

one simple action, or inaction, that meant more to me than anything she could have said.

I hugged her tightly for a brief moment, not wanting to cause any more pain. "Thank you, Ben." I whispered into her ear. She smiled as I released her and backed away. "You know, even if you aren't going, we still need some help." She gave me a look that could only be read as "no shit," before asking what she could do. "To start with, I need to know about this store. It would also be helpful to tell me everything you know about Manuel and this guy we're about to meet. Then I'm also going to need the knife back. We all know this is going to be a trap, but that doesn't mean we can't get a few answers out of the deal before things go sideways." Benny started to walk toward her room where she had the knife stashed, but not before turning back towards us. "Easy enough. What else." I took a moment to build up the courage to ask. "That's pretty much it," playing it off as nonchalantly as possible before finally blurting out in a way that stopped her dead in her tracks. "That, and I guess I'm going to need your keys."

XXIV

Talking Benny out of her keys turned out to be easier than I expected. We can chalk it up to my heartfelt speech mixed with a bit of guilt, but in the end all I had to do was promise that beyond the kid first and myself second, her car would be third on my list of what to protect. It was a sweet gesture until I saw her give Anael a sideways glance as she made me promise. A sly jab that let the angel know that they didn't fall anywhere on her list of priorities. That was Benny in a nutshell, a demonic kind of sweetness.

Getting the car was easy, but actually fitting a six-foot armor-clad angel into the narrow seats of a vintage sports car turned out to be a much more difficult task. I pulled the convertible top off and helped wedge Anael into the passenger side. Being a warrior angel, they weren't accustomed to needing assistance to sit down. There were a few bent wings, but I'll credit the angel for sticking to our *no-hitting* agreement. "Do not touch me. I will manage on my own." They insisted, fighting the urge to hurt me. Now that I knew they wouldn't be taking any swings at my face, I had a little more confidence as my mouth got a little loose. "Then hurry up. These aren't the type of people you keep waiting. Either squeeze your pale ass into the seat or curl up in the trunk. It's your call." To my benefit, they ignored me as they shimmied into the seat in a way that looked exceptionally uncomfortable. As I shut the door, sealing in the sardine-packed angel, I could see the kid standing behind us, amused at the situation. I couldn't help but laugh. "Alright kid, you know the drill. It's gonna be a little tighter this time; wedge into the center and let's get moving."

It was my first time behind the wheel since Anael revoked my ability to manifest the taxi and my first time driving anything other than the cab since starting this job. (Unless you count the moped situation, which I wasn't.) Everything from the driver's seat felt familiar. The wheel, the pedals, the seatbelt click, but it still felt unnatural despite familiarity. I had the weird feeling that I was cheating on my car. I popped the keys into the ignition and tried to shake the strange feeling, pulling the crumpled paper directions from the jacket's pocket.

Benny had spent many more years on this earth than I had, but unlike me, she tried to keep with the times in a way I was resistant. She jumped headfirst into the technology pool and embraced things like cell phones and the internets. So it was understandable that when I asked her for directions, her first instinct was to pull out her phone and start tapping away. It took her a moment to realize she was standing next to one of the only people left in this world not walking around with a minicomputer in their pocket. She gave up and tore her apartment to pieces trying to find a pen that she used to outline the short directions in elegant calligraphy. The words that looped across the scrap of paper were beautiful to look at but hard as hell to read. I pictured the city's roads in my mind and memorized the key points she had written before reaching the final line that simply read "Love, Benny." Complete with a devil tail trailing from the back half of the "Y."

Five Point Star Books was a run-down shop sitting on a side street in one of the city's oldest and trendiest parts. It is an area as old as the city itself but currently undergoing the series of face-lifts they called gentrification. A pretty modern idea where artists and trendsetters move in and change terms like "poor" into "minimalist" and "old" into "storied." The perfect camouflage for the little occult shop that added a touch of eccentricity to the area without being dangerous, at least as far as the residents knew. I had only recently heard of this place, but just like everything else in this world outside of my small area of responsibility, I just didn't give a shit to know it was there.

Things changed quickly as I drove the sleek antique through the city streets, trying to remember everything Benny had told me. She gave me a rundown of the store itself. Essentially a bookstore and bric-a-brac shop that sounded like a tourist trap you'd find outside the pit to Hell. She said he has a lot of *interesting* things but to stay calm and, no matter how odd something may seem, act unimpressed. She also warned me about the owner, a small portly man named Stewart who spent every hour either in his shop or the apartment above it. She described him as what happens when a kid raised on a steady diet of fantasy movies and role-playing games finds out that some of it is real.

As we rounded the corner to the small side street where the store was tucked away, I pulled the car to the curb and killed the engine a few buildings back. "Do you foresee a problem?" Anael asked, eyeing the storefront. "Nah, but let's just play this cool; fashionably late and disinterested in staying." The angel's eyes stayed on the door while the kid popped out from between us as I lifted the door handle and stepped into the shadowy alley. The kid, now free, stretched as he stood alongside me. "Same move as last time. It should be second nature by now. Drop from sight and stay close. I don't know who's going to be

in there but let's hope it's not another clairvoyant-for-hire."
The kid looked up at me, puzzled. "A clairvoyant. You know,
the weird skinny guy at the last place. Someone that can see
spirits." It didn't take him long to catch on. "What if someone
does see me?" He asked, trying to prepare.

"Some people might be focused on me, but most will
probably be staring down our big bald friend over there. We
should be drawing all the attention between the two of us. You
know what that means?" The kid nodded in a way I didn't feel
too confident about. "If you notice anyone looking at you
instead of the two of us, then that's bad. Find something big
and hide behind it. If things go wrong, stay put until I tell you
to come out. All good?" I held my hand out for the kid to slap
it in the way I've seen teenagers do on the street. He looked at
me a little suspicious before finally conceding to a pitiful
low-five. It was the type of uncomfortable exchange we both
immediately regretted before moving on.

"You ready?" I yelled to the angel, who put their hand
up to silence me. I could see them analyzing our surroundings,
trying to inspect everything before going in. "I could grab you
an oversized magnifying glass and a pipe, but I still don't think
it's going to help you find anything out here. What we're
looking for is inside. Let's get it over with." Anael took another
moment to peer up each side of the dead street before giving me
the go-ahead. With that, I flipped up the collar of my coat and
tucked my hands into the pockets. It wasn't much, but it was
time to look serious and, if possible, slightly dangerous.

The door to the musty shop creaked open and I
stepped in first. The kid was now incorporeal and stuck close
behind as our pet albino brought up the rear. I took in as much
about the shop as I could in the short time for us to reach the
front counter. It was like something out of a Hollywood
soundstage. A mixture of antique store and library focused
entirely on the metaphysical. Extensive selections of books in

languages I couldn't begin to recognize sat crowding shelves scattered with an array of roots, skulls, feathers, and anything you could file under the heading "Weird shit." Stepping up to the counter, I found a small silver bell and beside it another severed hand candle like the one I saw in Whitehall's library. I pointed to the candle-hand and looked back at Anael, who was not amused. The angel's pale lip curled as if there were a noxious odor in the room, but as their eyes traced around the items I could tell their discomfort wasn't anything as simple as a smell. I yelled a particularly obnoxious "Helloooooo" towards the curtained-off back room behind the counter. As footsteps made their way towards us, I decided to give the bell a few rapid "dings" for extra measure.

Anael stepped closer with the kid finding a safe spot nuzzled between us as the curtain withdrew in an overly dramatic fashion. Standing behind it was the round pink-cheeked face of a man anywhere between his early twenties to his mid-fifties. He wore the kind of large framed bifocals that were popular with mechanical engineers and had a closely cropped haircut that simply said, "I can't be bothered with styling." His clothing told a different story. He was draped in a thick earth-tone monk's robe, expertly folded and held firmly in place with sizable wooden prayer beads. His look in total felt forced and uncomfortable, a costume meant to impress us. His wooden sandals clicked against the floorboards as he stepped into the room. "Mr. Austin. I have heard so many things about you." His words drawn out and theatrical, showing he had practiced them before we arrived. "I am a great admirer of the *Manannán mac Lir*. I have done a great deal of research on your kind, but I never expected to actually have one present in my humble shop."

In his hands he held a black stone teapot steaming from the neck. He placed the pot on the counter along with two cups he pulled from underneath; his interest focused on something other than tea. He sidestepped the counter with his full attention towards us. "And yet, as delighted as I am to have you in my modest boutique, please forgive me as I am simply enthralled with the company you keep." He stood directly in front of Anael, looking her over as if she were an item I had brought to trade. "Anael of the heavenly choir, Ancient seraphim power, in my store." He pulled a jeweler loop from a small chain under his robe and closely inspected the angel's skin. "Or at least the temporary mortal vessel Anael is utilizing." He dropped the loop as it hung from his neck and broke his gaze away. "Truly amazing. Once it has transcended this form, you simply must allow me to purchase the remains. An Angelic carcass is not a treasure you come across very often." His words turned my stomach. Admittedly, I wasn't the biggest fan of the big ivory nightmare, but the sleazy way the little twerp spoke made my skin crawl. Anael was an angel, for God's sake, and despite their insistence on carting me off to Hell when this was all said and done, I still believed some things were sacrosanct.

Anael stood emotionless, a silent dignity in cold eyes that stared into the distance. On the other hand, I placed my palm on the little man's robed chest and eased him back. "Woah there, let's not start this off on a bad foot. Have a little more respect for my associate here; otherwise I can't be held responsible if they feel it necessary to correct you." He wiped away a nonexistent crease from where my hand had touched him before pursing his lips. He looked Anael over again with a playful expression. "I don't believe that will be of any concern Mr. Austin," he said as he turned back towards his counter. "I don't believe you know much about *it*, do you?" He set one of the cups in front of himself and began to pour from the steaming pot. "You see, angels are strictly forbidden from harming humans in any way. As such, I could do as I wish to the mortal vessel that stands with us and it wouldn't lift a finger in opposition. Would you, Angelic one?" He pushed a cup of tea towards me, motioning to take it. "That's an excellent theory. Sadly, despite what you've read in all these books I have a few bruises on my ass that would beg to differ."

He nearly spit his tea as he laughed. "Oh heavens. You don't still consider yourself to be human, do you, Mr. Austin?" I didn't want to give him the satisfaction of an answer. "You do! How delightful," he exclaimed in a way that I might as well have told him I still believed in Santa. "You ceased being human the moment you signed your eternity contract. You became one of the preternatural, a lap dog of the spirit world. The angelic one is more than within its right to smack you on the nose with a newspaper any time you get out of line." The analogy crept up my spine with irritation as I tried not to let it show. "Sodom and Gomorrah?" I asked, trying to divert the attention from myself. This time Anael spoke first. "We are avatars of the Father, including avatars of his wrath." Stewart snapped his fingers and pointed in agreement. "In those rare cases, they are not the ones perpetrating the harm, simply the tool." He looked far too smug for my taste. "I think *you-know-who* is taking a more hands-off approach these days, don't you agree?" He said, looking towards the sky. "Let's test it."

He stepped out from behind the counter and began speaking loudly, staring into the face of Anael. "All the items I have collected, all the forbidden knowledge I have read, all the dark transactions I have facilitated, and that's only the beginning." His predatory eyes narrowed, "Oh, my sweet angelic beast. I would have such fun with your physical being..." He stepped away and continued speaking, turning his voice towards the sky. "...and with all these impure thoughts and actions, I am more than deserving of divine retribution. So here is your opportunity. Your soldier is standing within striking distance. If I am to be punished, let it be now!" He shouted as a loud clap shook the room.

XXV

A second clap echoed through the musty store, soon followed by another. Stewart opened his eyes, looking dejected as we heard a familiar smarmy laugh. "Mr. Sangre. We had an agreement that I would be receiving our guests in private." I followed his eyes as they traced back towards the room behind the counter. Manuel stepped from the shadows clapping his hands as his serpentine smile gave away his amusement. "Forgive me, but your flair for the theatrics is truly inspiring." He took one of the steaming cups of tea and lifted it towards Stewart in salute. "Please feel free to finish your production. I will wait quietly."

The little man turned towards us as the wind had been pulled from his sails. "I think you get the point," he said meekly before stepping back. "Mr. Sangre here is a valued customer of mine, his willingness to vouch for you holds a lot of weight in my eyes." Manuel smiled at the compliment but continued sipping his tea. "He said you have questions regarding a certain object you have come across. An object that may be within my area of expertise." I felt the knife's weight as it rested in my coat pocket, not yet ready to show it off. "I found something alright, and Manny over there told us that you're the master of weird shit. So how are we gonna do this? I get the feeling that you're another one of these *"nothing's for free"* assholes."

Stewart dramatically clutched his chest as if struck by an arrow. "Charm that cuts like a knife, Mr. Austin. If you would please, take a look around you and tell me what you see?" I didn't bother since I wasn't interested in playing his games. "Exactly what I just said. Weird shit." He laughed. "I'll accept that, but to be more precise, let's call it weird and powerful shit." He picked up a small box covered in satin from a table beside him. "Take this, for example." He popped the lid off the box before placing it on the counter. "This is a preserved rat king. An interesting phenomenon where the tails of a colony of rats become intertwined and permanently fused together. They survive only through other rats bringing them food." He tilted the box in my direction. Inside I could see the small, dried bodies of more than a dozen rats tangled together. "Now, with the right knowledge, this can be a very powerful talisman." He snapped the lid closed. "Without that knowledge, it is nothing more than a box full of dead rats. That's what we value, the knowledge to accompany the trinkets. I don't believe it makes us *assholes*, as you say, to feel that knowledge begets knowledge." He turned back toward me. "Quid pro quo."

I could tell he was stalling. "So let's make a deal and tell me what I need to know. Then you can get back to playing with your rat boxes. What do you want?" He tucked his hands into his robe in an effort to look deep in thought. "*It...* is out of the question, I suppose?" he said, looking towards Anael. Silence was the only answer he needed. "Then let's trade knowledge. If the item you have brought is as powerful as I have been told, then that's very pricey information." He pulled his hands from his robe and began rubbing them together. "I will tell you everything I know about your object, and in return, you answer two questions of my choosing. No matter what the question is, you may not refuse to answer. Make that agreement, and we have a deal."

Knowing he had this all planned out, I forced myself to shake his hand, feigning the enthusiasm of a used car salesman. "Two," I said mid-shake, "My going rate with your friend over there is one, so I guess you cut yourself quite the deal." Stewart dropped his hand and made a production of wiping it clean with a handkerchief he lifted from the counter. "Yes, well, Mr. Sangre was polite enough to share that bit of information with me. In return, he gets to observe our conversation. Share and share alike I always say." I looked over at Manuel, who listened intently as he poured more tea. "Mr. Sangre was able to confirm that you are, in fact, one of the Manannán mac Lir" I stopped him before he could continue. "That's the second time you've called me that. What the hell is it?" Stewart gave me a look as if I had shit on his carpet. "Mr. Austin, let me give you some free advice. If you ever want to know if a myth is based in reality, you only need to search across cultures. If you can find the same stories existing among peoples with very little else in common, then there must be some level of fact involved. For instance, I have heard you call yourself a Charon from the Greek tradition. My Irish forefathers called your kind the Manannán mac Lir. Still, others call you reapers." He leaned in close as if he were telling me a secret. "If you're going to do the job, at least learn the lingo." He backed away again, continuing his thought. "Now that we have confirmation as to what you are, we can get into the more important questions." He strolled over to one of his bookcases and began to browse through it. "I have spent my entire life researching what comes next. Collecting books and objects with some connection to the afterlife. To support my research, I opened this little store. It allows me to buy and sell these items to people with similar interests. Along the way, I have done things that many would look down on." He reached into the bookcase and pulled out another dusty box. Bringing it over to us as he lifted the lid. "The heart of a sacrificed virgin. I had a customer come in last week and buy one just like it." I could see a delicate object wrapped in antique linen. "He could have been using it to summon a mighty demon. Then again, he may have been concocting a potion to increase the size of his *appendage*." His eyes gazed down the length of my body. "I'll never know because I never ask. Therefore, after years of being a facilitator for such acts, I know my soul is tainted. My place is secured in Hell, I have accepted that, but before I go, I want to know what it is like." He placed the box back on the shelf and quickly moved in close, licking his lips with anticipation. "So tell me. Tell me what I'm in for. You've been there. You've taken countless souls. Tell me."

His eyes had a crazed look, telling me he wouldn't like my answer before I began. "I can't answer that." He lunged towards me but caught himself to regain his composure. "You must. We have a deal!" "I'm not saying I won't," I interrupted, "I'm saying I can't. I'm not allowed in. Come on, think it over. Does the limo driver ever get invited into the reception?" His face flushed with embarrassment as he realized I was telling the truth. "You want to know the ins and outs of downtown, then ask Professor X over there," I said, pointing towards the stoic Anael. "All I can describe is the lobby."

Stewart waved his hand in front of the unresponsive angel. "I think we both know this one isn't about to do me any favors. That being said, you know more than you realize. Tell me about the crossing. You've seen more than most in this world; you've stood at the doorstep of damnation. Tell me what you do know of Hell." He was right of course. I may not have seen the entire show, but I saw enough to carry the stain. The fear you couldn't shake as it made itself at home within your bones. I thought for a moment. "It's quiet," was the only way I could describe it as I tried to put words to feeling and could see the little man getting angrier. "It's quiet! That's all you have?" It was amusing, for all the books he's read and things he's collected, he was still a naive baby in a world he knew nothing about. "You were expecting fire and screaming. Giant demons and torture devices beyond even your most chilling nightmares. What I can tell you is that I've never seen any of that. I don't believe you will either, that would be too easy. Torment would be a distraction from the worst torture that could ever be inflicted on you. The torture of your own thoughts. That's what I believe Hell is. An eternity of solitude, an eternity of loneliness, everlasting despair," I looked back at him, "endless knowledge that there's a place out there where beauty is limitless, and you'll never have to feel pain again; and that's the one place you'll never see."

Stewart stood staring back at me, fighting for composure yet betrayed by the heavy swallow of the lump in his throat. "Yes..." he said, much of the cocksure nature now drained from his voice. "That only leaves my final question, which I will hold for now. Please, Mr. Austin. If you would be so kind as to show me what you have brought." Stewart moved back to his sales counter and shooed Manuel away. The kid was still sitting on the floor incorporeal, unmoved by anything going on around him. I reached into my jacket pocket and grasped the knife as I moved to the opposite end of the counter.

Feeling the smooth cloth that Benny had wrapped it in, I placed it in front of Stewart as He pulled a set of black latex gloves onto his chubby hands. With a pop of electricity, he flicked on a bright magnifying light extending from a hinged arm attached to the desk. "Let's see what we have here," as he gently unwrapped the cloth. With the knife exposed, he looked up at me from under his glasses as if he was caught in an elaborate practical joke. "You really do not know what you have here, Mr. Austin?" I poured myself some of the tea sitting beside him. "I know I found it with the body of a friend of mine, and I know whoever put it there is going to pay."

He looked at the now fully exposed knife and picked it up delicately. "In that case, let's start from the beginning. It's an exceptionally rare object indeed, supposedly made from a metal that cannot be found in this world. Inscribed onto it is detailed lettering from a language that existed before man." There wasn't enough time left for his theatrics. "I get it. It's a knife made from Unobtanium and covered in words no one speaks. Why was it there?" He gripped it by the handle and pointed it at me. "You are partially correct. I'm assuming when you say you found this with the body of a friend, what you meant was you found it *in* the body of a friend. Right about here, I suppose." he pointed the knife at my forehead, slightly above my eyes. "Something like that. What I want to know is why they killed him with it?"

Stewart laughed with condescension. "No one was killed with this object, Mr. Austin, I can guarantee that. It's the same way you wouldn't use The Shroud of Turin to clean up a coffee spill. This object is far too precious for something so mundane." He placed the knife back on the counter. "Look closer. What is it that you see?" Knowing we were on the border of finally getting answers, I practiced self-control. "An overpriced magical letter opener that is starting to cut through my patience." He spun the knife around so the tip now faced him. "And that's what makes you stupid. You look at an object and never bother to consider that it may be anything more than your first poorly conceived assumption. Allow me to blow your mind. This isn't a knife at all."

I lifted it from the counter and gave it another quick once over, trying to see what I could have missed. "Forgive me if I don't get offended that the guy in a Halloween costume called me stupid, but if this knife isn't a knife, then what the hell is it?" He pulled it from my hand and turned the handle towards me. "You're focusing on the blade. I can't blame you, of course. As far as you know, it's the most important part of this object.

That is where you are so fundamentally wrong; this is." He pointed at the tip of the handle and the small, roughly cut jewel set into it. "It's called a blood gem. There's not much written about it. I've seen a few minor references hinting that they're formed from the ichor of an angel's essence. I must assume that you're not going to confirm that for me, will you?" He looked toward Anael, who gave him nothing.

"Well then. Let's take that as confirmation by omission." He rubbed his thumb over the jewel trying to wipe away a smudge. "No matter its origin, it is still an implement of great power." He placed the knife back on the counter and turned towards one of the bookcases behind him. "Did you know that the written word is only about 7,000 years old? That's amazing, isn't it? When you consider how long humans have puttered around on this giant rock, we've only been recording our knowledge for the most minimal fraction of that time." I felt the conversation veer off course. "Fascinating," I said, trying to reel him back in, "But it doesn't tell me what this thing is."

With another rehearsed speech chambered, Stewart's ego took a blow from the interruption. "It's a tap stupid. That's what I was trying to explain." He marched back to the counter as I tried to figure out precisely what he meant by tap. "As long as there have been humans, there have been those of us trying to gain knowledge of whatever lies beyond. Witches, Wizards, Warlocks, Shaman. Call them whatever you want, but they've been around since we first crawled from the oceans. Do you think knowledge like that just gets passed around from person to person through stories? It doesn't" He answered his own question as he lifted the knife from the table and held it towards me. "The unexpected can always occur. Sometimes knowledge had to be taken. Hence the use of this particular item, a tap."

I paused for a moment, unsure if I heard him correctly. "A tap? like the kind you hammer into maple trees?" "Yes. Only instead of syrup this one is used to funnel memories into this little guy right here." He pointed toward the small red jewel. "Right before the moment of death you tap into the root of the person's being. The third eye, the Ajna chakra." He placed the silver tip against the center of my forehead. "Piercing the pineal gland and draining the most important aspects of that person's memories into this pretty little stone." I pinched the blade of the tap and lifted it away from my head. "I found this thing in the head of a child. Not some mystical librarian. Why would someone use it on him." From the corner of my eye, I could see the kid standing. He stared at us as something caught his attention. "Knowledge, memories, two sides of the same coin Mr. Austin. In my best estimation, I would assume that this object was used because someone didn't want the child crossing over with a particular set of memories."

An idea was beginning to take shape in my head. "Are you saying the memories of what happened to the kid are still inside that stone?" Stewart bowed his head in agreement, apparently proud that I was finally catching on. He placed the knife back onto the counter before it was scooped up by a suddenly interested Manuel. "If they have not already been drained from within the jewel, then yes. I assume, of course, your next question will be whether or not I know how to retrieve them. Let me save you the time and say yes, but that's an entirely separate agreement. I still have one question left to satisfy this transaction."

Anael's gaze remained set in stone even though I could somehow feel the anger begin to burn over inside them. "Then ask. No more games." Stewart turned back to his bookcases as I felt another speech coming on. "I never had any illusion that Hell would be an enjoyable place. At most, I had hoped it would be only slightly less disdainful than I had anticipated. You confirmed for me, however, that this is not the case. So now I put this to you." He turned back towards me, his face sincere. "How do I stay out of Hell? I'm not naive, nor am I asking how to earn my way into Heaven. I simply want to know what I can do to prevent an eternity of torment?" For a moment, I sympathized with the little man. It was the same feelings I had expressed to Anael only a short while before. Hell was so drastic that it was human nature to look for any option out, never considering just not being a dick.

"Souls only have three destinations. Heaven, Hell, or the Gray. If you have really earned your ticket to the hot seat, then there's no other option for you." The sincerity in the man's face flushed with anger. "Our agreement was for truth. Not semantics, not canned responses, truth." He moved in closer as Manuel still played with the tap, grinning at the tension in our conversation. "I promise you this, Mr. Austin. If you withhold this knowledge from me, then you will never find out how to release what is contained within that stone."

He was right of course. There were other options; although I could see Anael shake their head slightly in disagreement, I knew now was not the time to burn a bridge. "Those are the only three eternal destinations for a soul," I said, reiterating my earlier statement, "but there are two other possibilities." Stewart laughed in relief and clasped his hands. "Excellent. All the studying. All the research. I knew there must be something else out there. Tell me, tell me now, what other choices do I have?" I felt slightly disgusted by his enjoyment. "If a soul is judged unworthy of any eternal option, then there are powers with the ability to choose dissolution. Destruction of the soul. This one won't even acknowledge your presence, so I think it would be smart to bet against that option." Stewart gave Anael an angry stare before turning back towards me. "With the right motivation, I'm sure it would be much more open to discussion. There's no need for us to jump to the messy options just yet. What is the other choice?" I felt a cringe at the masochistic tone in his voice. "Refusal," I said quietly, wishing I could keep it to myself. "We call them runners, ghosts. Souls that separate after death and run from their crossing. It's self-imposed exile." Stewart paced around us as he listened closely. "By refusing to cross over, you are rejecting the natural laws of the universe. You will forever be banned from leaving this existence. You will exist alone in this world for the rest of its days, and when the world takes its final breath, you will simply cease to be."

He steepled his fingers and placed them against his mouth, deep in thought. "So countless lifetimes as an invisible voyeur before a final poof into nonexistence." He looked up, almost giddy. "That's wonderful. Oh, Mr. Austin, you have really made my day. Thank you so much." He reached both hands out and shook mine enthusiastically before I recoiled. "Don't thank me. Ghosts are the lepers of the spirit world. I was only keeping our agreement. Now we need to negotiate another." He took a few steps back and smoothed the wrinkles of his robe. "About that. It seems we have a bit of a problem, Mr. Austin. Unfortunately, you don't seem to have anything else I want at this point." He positioned himself behind his sales counter, leaning over it towards me. "Don't get me wrong, I'm sure you have some fascinating stories that I would love to hear, but as for real knowledge, valuable knowledge, I don't think you have much more to offer. So in situations like this, it really just comes down to money." I stepped closer to him. "How much? Money isn't a problem." He tossed his head back with a fake laugh. "I'm sure you've got quite the little nest egg, sadly I just don't believe you have enough in this situation. At least not compared to your competitor." "What competitor?" I asked incredulously, noticing his smile as he began to bare his wolfish teeth. "Your only competitor Mr. Austin. The man I sold that tap to originally."

The words hit like a blow to the stomach. "Whitehall," I said softly as the little man gestured to something behind me.

The pieces fell together as I felt a hand on my back and turned sharply to see Manuel had quietly made his way to my blind spot. With the speed of a striking viper, I barely made out the blur of the silver-bladed knife before the world went dark.

XXVI

"To Sleep. To sleep perchance to dream. Ay, there's the rub, for in this sleep of death what dreams may come..."

That was Shakespeare's attempt at being poetic about the afterlife. We've all heard it, the favorite soliloquy of every hack actor. The romantic notion that maybe there are only dreams waiting for us on the other side of death. Take my advice and don't think about it too deeply. I can tell you from experience that Shakespeare was utterly full of shit. You can try to romanticize it in any way that kills the butterflies in your stomach, but take it from someone with firsthand knowledge. Death is death, sleep is sleep, and dreams are a luxury of the living. Right now, I was experiencing something that didn't seem to fall into any of those categories. There was no peace, and there were no dreams, just unforgiving darkness.

Within a silence that lacked serenity, I found myself in a place that was cold and ruthless, my soul encased in a cage of ice I couldn't escape. It was a personal prison where the last thing I felt before this stark void was the point of a blade puncturing its way through my forehead before I fell from the world around me. It was a painful way to drop from existence and worse when I was brought back as the same blade was removed. I could feel the pressure of the metal as it was pulled from my skull, but my senses were slow to follow. My hearing returned first as my blurred thoughts tried to make sense of the smooth Latin voice. "The little man did not know what this would do to a creature such as you," he spoke softly. I could tell from the sound of his breath that he was close. "He said if we were lucky, it would... how did he word it?" The voice hesitated. "Yes, he said it would push your pause button. He also said if we were unlucky, it would just piss you off. Well, friend, I am a great many things, and *lucky* has always seemed to be one of them."

My sight began to return. Unfortunately, hazy vision and a foggy mind meant the world around me made very little sense. My cheek rested against cold stone as the outline of expensive brown leather shoes began to take shape. My instincts took over, reeling back as hard as I could. Like a turtle in its shell, I tried to reach inside myself and fall into my non-existent state of being. I kicked with what little of my legs I could feel and thrashed every ounce of my body, focusing the few clear spots of my mind on just fading away. After a few more seconds of trying, I had only managed to give myself a terrible headache. A vice-like grip on each shoulder hoisted me to my knees. The figure in front of me came into focus, the one who had helped me up. "Relax yourself, Senor Austin," Manuel said. "Take a deep breath; look at your hands."

I had very little reason to trust him, but as my vision became usable I lifted my hands and heard the unmistakable sound of chains rattling. My wrists were bound together by thick cast iron shackles, while an intersecting chain led to a collar I could now feel around my neck. With a futile scream, I pulled at the chain, unable to break it. "I'm sorry. I really am. Please understand that I respect you and your position very much." He leaned down so our faces were even. "But this is bigger than both of us. Had I not done as I was told, I would be in the same position as you and your companion here. Perhaps even worse."

It took a moment for what he said to click, but as it did I hesitantly looked to my side. Behind me was Anael, their once pristine white cloak now stained from the soiled blacktop we both knelt on. A similar set of shackles restrained the angel as they hung their head in a gesture of peace and shame. As I stared in frustration, I could feel Manuel grip my shoulder once more. "For what it is worth, I am genuinely sorry. It is my hope that you both go with God.

With impotent anger, I spit on the ground. "God doesn't want me right now, so I can promise you this. I don't care what Hell is like; I give you my word it's nothing compared to what I'm going to do when I find you. Here or there, I will be waiting for you." He bowed his head, accepting what I had said as truth and walked away quietly. As he left, I turned toward Anael. "Annie, you doing ok?" We weren't exactly best friends, but if you can't give a fellow prisoner a nickname who can you give one to? The angel spoke softly without raising their head. "When my kind enters this world, we are bound by enduring laws. I am here as a vassal of the Father and a servant of man. These men knew that, as they knew I could in no way harm a living soul." Even in a situation as shitty as this one, it still struck me as funny. "Living being the keyword. You certainly kicked my ass." Anael's head rose towards me, and for the first time, I could see a rare smile. "That was no challenge," they said before dropping their head again. "If you help me figure out how to fix this little issue, I promise to put up more of a fight next time. What happened to the kid?" Looking up, Anael gazed sharply past my right shoulder. I followed the stare while trying to figure out where we were.

I could tell it was a parking lot, isolated but well-lit by large poles that fought against the deep night sky. In the sky the occasional star in the cloudless black meant I must have been out of commission for at least the rest of the day. Judging from where the moon hung, it was getting close to dawn. The smooth blacktop stretched from north to south for as far as my low position could see, only interrupted by what seemed like miles of chain link fencing running along its edges. "We were taken here in a mechanical wagon," said Anael with all the worldly knowledge of the dark ages. "The child remained in his ethereal state as you had instructed. When we were loaded onto the transport, he stowed away with us. I saw him remain by your side even while you were incapacitated." The angel raised their shackled hands and pointed a long white finger towards the fence. "When we were removed from the transport, he again followed your instructions and found the only possible hidden location around us. Somewhere beyond that perimeter." My vision wasn't strong enough to see clearly in the distance, but I was confident that he was still there. I lifted my heavy chained hands and placed two fingers into my mouth, whistling as loudly as I could. It took a moment, but even with my blurry sight I could see the small head of the kid pop up from his hiding spot and wave excitedly towards us.

A sense of pride fell over me. The kid stuck with the plan, even when I didn't know what the plan was myself. A quick glance around found that the three of us seemed to be completely alone. "Hey," I yelled toward the kid, seeing his head bob up and down. With a loud *clank* of the chains, I motioned him over hoping it was best to stick close together. The kid passed effortlessly through the chain-link fence while jogging towards us. He plodded along the asphalt, growing louder as he drew closer, yet the cadence of his steps seemed slightly off. I heard thump after thump before his foot hit the ground. It took another moment before my apparently concussed mind made that obvious connection that immaterial feet shouldn't be making sounds.

The rhythmic thuds grew louder as the kid stopped in his tracks a few yards from us. I felt a sudden cartoonish sense of dread as something approached over my shoulder. Taking a resolute breath, I turned my head towards the sound before a rush of wind caught me in the face from the oversized helicopter hovering above us. I knew a little about military equipment from late-night boredom, and I could tell that this one was a twin-engine Chinook. A heavy-duty aerial transport reserved almost exclusively for military use now upgraded to a sleek, highly glossed white paint job.

A few years back it was in the news how a rich action movie star decided to buy a decommissioned tank for his own personal use. At the time, it struck me as an impractical waste of money, but now I think I understood it a little better. It was a display of wealth that even the rich could only aspire to. A power play to set himself apart from everyone else. When the rich bought mansions, the powerful bought compounds. Some bought limos, while others bought tanks, and as I could see right now, when the wealthy purchased jets, modern-day kings hovered in their own chinooks. As we stared, kidnapped and kneeling in the middle of nowhere while a helicopter parked itself only feet away, I realized "You dumbass. It's not a parking lot. It's a landing strip."

The wheels made contact with the blacktop before the rear door of the chopper dropped open. A half dozen masked men funneled from inside, suited in a paramilitary fashion and carrying assault rifles. Right now was one of those moments that Benny would say, "shit just got real." Unable to move I was thankful that, as a dead man, I didn't have to worry about pissing my pants as the men surrounded us. Two more figures emerge from the rear door. A familiar frail man in a cheap dark suit and an overly tanned playboy with a blindingly white smile.

As he flashed a mouth of ivory in my direction, I spoke loud enough for everyone around to hear. "You're not still pissed at me for blowing up your library, are you Tommy boy?"

XXVII

"Don't be silly, Austin," Whitehall said as he pulled a piece of candy from the pocket of his khakis. "That's the great thing about privilege. You find that with the right number of zeroes, nothing is irreplaceable." He untwisted one end of the wrapper and popped a hard candy into his mouth. "Forgive and forget, water under the bridge. I never really liked that old place anyways. It was a stuffy old tinderbox that only my father cared about." He balled up the wrapper and tossed it into the light wind of the slowing propellers. "He's dead and the house is damaged. So let's all move on, agreed?"

I gave him a half-hearted thumbs up from one shackled hand. He was out of place in his well-pressed khakis and golf shirt more at home at a country club than out here doing whatever it was he was about to do. I guess there really was no dress code for angel kidnapping. "And how could I stay mad at you? I mean, after all, would you look at what you brought me," he said as he moved in close to Anael. He crouched on the balls of his heels and inspected the angel closely. "It's beautiful, isn't it? and from what I've been told, priceless." Still at eye level, he gleefully peered over at me. "This one is all dirty, though. Do you think they make them in other colors?" He let loose a forced chuckle as the guards joined in on the joke. It was clear who signed their checks and who owned their allegiance. "Beggars can't be choosers," he sighed as the chorus of laughs came to an abrupt stop. "I'll just have to make do with what I was given." I watched as he placed an index finger under Anael's chin attempting to raise their face. A mistake that led to the first interaction I had seen between the angel and a living human. Anael snapped forward with otherworldly speed, closing the short gap between their faces and staring silent murder into his eyes only a few inches away.

The quickness of the angel startled me, so I forgave Whitehall's fumble as he fell backward onto his ass and gasped heavily. His face set in a look of fear before quickly evolving first into embarrassment and finally settling into anger. He lifted himself from the ground and grabbed the chain hanging from Anael's collar, jerking the angel to all fours like a disobedient dog. "Well played." He said as he looked down, "but you've shown your hand too early. You got a good jump from me. I'm big enough to admit that, but now I know what they say is true. It doesn't matter what I do; you can't harm me." He knelt again as a sinister tone entered his voice. "I think we're going to have fun testing whether that rule has any limits."

Unable to see Anael like this anymore, it was time to jump in. "Hey, TomTom," I said, snapping my fingers to get his attention. "Since we're such good pals now, what say we pop these chains off and talk this through?" Whitehall visibly took a moment to collect himself as a dark piece of his personality had momentarily taken over. "Yes, that would be the gentlemanly thing for me to do, wouldn't it?" He wiped some non-existent dust from his pressed khakis. "However, you are not a gentleman. So forgive me for keeping you bound. I hope you can appreciate those manacles you are wearing. They were challenging to produce. Very expensive." Moving with the flow of the conversation, I lifted my hands so I could inspect the shackles "Yep, nice stuff," I said, eyeing them over like a fine watch as he narrated their features. "The power goes straight down to the metal itself. Iron forged with carbon from the bones of another heavenly creature I acquired some time ago."

He pulled a silver pen from the chest pocket of his polo and tapped Anael's collar, letting the sound ring out. "You heard that correctly. Angel bones in there, cool stuff, right?" He was eager to brag and there was no reason to stop him. "The inner cuffs are inscribed with a whole series of binding spells. I mean, it may be overkill, but come on. It's not like there's a recipe floating around for angel cuffs." He placed the pen back in his pocket. "So I hired a few high-priced alchemists, real creepy fellows, and said fuck it. Let's throw everything at the wall and see what sticks." He moved over to me, jerking the chain that connected the cuffs and collar, sending me sprawling onto my stomach. "I can't explain how they work, but they do seem to be working well. Don't you think? Be honest with me. You can't phase out of them now, can you Austin?" He gave the rhetorical question a momentary pause. "No, I don't believe you can. If you could, then we clearly wouldn't be having this conversation right now." I pushed myself back to my knees, raising my hands to brush my hair back into place. "Money well spent," ignoring his attempt to humiliate me. "Unless I'm just buying time of course. Are you willing to roll those dice?"

Without an answer, the strange man in the cheap suit leaned into Whitehall's ear and whispered something that brought a smile to his face. "A real tough guy aren't you, Mr. Austin. A tough guy with a soft heart. My associate here has informed me that the child is still with us. Standing right behind you, actually. That tells me you both have a mutual weakness for one another. If you were just buying time, you wouldn't be willing to risk the child in such a way. It seems things are going my way." He turned towards the small group of armed men behind him and pointed towards the helicopter.

Apparently expecting the order, they turned in unison and jogged to the rear ramp. "These aren't the only presents I brought for you, Austin. They were just the appetizer. Your real gift is arriving momentarily. I think you'll get a real kick out of this one."

The men emerged from the rear door hauling a large cement crate like pallbearers shifting a casket. They moved the large stone box in lockstep to only a few feet from where we knelt, dropping it with a cracking thud. Whitehall pulled a silk handkerchief from his pocket and made a show of polishing a section of the top as the mercenaries resumed their positions around us. "You're probably wondering what's inside, aren't you. The suspense must be overwhelming." He shoved the silk back into his pocket before jumping onto the lid of the crate, sitting towards the edge as his feet dangled. "There are so many more questions I bet you want answered also. Who's the kid? Why did I choose him? All the stuff you've been chasing your tail trying to find. Well, let's make a deal. If the kid agrees to show himself right now, I'll tell you everything you want to know."

An unexpected proposition as my expression gave me away. I turned back toward the kid who still stood silently behind us. He looked as confused as I did, but this was our chance. Our eyes met, and without words I knew he was asking if he should. Out of options and hoping that answers would be some consultation for my failure, I said softly, "it's ok to come out." Whitehall's grin doubled as the kid snapped back into existence in less time than it would take to blink. "That is one hell of a trick; I'll give you that." He slapped his hand on the cement crate. "Well, a deal is a deal. One thing though..." One of the guards stepped forward and snapped a matching set of shackles around the kid's wrists with one quick motion.

My movement was limited from where I knelt as anger took over. I twisted fiercely, headbutting the guard in the groin and feeling that the one piece of armor he overlooked was a cup. He dropped the collar he was about to place around the kid's neck while Whitehall clapped loudly. "Excellent. Pain really is the best learning tool, isn't it? Next time I imagine he'll be more cautious." I could see the fire explode in the guard's eyes before Whitehall intervened. "Leave him," he demanded. "That was your own stupidity. Let's forgo the collar on the child. The manacles are all we need to keep him solid." He turned his attention back to us. "I apologize for the surprise but look at it as an insurance policy. After I say my piece, this prevents the child from once again going *poof*."

　　Looking at the kid, I chose the best lie I could think of, "I've got this under control." Whitehall listened from his perch as he pulled another candy from his pocket. "I'm sure you do," he said as he slowly untwisted each end, "and now that we're all here, I do believe I promised you an explanation. Always keep your promises. That was one of the first lessons my father ever taught me. Power comes and goes, money is earned and money is lost, but a man's word is something no one can ever take from him." He chewed on the candy, tossing another empty wrapper into the wind. "He taught me a lot of things, my father, and almost all of them were double-edged swords. On my thirteenth birthday he called me into his office and told me something that changed my life forever. He told me that with my name, the very lineage I was born into, I could do anything I wanted in this world, and no one could stop me. Looking back on it now, I know he was telling me to not let anything stop me from being the man he thought I could be."

　　He hung his head and shook it slowly, laughing at an inside joke. "I took it to mean that laws didn't apply to me. What made things worse was apparently, they didn't." He looked up, staring daggers into my eyes. "Do you know what kind of impact that knowledge has on a young man? To know that you have unlimited resources and zero consequences? By the time I was leaving my teens, I had tasted every drug this world had to offer, coming and going from rehab the way many teens treat the mall. I consumed anything I could find, and after running through it all, I still felt so empty inside. I learned that drugs weren't the answer I was looking for."

He jumped down from his seat on the cement crate, eyeing us like insects. "So I started to look for satisfaction in other ways. I gambled away more money than most men would see in their lifetimes. I bought priceless art and hung it away, never noticing it again. Nothing I did ever seemed to feel right, so things turned darker." He stepped past me and towards the kid. "After a while, my tastes became more ... eccentric." His finger ran softly along the kid's smooth cheek as he stared down into his face. The implication made me nauseous. "I broke every commandment, defied every law, each time in more intricate ways. Not only for my enjoyment but also just to say I had done it. Proving time and again exactly what my father had said, never facing punishment." He dropped his hand and stepped away.

"Then one day, while I was tasting some of the more *interesting* experiences Eastern Europe had to offer, I received a call to come home. No one had bothered to tell me that my father had developed terminal cancer. Apparently, things had taken a turn for the worse. I rushed back and found him in that large mansion of his. He was surrounded by servants but couldn't have been more alone." As he spoke of his father, I could see genuine emotion in his face. "In his final moments, he reminded me of those words that had shaped my life so many years before. *You are a Whitehall, and in this world your potential is unlimited. No man can judge what you choose to do.* I remember his face growing cold as he added the amendment that would change everything. "*Yet man is not our only judge. When our time comes, we will be judged by something greater than us.*" He brushed what could have been a tear from his eye as he turned away. "That was when I saw something in his face I had never seen before. I saw fear. It was a fear I didn't know he was capable of, and the last thing I saw in his eyes before he died."

XXVIII

Enough of his self-indulgent one-way conversation already. "A rich kid with daddy issues. How unique. Let me guess, did you get picked on by the bigger kids too?" My knees were starting to ache as they pressed against the blacktop. "You got all the money but not enough hugs, poor thing. Can we move it along?" It didn't spark the anger in Whitehall that I was hoping for. Nevertheless, it prompted him to act. The Snap of his fingers signaled the nearest guard who caught me across the jaw with the butt of his rifle. The force knocked me over before being forcefully lifted back to my knees. "You know Tom, if you keep playing so rough I don't think we can be friends anymore." I reached one shackled hand into my jacket pocket and pulled out the silver cigar case. Fumbling with bound hands, I refused to give him the satisfaction of knowing I was in pain, "I'll forgive you this time if you help me out here." Whitehall grabbed the silver case and inspected it closely, popping it open before taking a quick whiff of the small cigars. "Cheap, of course," he said as he tossed the case to the ground, "and shit quality too."

Insulting a man's cigars felt like a low blow but I kept my mouth shut, knowing he was inching closer to explaining why we were here. "Before I was interrupted, I was saying how with just a few simple words, my father managed to once again turn my life upside down. Those terrible things I had done came rushing back, and for the first time, I felt their weight. It was fear that set me on a journey of spiritual discovery where I intended to find a way to cleanse my soul." With a raised eyebrow, he attempted to turn this into a conversation. "Do you know what I found, Austin? I spoke with so many people who claimed to have the answer, and the one problem with their roads to absolution?" The question was rhetorical, but that didn't mean I couldn't take a guess. "You're too big of a piece of shit to be forgiven by any of them?"

He went to snap his fingers again, but my involuntary flinch must have been enough satisfaction. "No, actually. I found that all their great paths to righteousness didn't exactly fit my tastes. They were all about earning forgiveness and devoting your life to a straight and narrow path. Doesn't that sound boring? After all, old habits die hard, don't you agree?" He hopped back onto the cement crate, revving up the theatrics. "I decided to take a different approach to this whole judgment concept, breaking it down into ideas that I understood. It was straightforward when I took a step back and viewed it in a different light. The offer of eternal salvation, a reward pending approval based on defined criteria that had the addition of a penalty if such requirements are not met before a final expiration date." He looked down at us like we had somehow missed the big reveal.

"You don't get it? It's nothing more than a contract, and all contracts have loopholes. All it took was hiring a team of lawyers and occultists who combed through every religious text for something that worked in my favor. It didn't take them long before they found it, hiding in plain sight." I looked over to check on the kid still standing beside us, his tiny hands shackled in monstrous cuffs. "One simple line of scripture, the key to exactly what I was looking for." He held out his hands in mock religious devotion while looking towards the sky. "Truly, I say to you, whatever you bind on earth shall be bound in heaven. Matthew 18:18" He smiled as he spoke each word slowly, turning his attention again to us. "I had my legal team play with that one for weeks, reaching out to experts who all came to the same conclusion. Are you ready for it?" I felt a shiver run up my spine from his unbearable sense of self-satisfaction. "Agreements made in this world that are completed in sacrament are held true even after death. Let that sink in." In a more dramatic act than a 10th-grade production of Hamlet, Whitehall pretended to check his nails as he gave us time to ponder what he had just said. "I can break it down for you if you haven't quite grasped it yet. It means any contract I make with a built-in clause for the afterlife must be honored by the big guy upstairs." He paced along the top of the cement crate preaching the genius of what he had found. "I had to confirm it of course, which wasn't cheap since it required pricey experts who could orchestrate demonic possessions that could converse with my legal team. On a side note, did you know that in a room full of lawyers and demons, it's actually pretty difficult to tell who's who?" The joke fell flat until an unpleasant stare triggered a roar of forced laughter from the guards. "Yes, exactly," he continued.

"The next piece is something I think our winged friend here is all too familiar with. Have you ever heard of a *proxy* Austin?" Having learned his lesson, he didn't bother giving me a chance to respond. "It's when one entity acts as a representation of another. Like an angel acting as a proxy for the word of God." Anael stayed silent as he looked towards the angel for a reaction. "You're no fun," he pouted. "In business we use them all the time, which meant my ticket to a squeaky-clean soul was just that simple. I needed a whipping boy. Someone who could take the punishment for all my questionable deeds while leaving me looking like the innocent angel I am." He folded his hands in prayer as he looked at us. "I needed a literal sacrificial lamb."

"Bullshit!" I yelled as he looked down through half-closed eyes. "You can't just force your sins on someone. Things don't work that way, never have. I don't think they're suddenly going to make an exception for a shitbag like you" Ignoring the insult, he seemed to pity the small, chained simpleton below him. "I'm not asking for anyone to change the rules. In fact, I'm sticking to them quite strictly. I'm fully aware that I couldn't demand someone pay for my sins. That would be outrageous." He hopped down and moved towards the kid. "But no one said that a willing person couldn't ask me for them, maybe even beg for them. Do you remember *Peter*, the way you begged to see your mother again?"

I should have been relieved that we finally knew the kid's name. It was Peter. Not the Saint, or the rabbit, but the kid we were fighting to keep from Hell itself; Peter. It was too bad the only thing I could think of was how I wanted to smash this overprivileged asshole's face into the cement until his pearly whites came peeking through the back of his skull. My head sped beyond its usual cruise control setting. Without thought, I lunged from my knees towards Thomas's throat, looking to take his head off with the chains that still bound my hands. My emotions overruled my knowledge that an uphill battle is rarely won and by the time I rushed toward him, he sidestepped my attack as a guard's boot caught me in the ribs. "Don't get testy; you don't want to miss the best part." He turned back towards the kid, towards Peter. "You don't remember any of that, do you? Thanks to that wonderful stone I purchased from the little salesman, you can't remember anything. Let me help you." He backed away as I saw Anael look up, waiting for the next word. "I needed someone to carry my burden, someone to take it from me even if it meant toting it all the way to Hell. Do you know what would convince someone to do that?" I could feel the answer turn in my gut as I quietly answered, "love."

"That's right," he said, still staring at the kid. "Like the love of a child for his mother. I just needed someone who met all our criteria, and in a city like this, that was easy. It didn't take long for one of my associates to find the foster child of a junkie who may have loved her child, but not as much as her next fix. We found him, and lucky for us his foster family required a little financial assistance." Something was amusing him. "Nothing says *no questions asked* like the feeling of cash." "You can't buy a child!" I wasted my breath, knowing he would never see what he did as wrong. "I paid for their silence, not for young Peter here. As I was saying, once we had him, getting everything set up was easy. Apparently, all it takes is painting the right demonic gibberish all over a room to get a kind of spiritual privacy. Then, in our private little moment, I made you a promise Peter. You may not remember it, but I intend to keep my promise. I swore to you that I would make sure you were with your mother again. I didn't say how, I didn't say where, and I may have withheld the little part about her conveniently overdosing a few days prior, but I was true to my word that you can still be with her. You just had to sign our little agreement so the two of you could be together for eternity."

He pulled a few folded papers from his back pocket. "And you did. You begged me to see her again because of how much you missed her. I know it's cliche here, but you really would have sold your innocent little soul just to scrawl your name across the dotted line. I didn't need your soul, though. I needed the opposite. I needed you to keep it and all my baggage along with it. My lawyers called it *contractual immorality transferal in perpetuity*. Then for the right price, a very disreputable gentleman made sure we wouldn't have to wait long for you to meet your end." He stuffed the papers back into his pocket, seemingly pleased with himself. "I made sure that little deal was ironed out before you signed. I didn't want to taint this new clean soul of mine by involving it in a deal like that. You know what's funny, Peter? You might be the only person judged for the sin of their own murder. Wrap your mind around that one."

He turned towards me again, the thoughts of everything he had just laid on us still spinning in my head. "It was you, Mr. Austin. You were the wildcard. The one aspect of this whole thing I never could have accounted for. Until our young friend here reaches those fiery gates, our contract is incomplete. That means my soul isn't looking too bright, so you'll have to forgive me for taking drastic measures." He slapped his hand down on the top of the cement crate. The guards surrounding us took up their previous pallbearer formation without a word, lifting the heavy lid in unison and resting it on its side. Thomas peered inside the empty inner cavity of the crate, almost giddy. "I initially had hopes that the angel would succeed in taking you both to Hell, but I'm always prepared with a backup. The winged one doesn't concern me, and once this is over, I'll find a nice place where the two of us can have some fun. The kid can catch a ride with one of your peers Austin; I'll just have to make a few phone calls. That only leaves you. I've made people disappear plenty of times, but you're different. After all, how do you kill someone who can't die?" He was so deep in his own gloating he didn't bother waiting for an answer. "You don't," he continued. "So I'll have to take a more business-like approach. What do you do with a business rival you can't destroy? You bury them."

A pair of guards boxed me in, grabbing my arms. Pulled to my feet as they dragged me towards the crate. I didn't resist. I may have been defeated, but I wouldn't give Whitehall the satisfaction of seeing me struggle. He spoke louder as my feet scraped against the blacktop. "With that lovely set of jewelry you're wearing, you can't do your cool disappearing trick. So what do you think happens if I seal you up inside of this cement sarcophagus? I think it means you're going to have a lot of quiet time to relax." A third guard reached down to grab my legs only for me to boot him in the helmet, sending him spinning. It was enough to make me feel a little better but wouldn't change what was about to occur. The two remaining guards moved in, each grabbing a leg as they tossed me into the empty stone coffin.

The largest guard placed a giant palm against my chest as the others hoisted the lid half on. As the top slid slowly into place, Whitehall peered over the edge, grinning down at me. "I don't want to spoil the surprise of where I'm going to have you buried, but I hope you don't mind the cold." His head disappeared again as the lid resumed its slow scrape towards closure. "Thomas," I yelled from my back like a wounded turtle. "Yes? Is there something I can help you with?" I could see his amusement while trying to buy more time. "Why did you tell us all of that? I mean, wouldn't it be more torture to just lock me away without ever knowing why?"

He shrugged, looking down as if the thought never crossed his mind. "Torturing you was never the point. Maybe I just wanted to tell the only other soul who might appreciate the gravity of what I've done. Maybe I wanted to gloat, for you to know that I won. Hell, maybe I'm just a dick. You know what, it's probably all three." He reached into the pocket where he held the contract and pulled out a leather tube, uncapping one end as he removed a long hand-rolled cigar.

"I want you to know that this isn't personal. It's business. If you ever make it to Heaven, please come find me. I'm sure we'll have a laugh about this whole thing." He held the cigar under his nose and took a slow inhale, enjoying the smell before reaching down and placing it into my chest pocket. "This may not be something that you're used to, but that's a quality cigar. Consider it a consolation gift," as the lid began sliding again. It only took a moment to move past his onlooking face as he called down into my darkened tomb, "Make it last. It'll be a long time before you get another."

XXIX

When you're cut off from all stimulation, your mind decides it's a good time to start making its own entertainment. In the hollow space of my tomb, I watched colorful shapes dance and coalesce in a space that somehow existed a few feet beyond the lid. I remembered experiments in sensory deprivation and how the removal of all external senses causes the brain to go into a state of hyper-sensation. Your waistband can feel like a tourniquet squeezing your torso while the sound of your own heartbeat can turn into a deafening drum. I suppose I was lucky I didn't have a heartbeat. Unfortunately, I did have a hefty set of chains restraining me, which meant every slight twitch of my body resulted in a clinking that echoed through the box. I did my best to stay still and considered my options when the rotating shapes were suddenly overshadowed by a bright beam of white light. It began above my head, traveling the length of the lid before settling into a position that split the darkness in half. "It's a little soon to go insane, it's it?" I asked myself as an unmistakable *ding* rang out from somewhere on the other side of the light.

The sound was instantly recognizable as the tiny sliver of light grew thicker, revealing a set of elevator doors that drew themselves open. I laid in shock as the last face I expected to see looked down at me from inside the newly adjacent room. "Woah, Austin, you look like shit. Do you need a ride?" Andy grinned from ear to ear while I stared up at him with a feeling of vertigo washing over me. I could feel myself laying on the cold slab of cement, but as I stared up at his tilted hat and crisp uniform, he seemed to defy physics with his feet planted firmly on the wall. It took me a moment to realize I was looking into a room whose center of gravity was shifted entirely from my own.

I stared dumbfounded as his grip tightened on the brass control lever of the elevator. "Are you coming or not?" he asked as I pushed to get my brain to kick over. "I think my mind snapped, but how the hell can you come back to Earth?" He slapped his knee and laughed like I had said the funniest thing he's ever heard. "Yeah, you're probably slipping a little. I'm not imaginary if that's what you're wondering." He stroked the floral wallpaper of the elevator like a loving pet, "this old girl is special. You know she can take me anywhere I've been told to go? That's why I'm here; I was told you needed a lift. Besides, technically I'm not on earth; you are. I'm just hanging out in my little box."

His demeanor shifted as the joke ended. "Seriously, Austin. I was told to come get you. Someone Is anxious to talk, and I don't think it's a good idea to keep her waiting." It didn't take much to convince me, anywhere was better than a cement sarcophagus. I raised one leg up, feeling gravity shift as my foot crossed the threshold into the elevator. Reaching shackled hands into the room as Andy gripped them, helping pull as inertia and the odd shift in balance sent me slamming my shoulder against the wall. I sunk to the floor in a small pile as Andy cranked the brass control lever.

"You mind giving me a hand with these?" I said as I shook the shackles up towards him. "I really wish I could," never pulling his hands from the lever, "but my orders were to deliver you as is. Extra emphasis on not interfering with any part of your current situation. In fact, if you had chosen to stay in your little rock cage back there, I was supposed to just leave you." I pulled the cigar from the pocket where Whitehall had placed it and gave it a whiff. He was right about a few things, this was a damn good cigar, and he really was a dick. "Then it sounds like the prick back on earth isn't the only one who wants to see me chained up." I dropped the cigar into my inner pocket, saving it until I had more answers.

Another ding of the elevator signaled our arrival. "This is it. I wish I could help more." Putting my hand out, Andy shook it and helped me to my feet as a large open room beyond us gave me *interrogation* vibes. The sterile feeling of the white walls and green linoleum tile was only broken by a single table and chairs in the center of the room. Stepping out, I looked back at Andy, unsure of what to do next. "So, am I about to get my thumbs broken?" I asked. He could only mouth "good luck" while the doors began to slide shut.

I decided to do what anyone would in this situation and took a seat to rest the heavy shackles on the table. Time and exhaustion were taking their toll on me. I laid my head in my hands, closing my eyes and hoping for a second of peace. That's when a briefcase slammed against the table only inches from my face. With the spring-loaded action of a jack-in-the-box, I shot upright in my seat, startled.

"Maggie," I yelled with false enthusiasm, "just the person I was hoping to not see." She flattened the back of her matronly dress and sat in the opposite chair. "Did they give you a new office? Don't get me wrong, I like it. It's more fitting to your personality." Her face remained expressionless as she popped open the latch on the briefcase. "You have been judged for damnation, Mr. Austin. As such, you are forbidden from entering Purgatory. Despite that fact, I needed to speak with you. That is why you were brought here." She gave an off-handed wave around the sparse room. "This place does not exist within Heaven, Hell, or Purgatory. Hence why you are allowed here." "Cool. Secrete level."

I wasn't surprised a video game reference was lost on her in my attempt to lighten the mood. In the mid-80s, I got into arcade games since every late-night grease pit seemed to have a few lined up against a wall. I spent many nights and countless quarters trying to rack up high scores before my gaming days eventually went into retirement. Still, if you ever find yourself with an overabundance of dots and you need a larger dot to eat them, just let me know; I'm your man. Since she was obviously not interested in being playful, I redirected my approach. "Too bad it's not possible," I said, confident in my understanding of the afterlife. "Nothing exists outside of those three besides the living universe, and I know we're not there." She seemed to have anticipated my response. "It didn't," she said firmly, "and after we leave this meeting, it will cease to exist once again. That leaves you with this opportunity to do something completely out of character and shut up if you know what's good for you."

I bit my tongue as she stared at me, waiting for a retort that never came. "Very good. There may be hope after all." She pulled a small file folder from the briefcase and set it in front of her. "When I found out you had disobeyed your orders, I have to admit I was surprised." She smiled for the first time since entering the room. "Surprised that it hadn't happened sooner. That is why when I was given the report that you had not only failed to deliver your charge to damnation but also brought an unauthorized soul back across the divide, I was very pleased to execute the termination order on your contract. Believe me, it was a good day, Mr. Austin." The visual of wrapping the shackles around her small pale throat and squeezing until her head popped off like a tennis ball flashed across my thoughts as I sat staring at the floor and saying nothing.

"Yet it would seem new information has recently come to our attention. Information that would put your actions in a rather interesting light." She tapped on the folder that sat in front of her. "Do you know what this is, Mr. Austin?" I didn't feel like playing guessing games and only shook my head. "This is potentially your new case file. Your file was purged when your contract was terminated, sentencing you to damnation. Your slate was cleared, as we say. I am hoping you understand the positive impact this could have on you." I rested the shackles back on the table. "It sounds a hell of a lot like you're telling me I'm not getting shipped downtown anymore. Is that what I'm hearing?" "That would be entirely your choice Mr. Austin. You see, you are in a unique position. One where you could potentially renegotiate your judgment. That is if you are so willing." I felt a sense of vindication. I had been right all along. "Finally, someone around here is coming to their senses. Thank you. Just tell me where to sign and let me get back to work so I can get the kid to Heaven. I'm happy to forgive and forget if you are."

I held the shackles out towards her and shook them as she remained unphased. "I'm afraid it's not that simple. Nothing in eternity ever is. You are aware that the very nature of existence is based on one constant, God is omnipotent. That means God is all-knowing, and God is infallible. Forgiveness can be granted, but all decisions are perfect and true. Is this making sense yet, Mr. Austin." I felt the weight of the shackles and no longer held them out towards her. "From where I'm sitting, it sounds like you're telling me that my sudden damnation was not a mistake." She sat upright, offended. "God does not make mistakes. That is what I am trying to tell you." She relaxed slightly, about to admit an insider tip she didn't want to get out. "It is us who are not perfect, however, so it is understandable that our process for executing God's orders can become... *muddied* in some situations. That is why we are attempting to correct our error."

I did my best to repress the growing anger, "So a child being damned to an eternity of torture isn't a mistake? Do you feel good about that? Protecting a system where a child was nearly tormented until time ceases simply because no one wants to say there could have been a fuck up?" For the first time in all the years I had known Maggie, she was speechless. She adjusted her tight hair bun, breaking eye contact. "No one wanted to see the child in pain. I will admit that. We were pleased when we found out the nature of what had occurred. It brought to light a lot of very dark things that have been transpiring in the mortal world that we were unaware of." It didn't take a genius to figure out what she was talking about. "He outmaneuvered you, didn't he? Used your own rules against you. That has to sting a little bit." She folded her hands. "It is not the first-time souls have tried to manipulate The Word to justify their desires. The only difference is this time, an individual was nearly successful in forcing his way into an ascension. If that had occurred, the results could have been quite catastrophic."

The notion caught my attention as she continued. "Through our connection with the angelic emissary that is accompanying you, we were able to hear Thomas Whitehall's confession. We heard everything you heard, and I must ask. Did you ever question why demonic forces were so willing to assist him?" I didn't want to tell her that the only thing that occurred to me while Whitehall bored the shit out of me with his rehearsed speech was how great it would feel to toss him into the propeller of the helicopter, but on reflection a new thought clicked. "He was their guinea pig. If it worked for him, why wouldn't it work for them?" She must have felt a small sense of teacher's satisfaction. "The lines of salvation and damnation would break down. Judgment would become fluid and, therefore, meaningless. Everything eternity is built upon would begin to crumble. That is why you are here. That is why I have this."

She thumbed open the envelope. Inside was a single sheet of paper she reversed and slid towards me. "Once you disobeyed your order, your contract was terminated. That was a judgment that cannot be undone, I'm afraid. That does not mean you are above forgiveness." Sitting in front of me was what I could only guess to be a new contract. "We cannot offer you your position as a Ferryman back," she continued. "With the ending of your previous agreement, that position is already in the process of being reassigned. We can, however, offer you a new role." I skimmed through the writing, unable to make out most of the legal jargon. I read it out loud to ensure I understood the most important part. "By executing all duties as an official Charon of God's Will, you shall be granted ascension at a time when formal approval is granted." She pulled a pen from her hair, clicking it open as she handed it over. "You have always been so fond of that word. I found it only fitting to formalize the title. This situation has proven you are up to the task of resolving any future unfortunate occurrences where a traditional ferryman isn't enough."

I started to write my name on the paper but held back momentarily to weigh my options. I could refuse to sign and take the express elevator to Hell. Although I hadn't seen damnation in its entirety, the potential didn't seem too promising. I could also tell Maggie to shove the contract as far up her ass as it could go, but then I might end up back in the box until an archeologist dug me up. Since I was already hungry, a few decades of starving underground in the dark didn't sound too appealing. That left me once more signing away my life and hoping to earn a little time off for good behavior. The choice was clear. Still, I didn't want to let Maggie off so easily. "I'll sign, but I want a few things to go with it." She nodded her head in concession, apparently expecting to negotiate.

"First, I want my car back, and I want it exactly how it was. No changes. Second, I want one week of vacation a year. For one week, I disappear. Nobody bothers me no matter what." I continued to push my luck. "Third. Benny. She stuck her neck out for the kid when none of you would. You don't have to tell me *what* she is, *who* she is that matters more. I want you to look into how she could earn her ascension as well. At a minimum, a job offer to push papers somewhere in The Gray if she wants. Last, I want you to promise that the kid isn't going to be damned." She flattened small wrinkles that formed in the lap of her dress. "All reasonable requests. Agreed," she said as she tapped the signature line of the paper.

For the second time since a first death that I couldn't remember, I signed on the dotted line and pledged my time to serve the afterlife, thereby earning my way to Heaven one day. I handed the pen back to Maggie as she stuck it into her hair and placed the contract into the briefcase. "So, where do we go from here?" Shaking the shackles at her again. She stood from her chair, the restraints instantly dropping off without a touch. "I go back to my office and prepare for another century of dealing with you," she said as she lifted the shackles and placed them into the briefcase. "You go back to the mortal side. Andrew will be along shortly to take you." She walked towards the door on the opposite end of the room, turning before she opened it to pull something from the briefcase. "I nearly forgot. Once you return, give this to the angelic one." She tossed a tan scroll towards me as I caught it mid-air. "What is it?" inspecting the black ribbon that tied the parchment closed. Maggie stepped through the door without ever looking back. "New Orders."

XXX

With the click of a deadbolt, I was left alone in the bare room, the sound of my tapping foot only interrupted by the *ding* I was waiting for. A small section of the blank wall opposite the locked door slid open revealing the elevator. "She's gone, right?" Andy asked, standing stiffly to adjust the lapels of his doorman's jacket while his eyes scanned the room. Not feeling much like talking, I gave him a thumbs up as I stepped inside. "Good," He relaxed a little, gripping the control lever. "I mean, I'm happy to carry out any order she gives me. I just prefer she doesn't give them to me in person. She scares the hell out of me, you know what I mean?" I leaned against the back wall to take some of the weight off of my tired feet. "Just give it a little time. After you get to know her, you'll see that under that rough exterior is a woman you can truly grow to hate." Andy chuckled as he threw the control.

It only took another moment before I could feel the elevator come to a stop, the doors sliding open to the same darkened tomb I had left only moments before. I moved towards the door, looking down at the cold cement slab unenthusiastic about crawling back inside. "Let's say I refused her offer back there," looking back at Andy from the edge of the door. "Would you actually have taken me to Hell if they ordered you to?" His face looked puzzled as if I had asked why the sky was blue. "You picked me up when I bit the dust. If you had the order, would you have taken me?" The guy had a point. "I do as I'm told, and hope whoever's making the decisions is smarter than I am. If it makes you feel any better, I would have felt like absolute shit doing it. By the way, there's one last part of the order from Maggie I have to fulfill. I hope you'll understand." As he finished asking forgiveness, I felt the impact of his polished shoe against my back before I wound up face down in the tomb. "She said to kick your ass out," he said, calling into the cramped cement casket. "I'm pretty sure she was being literal." The doors slid shut as he let out a final "no hard feelings. I'm rooting for you," before leaving me once again alone in my custom-built stone prison.

Things were different this time. I was no longer restrained by Whitehall's magic bracelets and all the cement and rebar in the world had about as much hope of trapping me as a wall of smoke. With a familiar icy feeling, my body snapped into the incorporeal state that allowed me to spin out of the tomb as easily as rolling out of bed. On my stomach, face down against the asphalt, I heard Whitehall's voice not far from me as I pushed up to my knees remembering to stay hidden. With Thomas's pet clairvoyant watching his back I could still be seen even in this state. As he continued to speak, I peered over the lid watching as he gave orders to the guards circling Anael and Peter. Calling the kid by his name would take some getting used to, something I would practice later since the human Ouija Board in the cheap suit was standing close by.

The only direction I could move without being seen was opposite of where everyone stood. There wasn't much behind the cement crate besides the open blacktop, an oversized helicopter, and me trying to pull my head from my ass with the hope that a plan might just follow it out. The propellers of the chopper were still, which meant it wasn't yet prepared to take off. The faintest idea started to take shape while sitting on my ass, trying to scratch my head with a nonexistent hand. I decided to go with it and improvise. With one last peek above the lid making sure everyone's attention was still focused away. I jumped to my feet. Running towards the helicopter as fast as a set of immaterial legs would take me, I barreled headfirst through the side of the Chinook.

I passed through the shiny white steel with no resistance and braced myself to stop short inside the dimly lit cargo hold, where I found exactly what I was hoping for, nothing. Despite painting and chroming the helicopter's exterior, the inside was exactly as it had been when it ran missions for the military. The olive drab walls were covered in cargo nets and uncomfortable-looking jump seats; otherwise, the interior remained empty. I focused for a moment and felt myself take solid form once again, my feet producing a light *ting* sound as I walked across the metal floor. I quickly ran down the side, folding all the seats upright to maximize the space inside before settling in the back. A warmth I had been missing radiated through my head as if I was flexing a non-existent muscle that had atrophied. It took longer than I was used to, but I didn't care. I was too happy to see my old friend again as the car, *my car*, snapped into being.

I ran my hand slowly along the roof, squeezing between the folded jump seats and the driver's door. "Long time no see, buddy. I wish we had more time to catch up, but we're still in some pretty deep shit. Let's get to work, then I'll explain everything." The driver's door affectionately popped itself open. Constricting myself through the door and into the seat that still fit like a glove, I found the keys hanging from the ignition. A simple twist and a spark of life prepared us as we sat in the belly of the helicopter.

Drumming my fingers against the steering wheel, each second that passed felt like a lifetime. I waited, hoping I hadn't overestimated my own cleverness, when the sight of the guards approaching reminded me not to second guess myself. In the shadow of the cargo bay, I watched as they moved closer, Whitehall directing them as they carried the cement tomb. Anael and Peter were bringing up the rear with their shackles chained to long leads attached to the crate. Holding my breath, I knew it was now or never. Hitting the lights on the car, the brightness momentarily blinded the makeshift funeral procession as they tried to figure out what was happening. I threw the car into drive and gunned the engine, taking advantage of the confusion. I may not have had this all figured out but what I did have was almost three tons of otherworldly steel at my fingertips as we shot from the loading ramp like a bat out of Hell.

In less than the time it took to blink, I smashed through the sarcophagus sending Whitehall and his mercenaries scattering. I jerked the wheel hard to the right and spun the car to their side, coming within inches of my two captive friends. It didn't take long for the guards to collect themselves, looking to their boss for orders. With the car in park, I climbed out, slamming the door behind me. "Oh, Tommy. There are some people up there who are really pissed off about your business practices. You're in trouble, my friend." Confusion shifted to anger as he picked himself up, pointing towards me. "Take him out..." he barked before I cut him off. "Wait!" Trying to defuse the situation, I put my hands up in surrender. "You may want to consider this first." I pulled my jacket open so the scroll nested in an inner pocket could be seen. The guns stayed on me, apparently holding their attention since no one had shot yet. Moving slowly, I pulled out the parchment, knowing I only had one chance for this to work. I called out "Anael" to my side as I tossed the scroll over the car.

Without hesitation, the angel snapped the shackles as if they were made of plastic and caught the scroll mid-air. "Son of a bitch," I couldn't help but yell. "So while I was getting my ass kicked and locked in a coffin, you could have done that the whole time?" My frustration only triggered an unconcerned shrug as they unrolled the paper. With a silent audience, Anael read through the document before dropping it to the ground. The Angel's wings shot up to their full glory, spreading what must have been 15 feet across as they leapt onto the roof of the car. "Woah, watch the paint," I said quietly, knowing they were focused on the guards. "This sacrilege ends now," Anael's voice boomed with authority. "I, as a representative of The Father, have been authorized to offer you one final chance to lay down your weapons and repent for this vile demonstration you have chosen to participate in. Repent now, and you are free to go. Yet I warn you, should you choose to take up arms at this moment, you are doing so against divine providence itself. You shall be judged accordingly."

The guards stood motionless as the words sank in, the quiet night only interrupted by the snarky laughter of Whitehall. "Don't let the wings scare you. Remember, this is our world. As long as this thing is here, it's mortal. Who's the one paying your salary? Consider that when you make your choice." He turned his back towards the angel as a final insult. "Tell you what. An extra 50% to anyone that can bring me those wings." An evil smile grew on his face. "They really would look nice mounted above my desk when I rebuild."

The men surrounded the car, their guns trained on Anael from every direction. "Your choice has been made," they said remorsefully. Slowly reaching behind their back, the angel withdrew a small set of curved daggers. I made another pissed-off note to myself that Anael had them the entire time. The reflection from the blades danced off the guards' helmets, their trigger fingers steadily locked in a standoff. In the distance

I noticed Stallworth's slim silhouette running from the scene. The clairvoyant mercenary must have also been psychic enough to know it was time to get the hell out of Dodge. Whitehall, losing his patience, shouted a frustrated "Now," as I jumped to shield the kid from what would come next. A rapid succession of shots rang through the night as Anael took to the sky. The angel's movements were sleek and purposeful, but most importantly lethal. Helmets clang loudly against the asphalt as the angel dove like a bird of prey, moving in the fraction of a time between trigger pulls. My mind was too slow to process their speed, but I could hear the shots cease with Anael again perching on the roof of the car. The scene was eerily calm, the group of guards still standing steadfast as their heads spun at their feet.

Like dominoes, their balance began to fade as they dropped to the ground one by one leaving only the four of us standing. "It's over Tommy boy," I yelled out from where I had the kid shielded. "I think you might be a little out of your league. Take the deal. Admit you were being an asshole; you may still have a chance." My plea struck a chord as Whitehall walked towards the closest headless body, pulling a handgun from the guard's holster. "I apologize for nothing!" He yelled with a crazed look in his eyes. "You think that flying stunt scares me?" He kept the gun steady as he took long strides towards the car. I watched as Anael dropped from the roof, standing rigid as he closed the gap between them. "This is stupid Thomas. You have no chance here," trying to bring some sense of reasoning into the situation. Anael turned to me; eyes sullen. The angel faintly bowed their head, a silent gesture of gratitude. I felt the impact of what was coming as they turned back towards the gun. Gripping their blades, I watched the last confident step as Anael moved towards him before a loud bang confirmed my fears.

A guard's body was lying only a few feet from where Peter and I stood. It was a little morbid, but I grabbed the shackle keys inside one of his pockets along with a decent lighter the guy had tucked away. Hey, he wouldn't be using it any time soon so why let it go to waste? I unshackled the kid, reassuring him that the bad stuff was over. As I put my arm around his shoulders, a voice called out from behind us.

"You think you won?" Whitehall screamed, standing beside the slumped body of Anael whose wings stretched along the ground. "But it was never about winning the battle. It's about winning the war. He was just the prototype." Whitehall pointed towards the kid. "The beta test, and now that I know this works, I can have hundreds more like him lined up as soon as I want. So take him, it's no concern of mine. Just imagine the possibilities, a new child anytime I want. One that's ready to take my sins away whenever I decide to be a little naughty." He clicked his fingers, trying to look clever. "In fact, I think I've just stumbled onto a new business model. A whole production line of desperate mothers pumping out kids to be sold off as sacrificial lambs to wealthy clients looking for a little soul refresh. I'll have every world leader under my thumb before long," he said menacingly. "And you, you'll have to stand by impotently and watch. So in a way, you'll actually be working for me, won't you?"

I stood calmly, adjusting my jacket as I walked towards where Anael was lying. "You're almost entirely right. You've done your research, you probably know more about the afterlife than even I could, but you don't know it all Tommy. For example, did you know that when a soul separates from its body, they have no memory of how they died? It's to cut down on the trauma of what just happened." He looked at me, not yet grasping what I was saying. "An angel's wings really are impressive," pointing down to the lifeless body that was once Anael. "And they cover a lot of ground, don't they? You know, I don't think it's very respectful to leave one of God's emissaries stretched out on the dirty ground like this." I rolled the angel to their side as Whitehall leapt backward in fear.

He could see what I had expected all along. His limp body lay hidden under the massive wings, the blades of angelic knives piercing his neck. "I warned you that you were out of your league." I turned towards him as he continued to back away. "They knew what they were doing all along, but you didn't bother to listen. So let me ask you a serious question now that you're dead. With that clean soul of yours, do you think killing an angel without remorse is going to harm your chances of getting into Heaven?" He said nothing, his lip quivering as reality set in. I moved in close to him, grabbing him by the shoulders to stop him from backing away. "You were right about one important thing though, Tommy," with a genuine smile. "I can't harm the living," and with all the anger, fear, and frustration built up over the last few days, I clenched my fist and broke his fucking nose.

XXXI

This may be obvious, since I think I've made it abundantly clear, but souls like ours sure as hell feel pain. Pain was the result I was going for as Whitehall grabbed his nose in anguish and crashed to his knees. It was the beautiful reaction I was hoping for. He was in my world now, and I was about to show him it's a world where all the money on Earth couldn't save him from what would come next. I paid little attention as he cursed loudly through the pain, instead, grabbing his collar and dragging him roughly towards the car. I didn't like to slap around souls too often, but if I'm being honest, I was really enjoying it this time. We neared the car and without a word, the trunk fell open as the car read my mind. "Sorry there, Tom," I said, tossing him against the license plate as his head bounced off of the rear fender. "I know this may not be the first-class accommodations you're used to but it's nice and cozy." I grabbed handfuls of collar and belt to get the proper leverage and tossed him into the trunk like the sack of shit he was.

"It's gonna get a little dark in there but don't worry. You're in good hands. I promise to avoid as many potholes as possible," and before the begging could begin, the trunk slammed tight. Peter was now standing by the passenger's door holding onto the handle tightly. His large innocent eyes unsure of what to expect next. "I can't take you with me, kid. You're not supposed to go where I'm heading, not anymore." With a sullen look, Peter's hand dropped. "So, where do I go now?" He asked, confused. It took me a moment, uncomfortable with the possibility of emotion, when an idea came to me. "One sec, let me see what I can do."

Turning towards where Whitehall's soulless body still laid outstretched, I rummaged through his pockets. It took a little searching, but I eventually came across what I was looking for. The silver fountain pen that was probably worth more than most people's cars. As I examined it, I could hear a shuffle behind me. "So are we still getting paid?" came the unsure voice of a disembodied guard. Their souls had now separated and were looking around confused, trying to piece together why their heads were sitting so far away from their bodies. "Someone's gonna be here any minute to pick you up. They'll make sure you get everything you're owed." The guard smiled an unquestioning soldier's smile and stepped away to inspect the strange sights around us. With the pen uncapped, I returned to the kid. "Can I see your hand?" I asked as he stretched it out. I scrawled a note on the top of it with the smooth fountain tip.

To Heaven, From Austin.
Fragile. Handle with care.

"Now, any moment someone like me is going to show up to take these morons to the bad place. Does that make sense?" Peter nodded, having experienced too much over the last few days to question anything new. "Good. When they do, I want you to go with them. Make sure you show the driver your hand. If they give you any trouble, let them know that I'll find them and pull their tongue out through their ass. I'm pretty sure I'm allowed to do that now." The kid chuckled; an unexpected sound that made me feel very calm inside. Without much thought I gave him a tight hug, feeling the pressure as his little arms squeezed back. "I'll see you again, Peter," I assured him softly. "I may be a little behind getting up there, but I'll be there soon enough."

The kid dropped his arms as an unmistakable set of bus headlights approached from the distance. "There's your ride. That means I need to get moving too." I held my hand out palm up, never doubting how uncool I really was. Peter took pity on me and slapped his little mitt against it, embarrassed as he did. With nothing left to say, I sunk into the driver's seat and heard thumping coming from the trunk. It wasn't anything a little extra volume on the radio couldn't fix. When the engine snapped to life I pulled off down the long stretch of asphalt, honking a final goodbye at the kid in my rearview mirror. I gripped the steering wheel tighter as the images outside the windows zoomed by until the scenery became dark and misty with a silent pop between worlds.

It was odd being back in the Gray again; having only been away from it for a few days, it felt like a lifetime. Speeding south along the nothingness we were bound for the same destination that started this whole pain-in-the-ass event, only this time, I knew I had the right guy. I sunk down a little lower in the seat, feeling the comfort of the leather as it wrapped around my back and enjoyed moments of peace I didn't expect to ever have again. It didn't take long for us to get the dark edge of the Gray that dropped off to whatever torturous Hell laid inside the pit. I spun the car around and stepped out, preparing for what was about to happen. I knew he would beg, and I hoped he would cry. There was even a chance he might try to fight, which would be interesting. Laughing to myself, I took a moment to practice my response and stepped closer to the trunk, barely making out the whaling from inside. The loud moans sounded almost infantile and somehow satisfying. I knocked on the trunk with my knuckles, "Have some dignity and pull yourself together," I reassured Whitehall as I dropped the trunk open. "It's too late now; you're not going to solve any of this with..."

Inside, resting with his arms folded behind his head and more relaxed than you would imagine possible inside the boot of a car, Thomas Whitehall laid laughing under the dim trunk light. His deep sarcastic chuckles lit a fire on the shortened fuse in my soul. I grabbed him by a handful of his perfect hair and pulled him out as he tumbled to the ground, still laughing. "That's Hell," pointing to the ledge of existence, "it's your next stop." I placed a steel toed kick directly in his ribs to shut him up. "Now, would you mind telling me what exactly is so funny?" He rolled to his back, cradling the pain in his side but still laughing as he looked up at me.

"You honestly think you won, don't you?" He managed through giggles. "You see yourself as the hero, some sanctified avenger who's delivering the bad guy to his ultimate punishment. That's the joke. Your misguided idea that the world is so black and white that whoever you see as *bad* will eventually lose." On shifty legs, he raised himself to his feet. "Things don't work that way in the real world, and I hate to break it to you, but you're not a hero. You're a chauffeur, an hourly employee. Face it, you're the help." He moved past me, inching closer to the edge. "And more than anything else, you're naive. Do you think I honestly put all my chips on one number? You have to hedge your bets Austin, remember?"

He peered over the ledge of the pit and into the darkness below, still smiling as he continued. "You see, I have something that every being in life and the afterlife wants. I have wealth, resources, connections, which means above all else, I have power. When you have power, it doesn't matter who you're working with; everyone is willing to cut a deal for the right price." He turned towards me, his feet tightrope walking the edge. "I made a valuable deal long ago. I knew I had to have my bases covered. Think about it, Austin. Do you honestly believe I would risk eternity on just exploiting a loophole in death? Always have contingencies for your contingencies. With all the power I have on Earth, there are entities more than happy to trade that type of influence for my own little throne in Hell." He held his arms out in a cross and smirked. "I have always been good at brokering deals. The first human soul to be a crowned duke of Hell. That's what's funny; for all your anger and all your threats, I still have a welcome party down there waiting to receive me. So please, do your job like a good servant."

  I watched him anxiously balance on the edge of Hell as his confession still rattled my brain. Was he bluffing? I couldn't tell, but he seemed too relaxed about the possibility of Hell and there was no question that he had previously been in contact with something down there. "You're right," I admitted. "You've outsmarted us all on this one." He kept his balance and he continued to gloat. "I'm damned if I do, and I'm damned if I don't. So let's make the best out of it and please move this along. I'm sure they have business down there I need to attend to." I stepped over to where he stood when something he said suddenly blossomed into an idea. "You were right about it all." I reached towards him, placing my hand on his chest for the final push. "The world isn't black and white. Sometimes there are shades of gray." I grabbed a tight grip on his shirt and pulled him back from the ledge, tossing him to the ground as the trunk again dropped open. His usual smug expression was wiped from his face. "What are you doing? You have orders!" He said, putting up his hands to block his face. I lifted him by the neck and flung him into the trunk before answering. "My orders aren't as black and white as they used to be."

The Gray is a pretty simplistic place when it comes to directions. South to Hell, north to the pearly gates, Purgatory sitting smack in the middle. That left any other direction outside the specific straight line between realms home to limitless expanses of nothingness. This was precisely what I was looking for as I spun the wheel at random into any direction off the beaten path and gassed the engine. As we sped deeper and deeper into the misty fog of solitude, I stretched back and sunk snuggly into my seat, keeping the pedal firmly to the floor. I replayed everything that happened over the last few days and all the new information that had come to light as I questioned whether what I was about to do was right. The doubt didn't last long.

We drove through the mist until I had lost all track of time, my eyes growing dry and heavy. I gripped the wheel until my stomach was so empty it sent shooting pains through my body and drove until I stood at the breaking point of exhaustion; and then drove a little further. I continued until I knew I couldn't drive another mile, and without ceremony or grand theatrics, we simply stopped. I stepped out of the car, the foggy, dull surroundings looking no different than they had at the first mile, but that was the point. It was here in the silent, lonely void that I popped the trunk open to see a sight very different than I had before. Thomas was curled in the fetal position, fearful as his eyes darted around trying to figure out what was happening. Before he could speak, I pulled him into the gray, dropping him as he tried to make sense of where we were. "Please, Austin," he said in complete panic. "Whatever your plan is right now. You can't do it."

I leaned down in front of him. "I'm not doing anything; that's exactly the point. I thought about what you said, I told you that you were right. You can't go north, you can't go south, and I can't bring you back with the living. You could cause too much trouble as a ghost, and since I don't have the power of dissolution we're stuck. So instead, I'm taking you nowhere." I stood facing him. "Literally nowhere. You see, out here there are only a few places you could ever possibly find, all existing in one very specific direction. Do you want to guess which direction that is?" I pointed a full 360 degrees as he looked around. "Tell me, how long do you think it would take to find a needle in an infinite haystack? Don't answer that; let's just test it to find out." I started back towards the driver's door as he pleaded, "Please! You can't leave me out here like this. I have nothing. You can't leave me out here with nothing!" There was something to what he said that I couldn't help but agree with. I shut the driver's door and took a few steps back towards him. "You're right, you know. I couldn't live with myself if I left you out here with nothing."

A glimmer of hope flashed in his eyes as I reached into the inner pocket of my jacket. "So I'm leaving you with this." I pulled out the single cigar he had left me earlier. I ran it under my nose, smelling the rich scent before placing it behind his ear. "And a small piece of advice to go with it. Enjoy it slowly. It's going to be a long time before you get another." He hadn't quite processed what was happening as I moved back to the cab. "One more thing," grabbing his attention before tossing him the lighter I pulled from the dead guard. "Here, it's more than you left me." With a clear conscience I took my place back behind the steering wheel. From within, I could see Thomas in my rearview on his feet and screaming unheard threats as I began to drive in the wrong direction. I knew he would follow and lead himself further into a dull prison of solitude. After I could no longer see him, we circled back on the path to Earth. Was I an ass for leaving him to face an eternity of isolation? *Probably,* but at least he wasn't a concern anymore.

XXXII

Three weeks.

That's how long I had apparently been gone. Deep in the Gray, a place beyond the earthly ideas of science and logic, the rules of time don't really apply. The further you travel away from existence, the more those rules mean even less. At least that's what I found out as I finally crossed over into the warmth of the living world. It was early morning in my city on a quiet downtown street. Since I was still in the early stages of figuring out what to do now, I decided to grab the morning paper before heading back to my collapsed home and unmade bed. That's when I saw that I had spent three weeks in the empty armpit of the universe which, in the moment, only felt like an overtime shift. "Fucking purgatory," I said under my breath as I leaned against the idling car and browsed the news. Thumbing through the same old political bullshit that's been circling around for ages, I eventually found a small article on the third page that caught my eye. The bold headline read, "Search still underway for missing city magnate Thomas Whitehall."

I scanned the words quickly, a short piece that recapped the basics of his sudden disappearance but conveniently failed to mention anything about decapitated mercenaries. I wasn't surprised. Just his name being published in the paper was more press than his family was used to getting, and with whoever stepped in to take over his businesses, I'm sure they had the scene cleaned up quietly. The last sentence struck me as funny. "If you have any information that could lead to his whereabouts, please contact the city authorities." I folded the paper up and tucked it under my arm, "yeah. That ain't happening." I laughed before climbing behind the wheel. As I started the car, I heard the unmistakable clap of a file landing in the glovebox. "I didn't need rest anyways" I said as I popped open the small compartment. Inside was a white postcard that said very little aside from an address written in flowing cursive and the words "See you there."

The morning streets hadn't reached their busy point yet, letting me navigate along the back alleys as if I never missed a beat. It didn't take long before I was parked at the address on the card, one of the city's large brownstones that had fallen into disrepair. Killing the engine, I peered over the dashboard to figure out what I was supposed to be waiting for when a startling crash threatened to cave in the car's roof. "What the ever-loving fuck was that!" I yelled. Exhaustion had whittled my patience down to a razor thin margin as I stepped out into the street, ready for a fight "Someone's about to get their dick kicked in!"

"I believe you'll find that difficult to do…" came the soothing voice of Anael, perched on top of the car and more radiant than the first time we met. "I like you," I said, backing away slightly. "I assumed we were friends now, but if you're here to drag me Hell, I'm not going quietly." I put my hands up in a pathetic imitation of a boxer's stance and waited for a pain that never came. Instead, Anael's regal body let out a series of giggles as I heard the sweet sound of an angel's laughter. "Relax my friend. I am not here to wish you harm." The angel stood; wings fully exposed. "In fact, I am not here at all. I am a manifestation appearing only to you."

Stepping in closer, I inspected the top of the car. "Yeah, well, if you're not here then why are you denting my roof," pointing to their large white boots that left small impressions in the metal. Anael hopped down onto the street, still towering over me but slightly less intimidating. "Dramatic effect," the angel said as their wings tucked themselves away. "I am here as a messenger. Since you have been granted one of the first new positions for a soul in centuries, we are still trying to understand how to best utilize you." A little more comfortable knowing I wasn't about to be hit, I moved in closer to sit on the car's hood. "Well then, let's figure it out. Are the choirs pissed about Whitehall?" Their smile faded. "No. It is agreed by all that your actions are regrettable but necessary under these unexpected circumstances. A new plan is being prepared if a situation like this arises again." With a lowered voice, the angel continued. "It will happen again, Austin. That is why they granted you this new title. The soul you have diverted into the great nothing is only the first of what is to come. That is what we fear."

There was something unsettling about the sight of genuine concern in an angel's face. "A door of possibilities has been opened, one that can never be shut again. There are those with dark intent who now know the laws of this universe are not as rigid as we once thought. We must be prepared for when they attempt to exploit them." I was too tired to worry; that would come later. "So a promotion without a raise and a lot less sleep. How did I get so lucky?" I asked facetiously. "I only have one question." The angel was prepared, "and that is?" I moved back to my feet, patting down my pockets before remembering I gave Thomas the last cigar. Sometimes I think I'm too nice.

"You said I was *one* of the first new positions in centuries. That seems wrong. Shouldn't it be *the only* new position in centuries?" Anael motioned towards the building over my shoulder. "Yes, about that..."

Two small figures came slowly from the front entrance of the brownstone. First was a small elderly woman who appeared frail in her floral nightgown. She was beautiful in the way only a grandmother could be, and as she smiled at the morning sun I could see that she was also dead. After acknowledging her, it took me a moment to place the second figure. Not because I didn't recognize who it was but because I didn't want to believe it was Peter.

He held onto the elderly woman's arm and helped her soul down the stairs. He was clean and confident, wearing the brown knickers and matching dress cap of a newsie ripped from the turn of the century. As they moved onto the sidewalk, the kid spotted me and waved enthusiastically. "Why is he here?" I turned to Anael, asking through clenched teeth. "Everything that happened. All we went through. He's one of the innocents!" I spat. The angel hung their head in agreement. "Yes he is, but I'm afraid we were left with no choice. This is not a time when we can show weakness in our decisions. The child was judged unworthy of salvation. I'm afraid at this time that judgment, no matter how unjust, cannot be overturned. As such, he will earn his ascension in the same manner as you, only slightly different." It was unfair, but I knew arguing would only make things worse. "What is he?" I said quietly as they moved closer to us. "He looks the same, but he's different. He seems...mature" The angel nodded. "He is not a ferryman or a Charon as you are. He is different. He functions as a comfort for those who deserve a gentler crossing than your kind can offer." I kept my thoughts to myself, not wanting to admit that it made sense. "Since his situation is different, we were able to give him a small insight into the universe itself." "So you gave him a piece of the alpha and omega?" I asked, trying to smile as the angel returned the look. "A sliver."

Peter stood beside the car, the passenger door opening itself to him as he motioned the elderly woman towards it. "Susan, this is my friend Mr. Austin. He is going to take you to see Edward. He has been waiting for you for some time now." Her face lit up at the mention of the name as the kid kissed her hand gently, helping her into the back seat. "Please give us just a moment to catch up; I promise you my friend will get you to your Edward very soon."

The door shut itself as Peter looked up at us. "Hello Austin," He said softly. "I've been wondering how long it would take you to come back." The kid looked good as I took in his new clothing and persona. "You clean up nice. Maybe a little outdated, but real nice either way." I knelt down, so we were again at eye level. "I'm really sorry for everything that happened. I want you to know that. I want you to know I wish I could have done more. You deserve more." Peter smiled and placed his hand on my cheek with the comfort of a father. "Don't apologize, Austin. You have done more for me than anyone could have asked, and pity is the last thing I would ever want. Instead, I choose to cherish what memories I have and enjoy the moments as they come rather than cry for what could never be." His words stirred something in me, the soft feeling of his fingers against my face. "Some of us don't even have memories," I said in a whisper as his eyes met mine. The soft glow of his soul seemed to radiate from within him. "You will one day. You will earn them all, plus more; and when you do, they will mean more to you than anything in this life ever could."

My eyes welled with tears before I forced myself to break away from his gaze. "Well, that's good news then," standing up to play off the emotion. "So, what happened after I left?" The kid could see through my attempt to change the subject but was kind enough to go with it. "Another ferryman arrived to move the souls across the divide. Unfortunately, I was not on the list to go with them. I had to remain on earth for the time being. Luckily I remember a friend." Slung over his shoulder was a canvas messenger bag that he shifted, reaching his small hand inside. "Bernice was kind enough to look after me until Anael arrived with the offer of my current position."

He pulled a small black rectangle from the bag, a smartphone like the kind I had seen Benny use so many times. "She made me promise to give this to you next time we met. Her number is the only one programmed into it. She would like for you to call her; she's very worried." I took the phone from his small hand and looked it over, hitting the power button as the screen lit up. "I guess I should let her know I'm alright." The kid laughed, since I had unknowingly cut him off. "You didn't let me finish. She's worried about her car." The phone went into my pocket since I was not yet ready to have that conversation. Where to now, kid?" I asked, holding onto the phone. He shifted the bag back and manifested a beautiful cherry red antique bicycle directly behind him. "The same as you." He pointed towards the cheerful lady in the back seat. "More work. Would you show me this diner you're always talking about tonight?" He asked as he climbed onto the leather bike saddle. "The best idea I've heard in a while."

As the kid pedaled away, I turned towards Anael who stood silently. "It's not going to take him as long as me to earn his ticket, right?" The angel shook their bald head with confidence. "His contract is short, but he is a kind soul. He may choose to continue of his own accord." I shrugged, almost forgetting the passenger in the back. "Kind and maybe a little stupid." Anael laughed again as their wings unfurled to their full size, calling down as they flew away. "We will be in touch soon. Best of luck Charon.".

I pulled the small phone out and turned it over in my hands a few times, finally getting the courage to dial. The other end rang as I held up a finger to mouth the words "one moment" to Susan. "You Dick!" came the immediate shriek from the other end of the line. "Hi Ben, I missed you too," trying to calm the situation. "You realize once I kick your ass, you're going to wish you had stayed gone!" It was a threat I knew she would make good on. "I'm sure you will, but I've got a lot of great stories you might want to hear before you kill me. Deal?" She huffed a monosyllabic agreement. "First, did the kid tell you I got a new title? New job and everything. I'm kind of making it up as I go along. That means I might need an assistant." I was rather proud of coming up with that one on the spot, even if it was bullshit. "Yeah," Benny said, the grin audible in her voice. "Sounds really neat, but one question. You hate being called a ferryman, right?" I gave a drawn-out "uh-huh..." not sure I liked where this was going. "So instead, out of all the titles you could pick, could you explain why the fuck you settled on Sharron?"